Humphrey and Me

Stuart H. Brody

SANTA
MONICA
PRESS

Advance Praise for *Humphrey and Me*

"In this heartfelt account of a crucial period in American history, an idealism that can sometimes seem lost today comes alive again."
                                                    —ANDREA BARRETT,
                        National Book Award-winning author of *Ship Fever*

"*Humphrey and Me* is a smart and thought-provoking story—made even better by knowing it's based on the author's own experiences."
                                                    —STEVE SHEINKIN,
                                    three-time National Book Award finalist

"Democracies are strongest when they produce leaders who can inspire the young. Stuart Brody's engaging and entertaining novel *Humphrey and Me* explores this crucial and timely dynamic between a young man and an idealistic politician. It reminds us that Hubert Humphrey, despite his flaws, was a virtuous and important 20th century figure, one deserving of our admiration and respect."
                        —THURSTON CLARKE, author of the *New York Times*
                                bestseller *The Last Campaign: Robert F. Kennedy*
                                        and 82 Days That Inspired America

"Brody, who was inspired by his own relationship with Humphrey, packs the novel with significant historic details . . . . An important chapter in American history told with clarity and honesty."   —*KIRKUS REVIEW*

"In this thoughtful and moving novel, Brody illuminates in fiction what he explored in his wonderful treatise *The Law of Small Things*—how we learn to be good. He demonstrates why choices matter in the formation of character, and in so doing, he helps us understand the basis of human freedom."
—LARRY ARNN, president of Hillsdale College

"By paralleling first person accounts of a young man's political awakening with that of his indefatigable mentor, Stuart H. Brody has rendered a timely affirmation of how enduring societies depend upon an apprenticeship of values. Most importantly, he has resuscitated for our cynical age a uniquely American notion of leadership and service."
—AARON WOOLF,
Peabody Award-winning documentary filmmaker

"Politics may be a dirty business, but there are still people who get in the game for the right reasons: to do what's right! In *Humphrey and Me*, Stuart Brody highlights one of the good guys—not because he was perfect, but because he genuinely believed in doing good. It's a great reminder of the complexities needed to understand people on a deeper level, and while it can be complicated, it can also be rewarding. It's a journey about finding consensus and alignment as opposed to agreement. Get started!"
—JEFFREY HAYZLETT, Host of *C-Suite with Jeffrey Hayzlett*

Published by:
Santa Monica Press LLC
P.O. Box 850
Solana Beach, CA 92075
1-800-784-9553
www.santamonicapress.com
books@santamonicapress.com

Printed in the United States

Santa Monica Press books are available at special quantity discounts when purchased in bulk by corporations, organizations, or groups. Please call our Special Sales department at 1-800-784-9553.

ISBN-13: 978-1-59580-125-8 (print)
ISBN: 978-1-59580-766-3 (ebook)

Publisher's Cataloging-in-Publication data

Names: Brody, Stuart H., author.
Title: Humphrey and me / by Stuart H. Brody.
Description: Solana Beach, CA: Santa Monica Press, 2023.
Identifiers: ISBN: 978-1-59580-125-8 (print) | 978-1-59580-766-3 (ebook)
Subjects: LCSH Humphrey, Hubert H. (Hubert Horatio), 1911-1978--Fiction.
| Political campaigns--United States--Fiction. | Presidents--United States--
Election--1964--Fiction. | Presidents--United States--Election--1972--Fiction.|
Bildungsroman. | Political fiction. | Historical fiction. | BISAC YOUNG ADULT
FICTION / Politics & Government | YOUNG ADULT FICTION / Historical /
United States / 20th Century | YOUNG ADULT FICTION / Social Themes /
Activism & Social Justice
Classification: LCC PS3602 .R63 H86 2023 | DD 813.6--dc23

Cover and interior design and production by Future Studio
Cover photo courtesy of Independent Picture Service / Alamy Stock Photo

To Ruth

Contents

PRELUDE
Looking for Someone I Could Trust

PEOPLE SAY I'M A SHY KID. They're right. I admit that. Not that I like being labeled. But that one is fair—about being shy, I mean—so I can live with it. But labels sting. That's what my father is always doing: labeling me.

He says I'm moody, impatient, and defensive. But I think he's those things more than I am. I don't think it's fair being labeled, especially if people do it behind your back, the way I'm sure my father does to my mother. Mom would never use harsh words against me. Anyway, I don't mind being called defensive if someone is labeling me wrongly. So I guess I admit I'm defensive.

To defy my father and his labels, I tried to think up words that correctly described me. Words like "sensitive," "respectful," "talented." Or "good listener," "well-intentioned," "good-natured." I liked those words, but they didn't seem to fit just right. It felt phony to label myself.

So I thought a better way to define myself was to list all the things I liked. I like playing soccer and I like girls, but I'm not very good at soccer and I'm not very good with girls. I don't see how I can define myself by things I'm not even good at.

What I'd really like to be good at is looking deeper into who I really am, beyond labels, words, and forced descriptions. To know the truth about myself? I know I can't do that alone. I need people who I can trust to help me. But I'm defensive, so I have a hard time trusting people.

In the fall of 1963, I began looking for someone I could trust.

PART ONE
Fall 1963

Chapter One

MY TEAMMATES AND I surged out of the high school gym like a herd of wild mustangs on a western range. We were primed for the soccer match against our archrivals two towns over. South Side Cyclones, in bright red-and-blue lettering, blazed across our jerseys.

"Let's get a move on, you turtles," the coach—and geometry teacher—shouted from the steps of the school bus. "We got a match to play."

A gaggle of pretty girls paused to watch as we raced to the bus, showing off by hitting each other as we ran. Amy Carlson was the cutest. She had pale blue eyes, freckles, and thick red curls rolling off her shoulders. She caught me looking at her and smiled. I looked the other way, nervous that the other boys might notice.

On board, the boys hurled insults at one another, belittling each other's skill with girls. I wasn't comfortable with that banter. There was nothing wrong with it. It's just that I didn't have enough experience to talk about it, and the other boys knew it.

Arriving at the field, the South Side players charged onto the field; that is, the regulars did. I took my accustomed place on the bench with the other second-stringers and pretended to watch the game, thinking about Amy instead. *Would a girl like that ever go out with me?* I wondered. It was ridiculous just thinking about. *But she did smile at me.* I scoured the faces of my fellow bench jockeys, just in case one of them guessed what I was dreaming about.

On the field, the teams traded goals and regulation play

ended in a tie. As sudden death began, a commotion broke out. A South Side halfback was down. My teammates lifted him to his feet and walked him back to the bench. A tiny contingent of spectators applauded kindly from the sidelines.

Now someone had to take his place. The coach paced back and forth, mulling over his meager choices. I couldn't help staring at him, not wanting to play but curious if he would pick me. Then he did, motioning me in without a word. Nothing needed to be said; the coach didn't expect much, and neither did I.

Our forward line started the charge downfield, dribbling elegantly. I backed them up, running less elegantly but keeping up. As we converged on the goal, the goalie kicked the ball clear of the goal, but it deflected off one of our players and spun high in the air. I was the closest South Sider and moved toward the ball.

I timed its descent perfectly and hurled myself into the air, smashing into a defender, but managing to head the ball. I crashed to the ground, but the ball found the corner post and squeezed in. The winning goal! My teammates mobbed me, yanking me from the ground and showering me with congratulations. Dazed, I gave them a faint smile.

Chapter Two

WITH THE GAME WON, I pedaled my bicycle home, still in uniform, with my cleats slung over my shoulder. Oak leaves rustled gently in the fall breeze. The windows of stately homes reflected the soft late-afternoon light. "Unbelievable," I kept muttering, replaying my improbable triumph in my mind.

I felt I was floating in a dream, suddenly cast into an alternate reality of athletic distinction and the admiration of peers. Other boys lived in that world permanently. I just had a taste but wanted more. My life needed to unfold in a different way. Not so ordinary. I would have to think of something.

But first I had to get through the next few hours. Tonight was "current events night" at home. It was Dad's idea. At first I liked it, but then it turned into a kind of weekly cross-examination with me as the witness breaking down on the stand.

I rode up to our house, leaned my bike against the garage, and walked around back to the kitchen door. I paused for another mental replay of my soccer victory. "Unbelievable," I said one last time before walking in.

The kitchen was filled with sweet aromas. My mother seemed to glow in the flush of steaming pots on all burners. Mom ruled the kitchen with regal calm—that is, until I walked in. She threw off her apron and hugged me. At sixteen, it was embarrassing to be smothered with affection by your mother, but she really meant it and that made it okay. Our dog, Pepi, a Welsh terrier, hovered nearby, wagging his tail furiously and leaping into the air. My sister, Diane, a gawky eleven-year-old, bounded in and gathered up the good silverware to set the dining room table. It was a special night. Current events night.

"Ray scored the winning goal against Lynbrook today," Diane said casually, setting off another burst of enthusiasm from Mom.

"Why, that's wonderful, Ray." She kissed me again, so hard this time that I had to shield my face.

"Thanks, Mom."

"But you'd better hurry. Your father will be home soon."

I gave Diane a dirty look. I had wanted to tell Mom about the goal.

Diane shrugged. "Ginger told me."

Ginger's brother was my teammate. The news was getting around and, secretly, I was pleased. Diane probably knew that.

I liked my bedroom. It was something that made me feel special. From my bed, I had a view of a giant oak tree that swept up high above the house. A few months ago, a tree cutter—called a tree surgeon—cut down some limbs, and he said the tree was at least 175 years old. That meant it was around during the Revolutionary War. George Washington might have seen this tree, I thought.

A fish tank bubbled on my dresser top. Angelfish only. Thin and sleek, they darted with magical speed, especially when you tapped the glass, which you're not supposed to do. Angels are the essence of elegance. I would stare at them for hours. I used to have swordtails, neon tetras, and zebras, all the popular fish, but I decided to go for the queen of tropical fish: angels. I even tried to breed them, but it never worked. I guess I wasn't a very good fish breeder. Failed fish breeder! You could put that label on me and I wouldn't mind.

In the corner stood my double bass, which I played in the high school orchestra. I started in fifth grade, when I couldn't even carry it. But I loved the sound, so my parents paid for lessons and helped me lug it around. I was pretty good now.

But the most unique thing about my room was the closet.

It was big for an ordinary bedroom, and it even had a window. I know it seems funny to say, but having a closet with a window made me feel lucky. There was even a little desk in there where I could sit and do homework. In the late afternoon, when light poured into my room through the oak tree's leaves, I could work by sunlight alone.

On my closet desk, I kept a little blue-and-white box with a map of Israel on it and a slot at the top. Every day I put change in the box. I liked to see how fast I could fill it up so I could send the money to Israel to plant trees. Lots of Jewish kids did that. It was twenty years since the Nazis exterminated the Jews of Europe. Our parents told us we could honor the murdered Jews by planting trees in the state of Israel; millions of trees, at least six million, to commemorate the six million Jews slaughtered by the Germans.

Living in Rockville Centre—that was the name of my town, spelled with an *re* like the English do it—my friends and I could not imagine the horrors of World War II or the Depression. Our parents had lived through both and told us we were privileged. We knew that. How could we not know? Our dads wore suits and ties to work in New York City and drove nice cars. Downtown Rockville Centre had fancy shops and expensive restaurants, and the streets were lined with beautiful homes and gleaming lawns.

When our parents spoke of atrocities and hardships, they sounded like stories from ancient times in a foreign land, like a fairy tale with ugly interludes where the hero made it out alive. The villains of history and the calamities of the past seemed remote to us. We could not access our parents' emotion over these events. We had worries, doubts, and sadnesses of our own. Still, I listened with respect and kept depositing my coins in the little blue-and-white box.

Suddenly, Pepi started barking and then Diane screamed, "Daddy's home!"

"Quiet, beast," I heard Dad say to Pepi, who was yelping

with joy.

I dashed to the shower and emerged in world-record time, just as Mom called from the downstairs landing, "Rayyy-ee."

That was the signal I'd worked out with Mom. On current events night, I would wait till the last minute to come down, so I could avoid small talk before performing for Dad. When Mom called, that meant it was time, so I shot downstairs and slid into position to the left of Dad. Mom sat to his right and Diane across from him.

Food was crammed onto the dining room table: Mom's special pot roast with boiled potatoes, string beans with almonds, and the salad Mom insisted on having with every meal. We waited for Dad to serve himself, scrutinizing him to detect his mood. He unveiled a half smile as he looked first at me, then Diane, and then me again. "You kids ready for current events night?"

Diane waved a news article. "I'm ready, Daddy. My report is on the new bridge they're building across both halves of Michigan."

When she was done with her report on the construction of the Mackinac Bridge, Dad shed an indulgent smile. "Very nice, honey." Then, still looking at Diane, he said, "Now I'd like to hear from your brother." Slowly, his head turned, his smile evaporated, and his stern look settled on me.

I looked at Mom, seeking a confidence boost. She nodded and I forged ahead, reading from a folder of newspaper clippings.

"'Last week four Negro girls were killed in a bombing at the 16th Street Baptist Church in Birmingham, Alabama. They were murdered attending church.'"

Mom gasped. "Oh my God."

"Don't editorialize," Dad said. "Just the facts."

I kept reading. "'The sheriff of Birmingham announced on Monday that he has insufficient evidence to make arrests . . .'"

"And don't read."

Mom was biting her lip, holding back tears.

I shoved my folder aside, still looking down at the table. "Negro leaders are saying that the sheriff is refusing to investigate the case. They've called for a federal investigation, claiming that Alabama officials are biased against Negroes."

"Look at me," Dad commanded.

I looked up. Mom was staring at me through tear-filled eyes. Diane's eyes darted between Dad and me.

"Well, that describes what happened," Dad said. "Now analyze it."

In a desperate attempt to diffuse the tension, Mom motioned to Diane to take more string beans, then shoveled some onto my plate.

I took a deep breath. "Well, it seems that whenever Negroes push for their rights, the law doesn't protect them. I think the federal government should get involved."

"Okay. How?"

"By passing new laws against discrimination. Without laws, people just don't do what's right."

"Don't people always find ways around the law?"

"Yes, but if something's against the law, people will get used to seeing it as wrong and things will start to change. That's why President Kennedy announced a civil rights bill that could change the way Negroes are treated."

A slight smile creased Dad's face. I'd answered his tough questions. The worst could be over. But I wasn't sure. I wondered if his smile was a prelude to another round of questioning.

"So tell me how a law changes the way people think," he said. "Even President Kennedy acknowledged that laws alone can't make people do the right thing."

I answered this, I thought to myself. *Is Dad provoking me, using President Kennedy against me?*

"I explained that. The law changes the way people act."

"Yes, you explained how laws change the way people act. I'm still waiting to hear how laws change the way people think."

Mom rushed to my aid. "Honey, please."

Dad turned to her calmly. "He needs to be clearer about what he's saying. I want him—and Diane, too—to be thoughtful about what goes on in the world."

"He sounds very thoughtful to me," Mom said softly.

"He needs to be more committed," Dad argued.

"Right," I muttered. "Always more."

Dad stared coldly at me.

"He *is* committed, honey," Mom said. "He has his soccer and his music, and he's closing in on being an Eagle Scout. What more does he need to do?"

"Yeah, and he scored the winning goal against Lynbrook today," Diane blurted out.

"Yes, Diane," Dad said dryly. "Your mother told me." Then he looked straight at me but answered Mom, referring to me in the third person. "Those are things he just *does*. I'm not discounting them, it's just . . ." He paused and drew his face tight, fixing a hard look at me. "Skipping a grade was all well and good, but you may be left behind in other ways. Frankly, you don't seem focused."

"Focused?" I shouted. "I'm focused!"

"I mean putting your heart into something you really believe in and going all out for it."

"For goodness' sake, Jim," Mom said. "He's got time for that."

Dad paused and looked down at the table. He no longer seemed present, as if he were being called by some distant voice or seized by a dark memory. I glanced at Mom nervously. She gave a quick shake of her head to reassure me.

Then, a few seconds later, Dad came out of it. "Look," he said, "you'll be going to college soon. I don't want to see you drift there."

He's accusing me of drifting, I thought. It made no sense at all. It was so wrong. It was just plain stupid. "Well, Dad," I exploded, "maybe I just won't go to college. Then you'll actually have an excuse to be disappointed in me."

I pushed my chair back abruptly, slamming into the breakfront and causing the dishes to rattle, and stomped off.

"Come back here!" Dad yelled. "I didn't say I'm disappointed, for God's sake."

"You're being too hard on him," I heard Mom say as I headed upstairs.

I slammed my bedroom door and hurled my current events folder into the wastebasket. I plopped down on the bed and stared up at the oak tree, with its massive limbs shooting into the night sky. I calculated that with one great leap from my window I could reach the branches and lose myself in their ghostly majesty. Of course, I would never attempt such a jump, but imagining that I could offered some comfort.

My parents were talking downstairs. I could only make out snatches of their conversation, a word or two said loudly. Dad's deep voice seemed to convey complaint and defiance; Mom was speaking calmly, her soft tones drifting upstairs and reassuring me. I imagined she was defending me.

I could hear Dad trudging across the kitchen floor. His step was naturally heavy—a clomping sound, especially when he moved fast, like when he was angry. He had polio as a child, and he walked with a limp. He couldn't serve in World War II like most of my friends' fathers, but he never complained about his limp. What he did complain about was his business, a textile wholesaling company his father had started in 1906, fresh off the boat from Lithuania. Dad called it the "rag business." He wanted to be a lawyer, but then the Depression came. He left college to help run the business and never went back. I wondered if being stuck in the rag business caused his bitterness, his hard rules and strong opinions—his current events nights.

I waited for the argument to stop, and then moved quietly downstairs to the phone and called my friend Gerry Moretti. Gerry might be someone I could trust.

Chapter Three

THE NEXT DAY, Mom drove me to school for orchestra practice. Instead of dropping me off at the school entrance, she pulled into the parking lot. This meant she wanted to talk.

My double bass sat between the back and front seat, but its long neck stuck out so far, we could barely see each other.

"Your father means well," she said, leaning over the neck of the bass.

"I know," I said without meaning it.

"No, Ray. It's true. Think about what he has on his mind. Providing for us, while the business is declining."

I winced.

"Haven't you noticed the signs?"

"I'm not sure, Mom."

"His complaints about work, and his moods?"

"Maybe."

"Well, your father and I have been talking, and I've decided to go back to work."

I shifted in my seat, stared out the window, and tried to figure out what to say. "What? What kind of work?"

"As a secretary. I did that before I met your father, you know. During the war."

"A secretary, Mom? What about your volunteer work, the temple sisterhood . . . and your hobbies, like ceramics? I mean, you just bought a kiln. And Rosie? Who's going to take care of Rosie?"

Rosie was my mom's sister and my favorite aunt. She was slow, Mom would say with a smile of benevolent understanding, and lived with my grandmother in Long Beach.

Grandma was less benevolent and in a state of perpetual irritation. At least, that's the way it seemed to me. Mom was Rosie's protector.

"Rosie will be fine. I've talked to Uncle Phil, and we've made arrangements for her."

I was trying to throw up objections, like a soldier at a barricade. Suddenly, my way of life was under attack; I was being forced to make room in my life for troubles in my parents' lives.

"Stop worrying, Ray. I'll find time for my charity work, and ceramics, too."

"So you've already decided?"

"Yes."

"Then I'll go to work, too," I blurted out. "I can pay for my bass lessons and other things."

"No, dear. You need to concentrate on school. And you're so close to Eagle Scout. How many more badges do you need?"

"Three more. But really, Mom, I can work and do everything else, too."

"Don't worry, Ray. We'll be fine. Your father will see to that. He always does, you know." Mom gave me a warm smile and squeezed my hand. "Will you be home after school?"

"Later," I said. "I'm going to practice soccer with Gerry for a while."

"That's fine, dear. Gerry's a nice boy."

I maneuvered the bass out of the car and into the school. As usual, kids made fun of me as I walked through the halls. It was all good-natured, but today I was more impatient than usual.

I began imagining how my life was about to unravel. It would start with the disappearance of small things, like Saturday night dinners at the local Chinese restaurant and nice gifts at birthdays and Chanukah, then the summer trips to Lake George. Finally, we'd be forced to move, maybe to a smaller house in town? I'd have to abandon my closet and leave the oak tree by my window forever. I started feeling nauseous and lightheaded, the way I did before current events night.

Suddenly, I heard a voice call out—Amy Carlson's voice.

I stopped and turned around, and there she was, eyes sparkling as she walked up to me. "Ray," she said, "do you know about the WABC Good Guy High School of the Year Contest?"

Like a lot of popular girls, Amy always seemed to be smiling—even at me—but we never exchanged a word. She lived in a world foreign to me: self-confident, admired, invulnerable to the insecurities most kids suffered. Or so it seemed.

I shook my head, blushing, thinking the contest was something I should know about.

She pulled a card from her pocketbook and showed it to me. I stretched my neck around the bass and read it out loud. "'South Side High School, WABC Good Guy, Amy Carlson.'" I looked back up at her, puzzled.

"Don't you know what this is, silly? You write your name on these cards, like a hundred thousand times, and the school with the most cards wins."

"Really? Wow. What do we win?"

"Well, I think they announce the school's name on the radio a lot—stuff like that."

I stared at Amy, hoping that the purpose of this contest would somehow reveal itself to me. The sound of instruments tuning up was starting to drift down the corridor. I glanced toward the orchestra room.

"Look, Ray, you and I could work together—sort of like a team. It'll go faster that way. Besides, everyone's talking about that goal you scored. Meet me at Roberta Stein's house tomorrow night, seven o'clock sharp."

"S-sure," I stammered. "Okay."

"Great. Gotta go. See you tomorrow." And she was off.

I stood in the hallway for a moment, basking in the glow of Amy's invitation.

Chapter Four

GERRY MORETTI WAS my next-door neighbor and the best soccer player I knew. But he didn't play for South Side. Gerry was Catholic, and the Catholic kids went to St. Agnes, the parochial school, so he played for them. Gerry and I used to hang out and we were still friends, but we belonged to different worlds now. The Jewish kids went to South Side with the Protestant kids, and never mixed with the Catholic kids who went to St. Agnes.

I called Gerry after current events night because I knew he could help me with soccer. Riding the bench for South Side, I was learning nothing.

First, Gerry showed me how to dribble a soccer ball. He seemed to fly right by me, but after a while I could predict his moves and slow him down. Then I tried. I couldn't get past him at first, but he taught me how to use my height, almost six feet, to feint left or right and fool defenders. I got past him a couple of times. I had a long way to go, but I saw that I could get better. A lot better.

After practice, Gerry came over for my mom's cookies. Mom was her usual gracious self, coaxing us to describe how practice went. When we were alone, I asked Gerry, "You work, don't you?"

"Yeah, at a bulk mailing business in South Hempstead. Every Saturday morning. It's pretty good. The fellas are Italian like me. And the pay is good, too. Three dollars an hour, which makes twenty-four dollars a day, and I still get off by two in the afternoon."

"You mean you start at six in the morning?"

"Yup. I leave here at five thirty and ride my bike up." He noticed I was staring at him, and chuckled. "It's okay, though. You're not interested, are you?"

"Actually, I am. Do you think I could go with you tomorrow?"

"Sure." He shrugged. "I guess so. We have to take off early, though."

"I know. Five thirty."

At 5:00 AM the next morning, I got up, dressed quickly, ate something, and left a note on the kitchen table: "Went with Gerry to see about a job. Be back at 2:30."

Gerry and I pedaled through the dark streets of Rockville Centre, across the tracks of the Long Island Railroad, and into South Hempstead. We dropped our bikes against the wall of a plain building with a sign that read South Nassau Mailing Company. Walking up to the entrance, Gerry explained that the company was a "junk mailer," which meant they mailed advertising circulars for department stores and grocery chains to homes throughout Long Island. Gerry's job was to load stencils into a machine that addressed the circulars as they shot through a chute into a bin for wrapping.

Arriving at 6:00 am on the dot, Gerry went right to work. He pointed me to the office and told me to introduce myself to the boss, Mr. Mele.

I walked into the office and saw a small, intense-looking man with a round face, curly gray hair, and large brown eyes sitting at a desk. He looked up at me, startled. "Who are you?"

"I came with Gerry, sir. He said you might need a wrapper. My name is Ray Elias."

The man's eyes brightened and his face relaxed. "Yes, we might need a wrapper," he said. "Are you a good worker like Gerry?"

"Yes, sir."

"Well then. All right, we'll see. Can you start now?"

"I guess so, sir."

My job was to grab a stack of circulars from the receiving bin as the addressing machine spit them out. Then I turned ninety degrees, placed them on a tying machine, and stepped on a pedal, which caused a long metal arm threaded with string to sweep around the stack of circulars and wrap them. All the while, more circulars were piling up, so I had to move fast to retrieve them before they jammed in the machine. Then I repeated the process. Gerry kept a watchful eye over me and pulled the circulars from the receiving bin if I fell behind. By the time our work day ended at 2:00 pm, I was skilled at my new job.

I'd also become acquainted with a new world of colorful middle-aged men. Mr. Mele had three brothers who also worked at the plant. There was Babe, the floor manager, who was the youngest and the shortest. His glasses were always slipping down his nose, which magnified his eyes, giving him the appearance of a giant fish. Little Richard, who was in charge of stencil management, was the tallest and the eldest of the brothers. He dressed all in white, which was odd because his job involved inking stencils. Yet somehow, he kept clean. Then there was Tex, a foul-mouthed truck driver with a busted nose who complained about everything. To Tex, the world was full of villains. Every social ill was caused by one group of scoundrels or another.

There were girls, too, pretty Italian girls who worked in a row on the other side of the building, poring over phone books, voting registers, death notices, and tax rolls to keep up with the changing demographics of the county. I noticed them eyeing me, but I didn't pay much attention because I was busy learning my job. I wasn't good with girls, anyway.

HUMPHREY
He cares.

"How was it?" Mom asked cheerily when I got back.

"Fine," I replied. "I like it."

Mom's eyes brightened and the corners of her mouth lifted in a smile. Dad tossed a look of approval at Mom. I think they were proud, but maybe a little miffed. I managed to land a job barely twenty-four hours after I said I wanted to—and after Mom told me not to.

That night, I watched television with Diane and basked in the cool pride of holding a job. I was now part of the world of working people earning my own way. At least, that's the way I looked at it. I was focused. But around eight o'clock, I realized I had forgotten about the WABC Good Guy party at Roberta Stein's house. "Seven o'clock sharp," Amy had said—or, more accurately, commanded. I totally blew it.

I found Roberta Stein's number in the phone book and called. Her father answered and went to find Amy. "She's busy," he reported back flatly. "Looks like they're filling out cards of some kind."

"Yes, sir. I know. Could you just tell her I'm sorry?"

"Yes, I will, son, but . . . she looked mad when I told her you were on the line."

"Okay. Thank you." My mood was wrecked; my pride dissolved into guilt.

"What's wrong?" Diane chirped.

I explained what had happened, and Diane jumped to the rescue. She found some index cards Mom used to write down recipes, and together we filled out every last one of them with the words: "South Side High School, WABC Good Guy, Ray Elias." Two hundred and thirty-five in all.

At school on Monday, I dutifully handed the stack of cards to Amy. She seemed annoyed, but she tucked them ceremoniously into her pocketbook and sauntered off without saying a word.

Chapter Five

ONE SUNDAY MORNING, Dad knocked on my bedroom door. "You up, son? I thought we might fix the picnic table this morning."

I jumped out of bed, gulped down a bowl of cereal, and joined him outside. I watched as he fitted fresh planks on the tabletop, pointing to where he wanted me to hold the wood while he nailed it down.

On the Sunday mornings that followed, we did other projects together, like reglazing the storm windows and rewiring electrical outlets. I don't know where he learned how to do those things growing up in Brooklyn, but I was happy to take orders and learn. Few words were said. I was grateful for the truce between us.

Mom took a job as a secretary at Dale Carnegie and Associates, an organization that promoted the work of the famous motivational speaker and writer. His book, *How to Win Friends and Influence People*, was a sensation. At dinner time, Mom told stories about Carnegie's legendary patience. She said that *he* never condemned anyone, and always praised and encouraged them.

I was sure Mom meant for these stories to be messages to Dad, but he listened without reaction. Or maybe she was aiming them at me! Not because I complained like Dad, but because deep down, I was not very patient. I knew that. Restless was probably a better label for it. Secretly, I feared that people could see that about me, especially Mom.

Everyone in our house was working now except Diane, who was too young, but she helped Mom with household chores. And every Saturday after work, Gerry and I played soccer. I improved so fast that he encouraged me to try out for a regular position on the team. I'd never thought of that. Even after my celebrated goal six weeks ago, the coach rarely played me. I figured it just wasn't in the cards. And whose place would I take, anyway? My teammates were friends. It didn't seem right to challenge them for their position. I wondered what Dale Carnegie would do, but I never asked my mother.

One day, one of our players, a forward, broke his ankle in a bicycle accident. When I told Coach I wanted to try out for the position, he thought I was joking. "Elias, do you seriously think you can go from a bench-warming halfback to a forward in six weeks?"

That made me mad. "Yes, sir, I do."

"Okay. Let's see what you can do. This should be interesting."

He set up a scrimmage with other boys. I dribbled past the defenders the way Gerry taught me and scored. The second time, the defenders tried harder to stop me, but I still got past some of them. I spotted the coach scratching his head, which was as satisfying as winning the position. Though the season was winding down, I became a starter. I had gone from a nerdy, no-talent benchwarmer to starting forward. *Unbelievable.*

I felt good about it. Proud. It was proof that I could do something nobody thought I could do. It was different than doing well in school, playing the bass, or earning badges for Eagle Scout. Those were accomplishments for sure, but in a way, they were things I just *did*, as Dad said. Trusting Gerry to teach me soccer taught me I could do something unexpected and learn something new about myself, the truth about who I was. Now I wanted to do it again, with something bigger.

On November 22, 1963, the Friday afternoon before Thanksgiving, I walked into social studies class and was accosted by my friend Ronnie.

Ronnie Klein was tall and dark with straight black hair, slicked back like an Italian movie star. The only thing was, he had acne, a bad case of it that marred the impression. But his brashness endeared him to everyone.

"Ray," he said, "you gotta help me."

"Why? What happened?"

"I didn't come up with a name."

"What name?"

"You know, the biography project. We have to pick a name."

"Oh yeah. I forgot about that."

"Can you think of a name? You're good with current events."

"What about Nehru?" I said absent-mindedly.

"What's a Nehru? C'mon, give me a real name."

"He happens to be the prime minister of India."

"All right, fine. I can go with that."

Mr. Francis, a balding man with horn-rimmed glasses and a permanently troubled expression, entered the classroom and plopped a stack of books on the desk. "I'm sure all of you are ready with brilliant topics for our biography project."

The class let out a collective groan.

Undeterred, he plowed on. "Maybe today someone will succeed in convincing me that teaching was a better career choice than my brother-in-law's plumbing business."

A few students chuckled, but his comments about his brother-in-law had lost their novelty. Mr. Francis pretended to be aggravated by his fate, imprisoned in a classroom of unappreciative teenagers instead of enjoying the lucrative rewards of the plumbing business. But he didn't mean it. A gleam in his eye betrayed his sarcasm. He made jokes, but he never raised his voice or looked bored, and he was never too busy to help a student after class.

"What's his first name?" Ronnie persisted in a whisper.

"Whose?"

"Nehru! Hey, what's the matter with you today, Ray?"

"Nothing, I'm fine. It's Jawaharlal."

"What?" Ronnie eyed me doubtfully.

"I said I'm fine."

"No, I mean the name. Jah something? What kind of name is that?"

"It's an Indian name, you nut. He's Indian."

"How do you spell it?"

Mr. Francis was glaring at us. "Mr. Elias and Mr. Klein. Would you mind suspending your deliberations while we proceed with class?"

"Yes, sir," Ronnie said with exaggerated deference.

"Thank you," Mr. Francis said and turned to Janet Abrams, who sat in the first seat in the first row. "Miss Abrams, let's start with you. Who have you selected for the biography project?"

"I've selected John F. Kennedy, president of the United States."

Mr. Francis eyed her imperiously, juggling a piece of chalk in his hand. "Miss Abrams, our president is a fine man, but have you considered someone a bit, shall we say, less obvious?" He surveyed the students' faces. "Hmm. All right. How many Kennedys do we have?"

Eight students raised their hands. A quarter of the class.

Ronnie was still pestering me for Nehru's first name when Mr. Francis's voice boomed in our direction.

"Mr. Klein!"

Ronnie leaped to attention. "Yes, sir, Mr. Francis."

"I'm very interested to know if your consultations with Mr. Elias have yielded anything of value to the rest of the class."

"Absolutely, sir . . . Nehru."

"Nehru?"

"Yes, sir. He's prime minister of India. That's an under-developed country."

"Okay, so what is it about Mr. Nehru that inspires you?"

"He's inspiring me to develop."

The class exploded with laughter.

"He's probably got an easier job reviving the Indian econ-omy," Mr. Francis said, shaking his head. "By the way, Mr. Klein, does Mr. Nehru have a first name?"

"Of course," Ronnie said confidently. "It's Jaywall."

"Jay what?"

"That's his first name. Jaywall."

"I see." Mr. Francis transferred his gaze to me. "Now, Mr. Elias, having collaborated with Mr. Klein so impressively, may I inquire what famous personality you have reserved for yourself?"

"Actually, I don't have one."

The class turned toward me in unison, then turned back to Mr. Francis.

"Surely, Mr. Elias, in the pantheon of world figures, there is someone who merits your admiration."

"Well, sir, I'm sure there is. But . . . I need more time to figure out who."

The class laughed, but I didn't mean to be funny.

Mr. Francis's tone softened. "Did you not understand the assignment, Ray? To choose someone—"

"I understand the assignment, Mr. Francis. But I didn't want to pick just anyone. I'm sorry."

Mr. Francis nodded. "Okay. Okay. See if you can resolve your indecision in a timely fashion."

"Yes, sir."

Just then, three sharp chimes rang out. Every pair of eyes in the room shot up to the speaker above the blackboard; announcements were never made while class was in session. A sharp, urgent voice broke in. "Attention, teachers and students. Attention please, attention." It was the principal.

There was a long pause, then shuffling sounds and indistinct voices in the background. "The president of the United States . . ." The principal's voice faltered. "God help us," he muttered.

We all looked at each other, some giggling anxiously.

"President Kennedy was shot in Dallas."

The girls gasped; the boys frowned. Another long pause. No one moved.

"President Kennedy . . . President Kennedy . . . is dead."

Shrieks pierced the room. Mr. Francis slumped into his seat and covered his eyes.

"Classes are suspended," the principal continued. "Proceed quietly to your homes."

We trudged in silence through the hallway to our lockers. Ronnie looked at me pleadingly. "What do we do now?"

I started pulling books from my locker. Ronnie was staring at me blankly. "Hey Ray, why are you cleaning out your locker? We'll be coming back to school on Monday, won't we?"

Confused, I looked at him, then put my books back and walked out of the school empty-handed.

When I got home, I retreated to my room and curled up in bed, listening to accounts of the assassination on a transistor radio and staring at the big oak tree. I felt as if my body and mind had separated, like I was watching myself listening to the radio and not actually hearing it. I felt myself sliding into guilt, not for anything I had actually done, but because I had failed to appreciate President Kennedy.

He was the first president I was aware of, but I'd never paid much attention to politics. I knew only the things that everyone knew. He was young, vigorous, and smart. He spoke intelligently to people. Even as a sixteen-year-old I could see that he tried to elevate and inspire people, not divide or talk down to them. And Jackie Kennedy was glamorous too, even to a kid. They were a romantic couple, dazzling in their perfection.

Now he was gone, permanently cut off, forever lost. All that was left were scattered memories of press conferences and speeches I'd seen, and a sense of longing for what I would never see again. I understood that life was not stable or predictable. Even the life of an entire nation could be upended in an instant by events no one could foresee or control.

I was lost in these thoughts when Dad walked in, pulled my desk chair over to the bed, and sat down. "Are you all right, son?"

Tears running down my face, I looked up at my father. "What's going to happen, Dad?"

"We'll get through it, son," he said, putting a hand on my shoulder. I felt consoled for a moment. Then he seemed to resume his role as the stern interpreter of reality: "Life goes on."

He was right, of course. Life *was* going on. Lyndon Johnson was the new president, and the country would dig itself out of the rubble of tragedy as it always had. But there was more to life than watching events unfold in predictable sequence. I wanted to be reassured that my emotions would settle down and the world would offer encouragement again. I didn't know how to get that reassurance, but I figured it was the job of a parent to know.

I pulled my shoulder away and put the radio earpiece back in my ear. Dad got up and walked out. I knew it was hurtful, but I was too angry to care. I refused to be part of such a cold vision and lifeless perception of things.

The rest of 1963 passed by like a dream. Thanksgiving wasn't much of a holiday; the nation was in mourning. Our family got together with Uncle Phil, Grandma, and Aunt

Rosie, but the day felt mechanical and cheerless. Holiday decorations showed up around Rockville Centre, but they were later than usual and less lavish. A Christmas snow brightened the neighborhood, but a pallor hung over the town.

As the calendar crept toward 1964, time seemed to slow as the year drew to a close. But the new year finally arrived, and with it, a feeling of relief. We could begin to think of the Kennedy assassination as "last year."

PART TWO

Winter–Summer 1964

Chapter Six

EARLY ON A COLD and still Sunday morning in January, I drove from my home in Chevy Chase to the United States Capitol. Muriel and the kids were still sleeping.

The Capitol police greeted me with a "Morning, Senator Humphrey," and puzzled looks. *What is a United States senator doing at the Capitol at 6:00 am on a Sunday morning?* I wasn't sure myself. But the Capitol was my workplace, and there was so much work to be done.

I took my seat in the Senate chamber, alone but for a single guard standing watch by the door. My mind tumbled through the tragedies that had befallen our nation. There had been other assassinations—Lincoln, Garfield, and McKinley—but this tragedy was deeply personal. John Kennedy was not just my president, but my friend.

Four years ago, on winter mornings just like this, we had faced off in West Virginia and Wisconsin, competing in the primaries. We were opponents for the presidency, but we were never enemies. He beat me with money and superior organization, but the truth is, I was whipped by an extraordinary man.

We were very different people, President Kennedy and I. He was Catholic, and New England nobility. His father was one of the richest men in America, with oceanfront homes on Cape Cod and at Palm Beach; all the boys went to Harvard. I was the son of Norwegian immigrants and Quakers, growing up amid dust storms and the haggard faces of hungry neighbors. My father moved us from town to town, always on the verge of going broke. I had barely enrolled at college when

Dad summoned me home to work.

Kennedy's life was a storybook; mine was a case study in hardship. But he had faced loss, too. And now he was gone.

Unsettled by this reminiscence, I pitched my chair forward, sending a loud creak reverberating through the empty Senate chamber. The guard took a step toward me, then halted when I offered a reassuring nod.

I began to think of my first years as senator, when few were willing to call me a friend. I was shunned by the Southerners for advocating civil rights; even Northern liberals thought I was pushing the issue too hard. My fellow Midwestern senators, nearly all Republicans, called me an unpolished upstart. I guess I was. I tried to help people who were deprived of the opportunities others took for granted. For a while, I was on everybody's blacklist.

Civil rights was in the news again. Dr. Martin Luther King Jr. had electrified the nation with his "I Have a Dream" speech, and John Kennedy had responded with a sweeping bill just before he was killed. President Johnson pledged to sign the bill if it passed the Senate and put me in charge of getting the votes for it. A surge of pride ran through me, a pulse of defiance. Yes sir, I was going to take on the prejudices of my colleagues once again, on behalf of my Negro countrymen.

Chapter Seven

ON A SUNDAY AFTERNOON in mid-January, Mom and Dad were taking down the holiday decorations when I walked into the living room. We were Jewish, but Mom's father, Grandpa Jack, was Irish, so we had both Christmas and Chanukah decorations over the fireplace. Diane was sprawled on the couch doing homework. Mom handed ornaments to Dad, who packed them in a large box with a special compartment for each one.

They performed this ritual every year, and they did it fast. But sometimes Mom got ahead of Dad and paused to let him catch up. I waited for that moment. Mom held a handful of tinsel while Dad finished packing up Santa and his reindeer.

"Am I going too fast for you, honey?" she asked.

"No, no, I've got it."

That was my moment. "Mom, is it okay if I eat dinner in the living room tonight? There's this show on TV." I thrust a newspaper in her hands with the TV listings.

I smiled nervously at Dad while Mom looked over the paper. This was her call. Dad ruled current events night and a million other things, but when it came to food—what was prepared, when it was served, and where it was eaten—Mom called the shots.

"Sure," she replied, handing the newspaper back to me.

Diane jumped up from the couch. "Me too."

"Thanks, Mom," I said. As I hurried upstairs, I could hear Mom say to Dad, "It's something about the Kennedy election."

"He's dwelling on the assassination," Dad sneered.

"It's fine, honey. He needs to go through this in his own way."

Before the show, I lugged my reel-to-reel tape recorder downstairs, a gift I bought myself with my mailing house earnings, plus a little extra Mom pitched in for Chanukah. Diane hovered while I connected the TV speaker wires to the recorder. I flicked the TV on, hit the record button, and waited. A soft green light began to flash on the recorder, which meant it was working. I pumped a fist in the air. "Yay," Diane said, pumping her fist, too.

The show's title flashed across the screen: *The Making of the President 1960.* The broadcast opened with a shot of the Oval Office and a soaring brass fanfare. "This is a story of power," the narrator began solemnly. "This room is its sanctuary. The man who occupies this desk directs the awesome power that defines the United States of America."

Mom called out from the kitchen, summoning Diane. My sister leaped into action and returned with two small TV tables. I noticed that the green volume meter was no longer oscillating. "This contraption isn't working," I whispered to Diane. "I have to record with the microphone, so be quiet."

Diane brought a finger to her lips and nodded.

The narrator continued. "In the one hundred and eighty-fourth year of their republic, the American people faced the quadrennial responsibility of investing immense power in a new leader in that tumultuous spectacle called a presidential campaign."

Dad walked into the living room and announced loudly, "You can get your dinner now."

Diane turned to him with a finger thrust against her lips. "Shush."

He shot her a look of annoyance and walked away. Moments later, Mom walked in with two plates of food and gently put them on the TV tables, then sat down to watch.

Amid a rousing patriotic melody, the screen depicted cold

prairie country. John F. Kennedy held out his hand to hard-scrabble miners and factory workers. The narrator somberly continued his description of the 1960 West Virginia and Wisconsin Democratic primaries: "In the winter of 1960, two Democrats vied for the mantle of power, Senator Hubert Humphrey of Minnesota and Senator John Kennedy of Massachusetts. Humphrey brings his homespun zeal to the effort, handing out recipes of wife Muriel's black bean soup."

Diane was plunging into her meal, but I was intrigued by the depiction of Humphrey, who was shown greeting supporters in his modest campaign headquarters. I was struck by his genial simplicity. He seemed warm and personal. A folksy background rhythm added to my impression of Humphrey as a sincere and humble man. His voice was gravelly with fatigue, yet buoyant with enthusiasm. Muriel smiled by his side.

"It's been Muriel and me," Humphrey said. "You see, I sort of feel like an independent merchant competing against a chain store when I run against the Kennedy family."

Dad drifted into the room and stood next to Mom, watching the television.

"Humphrey's campaign evokes America of an earlier day," the narrator continued, "of New Deal progressivism and the populism of old. He is the common man's candidate, and he speaks the language of the downtrodden and disadvantaged. The factory workers of Wisconsin and the unemployed coal miners of West Virginia are his people, and he presses his cause with down-home zeal."

On-screen, a singer with a guitar at the Humphrey campaign headquarters on primary night was trying to drum up excitement, belting out lyrics to the tune of "The Ballad of Davy Crockett":

Humphrey is a senator, a neighbor, a friend.
We're gonna stick with him all the way to the end.
He used to come over just to help us out.

It's our turn to help him without any doubt.
So vote for Hubert, Hubert Humphrey, the Democrat for you
and me.

"I'm not sure I've ever heard of Hubert Humphrey,"
Mom said. "Who is he, dear?" She asked me the question, but
Dad answered: "He's a senator from Minnesota. Very liberal."

I glanced at Dad. *He meant that as a criticism*, I thought.

The narrator continued. "On May 10th, 1960, West Vir-
ginians cast their ballots. By midnight, the verdict was clear. A
Kennedy victory, sixty–forty."

Diane cheered.

"And so, Humphrey spoke to his supporters for the last
time."

The documentary cut to footage of Humphrey making his
concession speech: "'I withdraw my candidacy for president
of the United States. I shall run for reelection to the United
States Senate and continue to work for progressive policies
that support the millions of Americans who have been left behind in the wake of this great nation's prosperity.'"

The singer onstage with Humphrey tried to raise spirits
with a tune but slumped over dejectedly. Humphrey walked
over and embraced him, then flashed a big smile to his campaign workers.

The narrator closed the chapter on Humphrey with these
words: "First casualty of the 1960 primaries, Humphrey leaves
a glow of devotion on his followers."

The show went to commercial, an invitation to "see the
USA in your Chevrolet." I sat motionless, fixated on the
screen.

I silently repeated the narrator's last words. *Humphrey
leaves a glow of devotion on his followers.* I could see that! I understood why he inspired devotion. There was something down-
to-earth about Humphrey. He was committed to regular
people in an honest way, with genuine emotion. He was not

polished like John Kennedy but still charismatic.

I could feel my parents' eyes on me, waiting for me to react. I smiled and they relaxed. Diane giggled. The spell was broken. But it wasn't President Kennedy who had moved me. It was Hubert Humphrey.

As I lay wide awake in bed that night, I thought about Hubert Humphrey. I wondered what caused my sudden attraction to a senator I had never heard of from a far-off state. I wasn't even that interested in politics. Politics was something that adults did. They always seemed so serious when they talked about it and most of the time wound up in an argument. I considered myself informed on the big issues—current events night took care of that—but I wasn't really interested in the lives of politicians. I didn't understand why people sought power. It seemed like pure ego, and when adults argued about politics, they seemed egotistical, too.

But Humphrey appeared to cut through that. He looked like a decent and caring man without pretenses. He broke the stereotypes. He was direct and accessible. Someone you could trust. I wanted to know more about him.

I got out of bed and tiptoed past my parents' bedroom and down the stairs to the basement. On a shelf between Dad's workbench and Mom's ceramics table was a stack of *Life* magazines. *Life* featured the most popular figures of the day on its cover, and I wondered if Humphrey had appeared there. Sifting through images of famous actors, politicians, sports heroes, musicians, astronauts, and writers, I came across the issue from March 28, 1960, featuring Humphrey and Kennedy. The cover story was the political primaries I had just seen on TV.

I kept going back and found the January 1959 issue with Humphrey on the cover dressed in a fur hat. The caption read, "Eight Hours with Khrushchev, by Hubert Humphrey." Humphrey described how a routine goodwill meeting with the Russian premier evolved into an eight-hour debate marathon over disarmament. I devoured every word.

As dawn was about to break, I was back in my room making a list of questions I had about Humphrey: Where was he born? What was his childhood like? What did he study in college? Why did he go into politics? But most of all, I wanted to understand what caused my instant connection to him. I decided to go to the public library where I could find answers. For the second time that night, I sneaked past my parents' bedroom and down the stairs, this time out the back door to retrieve my bike for the ride to the library.

Chapter Eight

"UP EARLY?"

My wife's voice pierced the pre-dawn tranquility as I sat at our kitchen table in Chevy Chase.

In the quiet moments of our lives—when the kids were at school or sleeping as they were now—we talked. Muriel's old-fashioned common sense could whisk away my woes and worries. She was fifty-two, with gray hair and a bearing that the press called stately, but I still saw the shapely coed with the self-confident smile I'd met in South Dakota thirty years ago.

Her parents looked down on me at first. We were new-comers in Huron, having struggled in Doland. Our house was modest and Muriel lived in a grand home on the better side of town; that is, until the Depression claimed her family, too. And of course, we were Democrats in a place where Democrats were looked upon as a ragged bunch of uncivilized rascals. The Humphreys were "different," her father declared.

It didn't help matters that I called for Muriel after midnight, when my work at Dad's store was done. Even so, we managed to get in a little dancing, sometimes until dawn. But I almost lost her, and work was the culprit. Soon after we were engaged, I had to work even longer hours because Dad gave employees time off for vacation. That was the last straw for Muriel and she threatened to leave for California. I came to my senses and, shortly after, we got married. In the tug-of-war between my love for Muriel and my loyalty to Dad, Muriel won. That time.

"I was just thinking . . . ." I began.

Muriel sat down beside me. "About what, Dad?"

"If I can get this civil rights bill passed for Lyndon, the vice presidency could be my reward."

"Get it passed for Lyndon? Civil rights is *your* life's work."

"I know. I know. I'm just saying that my best bet for another crack at the presidency is through the vice presidency."

"Lyndon is unpredictable, Hubert."

"After twelve years in the Senate, I think I know the man."

"You were equals in the Senate," she said flatly.

"What do you mean?"

"He's president now. Things are different. And . . ."

"What?"

"Lyndon has a cruel streak."

I got up, walked to the window of the breakfast nook, and watched the early morning light seep through the scarlet oak trees. Ambition ran through me like a restless prairie wind. I knew Muriel was trying to tame it. I would drop it for now.

"Okay, Mom. How about a little breakfast?"

"Oatmeal with brown sugar?"

"Yup, my favorite."

Chapter Nine

I PEDALED ACROSS TOWN through the early morning cold. It was Monday, so there was more traffic than on my Saturday bike rides to the mailing company. I arrived at the Rockville Centre Public Library, guided my bike into the rack, and walked in, the library's first patron.

By 3:30 p.m. I was hunched over a dozen books and magazines, delving deep into the life of Hubert Humphrey. Nicknamed "Pinky," he grew up working the soda fountain at his father's drugstore in Doland, South Dakota. Times were tough. Humphrey came home from high school one day and found his parents sitting under the big cottonwood tree on the front lawn, weeping. They told him their house had just been sold and they'd be moving to a small place on the other side of town. It was the only way to pay the bills, his father explained. Humphrey had never seen his father cry.

Then they moved again, to Huron, a larger South Dakota town. After high school, Humphrey enrolled at the University of Minnesota, living on ten dollars a week he earned washing dishes at the campus drugstore. But his father continued to struggle, and summoned Humphrey home to work.

It was hard for me to imagine that the man who debated Khrushchev and battled John Kennedy for the presidential nomination once labored in his father's drugstore, against his will, with no salary, swiping coins from the till to date his girl-friend, Muriel Buck.

Reading about Humphrey's boyhood, I felt lucky in a way. My father's financial hardships were nothing compared to what Humphrey went through during the Depression.

There was no doubt I would go to college. I applied early to the University of Chicago and was accepted. Still, I wondered. Would Dad summon me home to work in the "rag business," or stop paying for college because I wasn't "focused"? Maybe not, but I understood what it was like for Humphrey to have his spirit crushed by a demanding father.

Humphrey did find a way out, and Muriel stuck with him. She dropped out of college, worked, and saved enough in two years, $675, to set off for Minneapolis. Humphrey resumed college and began to make a name for himself in public life: first as a director of the Works Progress Administration, a Depression-era works program, then as mayor of Minneapolis. As senator, he had risen to the position of Majority Whip, the second highest in the Senate.

Pondering the bumpy trajectory of Humphrey's life, I was oblivious to a group of kids from school walking into the library until Amy pulled up beside me.

"Hi, Ray."

"Oh, hi, Amy."

"How long have you been here?"

"All day, I guess."

"All day!" she exclaimed. "It's a school day!"

"I know. I missed school today."

Amy took a step toward the table, boldly fingering the books in front of me. "What's all this stuff?"

"I'm researching a senator named Hubert Humphrey."

She giggled. "What a funny name. Is he from New York?"

"No, actually, he's a senator from another state. Minnesota."

"Minnesota! What class is that for?"

"No class. I'm just interested in him."

"Oh."

"I might like to work for him someday," I added.

"Work for him. How?" She narrowed her eyes.

"Well, I'm not sure. I haven't figured that out yet."

"I don't understand."

"I know. It's kind of hard to explain."

A moment passed. I gave Amy an imploring look, hoping she could somehow understand the raw inspiration behind skipping school to research some senator from Minnesota and not even for a class, just on a whim.

I broke the silence with another attempt. "I just think that people like Humphrey . . . you know, people who've accomplished something . . . can help us understand what we are meant to do."

Amy shifted her body, taking a step back and folding her arms.

"I mean what to strive for," I stammered on. "You know, and how to help fix things that are wrong."

"Sure, Ray," she shrugged. "I guess so."

"Like Hubert Humphrey does. For instance, take civil rights—"

"Maybe I'd better let you get back to . . . Herbert Montgomery."

"Hubert Humphrey."

"Whatever." And with a wave of her hand, she trotted off to her friends.

At 7:00 PM the library lights flashed, signifying closing time. I'd been there twelve hours straight. I hadn't eaten all day and had barely slept the night before. I was starting to fade. The librarian, Mr. Savoy, an elderly gentleman dressed in a suit and bow tie with a permanently worried look on his face, walked over to me, carrying a huge reel of film.

"You found it!" I shouted.

Mr. Savoy raised a finger to his lips to quiet me. "I did, son. But it's late. The library is closing. I just called your parents. They didn't know you were here?"

I felt guilty. I hadn't thought to call my parents. Now there would be hell to pay. I turned away from Mr. Savoy, embarrassed.

"But I suppose we could take a quick look before they get here." He smiled kindly. "I'm curious about what you see in Hubert Humphrey."

He led me into a small screening room and carefully threaded the newsreel of the 1948 Democratic National Convention through the sprockets of a 16 mm projector. The voice of the narrator crackled to life: "With Harry Truman's nomination a foregone conclusion, attention shifted to the fiery young mayor of Minneapolis, Hubert Humphrey, and his crusade to make Negro rights a part of the Democratic platform."

Humphrey looked boyish then; his primary run against Kennedy for the presidency was twelve years off. But his manner was the same: his head slightly cocked, his hand reaching out, finger pointing upward, eyes fierce with conviction and eyebrows arched for combat.

"There are those who say we are rushing this issue of civil rights," Humphrey said. "I say we are a hundred and seventy-two years late."

On the newsreel, cheers mixed with jeers throughout the hall.

"There are those who say this issue of civil rights is an infringement on states' rights," Humphrey continued. "Well, I say the time has arrived for the Democratic Party to get out of the shadow of states' rights and walk forthrightly into the bright sunshine of human rights."

Suddenly, there was a pounding at the door of the library. Mr. Savoy got up and returned with my father. They both stood silently, watching Humphrey conclude his speech.

"Let us forget the evil passions, the blindness of the past. That path has already led us through valleys of the shadow of death. Now is the time to recall those who were left behind on the path of American freedom."

As the audience exploded into a thunderous ovation on-screen, Dad walked over and put his hand on my shoulder.

"We didn't see you this morning; we thought you left early for school. But you've been here all day. Isn't that right, sir?" He turned to Mr. Savoy, who nodded. "What's this sudden passion for Hubert Humphrey?" he asked me.

"I'll leave you two alone," Mr. Savoy interjected, backing out of the room.

"I don't think I can explain it right now, Dad."

"I'm just trying to understand, son. Last night you'd never even heard of this man."

There was something less stiff and resistant in Dad's voice; he seemed sincere, so I opened up a little. "There's something I saw in him, Dad, a kind of honesty—"

"Honest! A politician? What do you really know about him?"

"A lot," I protested, sliding my chair back abruptly. "I've been studying him all day. I can tell he cares about people and he fights injustice. I feel I can trust him."

My father bit his lip, closed his eyes, and looked down at the floor. I had seen this look before: Dad's sudden way of retreating into a private world. What usually followed was reproach of some kind. Would he tell me again that I was unfocused? Instead, he turned sharply and walked out of the room.

I hastily collected my stuff and followed him.

Outside, Dad lifted my bike from the rack and put it in the car. "You know, son," he said, finally breaking the silence, "if you looked a little harder, you might find the qualities you admire closer to home."

I didn't know what to say. I didn't feel I was wrong in admiring Hubert Humphrey, but I felt guilty that I made Dad feel bad.

Chapter Ten

SOON, I BECAME an expert on Hubert Humphrey. I researched every Senate bill he was working on. I learned every Minnesota town and village he'd recently visited. I learned what he had for breakfast as a child—oatmeal and brown sugar—and asked Mom to make it for me.

I was living and breathing Hubert Humphrey, and it was contagious. Kids at South Side started calling me Hubert, and since my middle initial was H—as in, Ray Howard Elias—I just pretended that it stood for Hubert.

Studying Humphrey, I became confident in my knowledge of the big issues of the day. Current events night had been suspended after the blowup last fall, but I now had a new way to stay on top of national events: I subscribed to the *Congressional Record*, the official record of proceedings in the Senate and House of Representatives. It was delivered to my house every morning at 6:00 am by special courier, and I got up early to read it. Before long, I could name every United States senator—all one hundred of them—by state, and I knew where most of them stood on the main issues.

I was learning that getting involved in politics was more than watching the news or reading the newspaper. It meant taking a stand on the big problems facing the nation, even if you were a kid. It meant believing in America, and it meant being committed to building a better country.

I also saw lots of politicians talking about the ideals of our country, but not many of them were really committed to making those ideals work. Hubert Humphrey was, and he had been working for twenty years to make civil rights a reality for Negroes.

I also learned a lot about racism. I thought about those four Negro girls killed in the Birmingham church last September. I knew that four white girls would never be burned alive in a church just for being white, but those four girls were murdered just for being black.

Over the next several weeks, I worked out a plan: a campaign to make Hubert Humphrey vice president of the United States. Crazy, I know. But why not? The country had been without a vice president since the year before, when President Kennedy was assassinated. Johnson was running for president in his own right, and he needed a running mate. Humphrey was perfect—a civil rights advocate, great orator, and sponsor of more important legislation than any living senator.

But what could a kid do? Was anyone going to pay attention to a teenager campaigning for someone to be vice president? And how would I raise money? I needed advice from an experienced businessman like my father, but asking him was out of the question. "Overblown" was what he called my passion for Humphrey. He also called it an "affectation" and a "passing fancy." More labels!

Still, to launch my campaign, I needed help. Ronnie was a natural. He loved to create mischief, so I knew my plan would appeal to him. He came on board right away. Two soccer buddies were next on my list. Dave Browdy was our star forward, a great athlete and popular in school; I figured those skills would come in handy. Marc Snyder was a genius at logistics, and I knew he could help me plan the campaign. Marc and David signed on, and with Ronnie, I had my core staff.

One night in early May, the four of us gathered in Ronnie's basement for our first big campaign push: publishing our first campaign flyer. Ronnie found an old mimeograph machine from God knows where, and I got a stencil from the mailing house, one of the big ones that I could type the whole flyer on. I worked all day on it. I had to go slow, plucking one letter at a time: one mistake, and the stencil would be ruined.

But it was done and now it was time to print. The four of us stood over the machine, puzzling over its buttons and levers, terrified that this contraption would eat the stencil and doom our project. Finally, I pressed the start button, and the stencil started moving around the drum to ink up. It printed one sheet and then another, picking up speed until it was spitting out ten sheets per minute. After an hour, we had run off 500 flyers, enough for half the school.

As Marc and I monitored the printing, Ronnie and Dave rolled up a giant red, white, and blue banner made up of three bedsheets stitched together by Diane, painted with the words Hubert Humphrey for Vice President in '64. She wanted to help with the campaign, so Mom showed her how to sew the banner together.

"You boys ready?" I asked, as if we were launching a secret mission in enemy territory. Which, in a way, we were.

They nodded solemnly.

"Okay, let's go."

As we left the basement, Ronnie picked up the mimeograph machine.

"Why are you bringing that?" I asked.

"Let's just say I have to return it to school before anyone notices."

"Oh my God, you stole it from school?"

"I borrowed it."

"How are you going to get in? I mean, it's the middle of the night."

"You don't want to know."

I shook my head, and off we went to the high school in Ronnie's parents' car. We parked alongside the sweeping abutment on the west side of the building called the colonnade. Six oval concrete pillars held up its roof. On my signal, David climbed the oak tree that leaned lazily over the colonnade; in thirty seconds, he was at the top. I followed him up the tree. Marc and Ronnie heaved the banner up to us, and we quickly attached it to the building's facade.

As students and teachers arrived at school that morning, the first thing they saw was our banner. Ronnie, Marc, David, and I were stationed by the entrance, passing out our mimeographed flyers. A large white poster board sat on an easel—an improvised birthday card. Humphrey's fifty-third birthday was on May 29, barely three weeks away, and my goal was to get at least 300 signatures on the card.

Ronnie was in his element, hitting students up for donations to the Humphrey for Vice President Campaign Fund. "Look, Hubert Humphrey is going to be vice president," he shouted, "and he's gonna know who was too cheap to kick in for the campaign."

Amy, walking by with her girlfriends, strutted up to me. "So Ray, I see now what you were doing in the library that day."

"That's right, Amy," I said proudly.

"I get it. This is like the WABC Good Guy High School of the Year Contest, right?"

"What? No. I'm campaigning for Hubert Humphrey to be vice president."

"That's silly," she scoffed. "Everyone knows you can't campaign for vice president." She turned on her heel and went back to her friends.

Scores of kids were dropping coins in the donation jar and then shuffling into position to sign the giant birthday card. Marc decided it was time to step up the excitement, encouraging the crowd to sing. "You'll find the words to our campaign jingle on the flyer," he said, and then sang the first two lines: *"Humphrey is a senator, a neighbor, a friend. We're gonna stick with him all the way to the end."*

But only a few students joined in. "C'mon" Marc cajoled. "Sing so they can hear you in Washington."

More students began to sing, hesitantly. *"He used to come over just to help us out. It's our turn to help him without any doubt."*

More joined in, and the chorus swelled.

"So vote for Hubert . . . Hubert Humphrey, vice president for you and me."

More students lined up; the birthday card was filling up, and so were the coffers. Teachers passed by, puzzled by the activity.

"What are they doing?" one of them asked Mr. Francis as I thrust a flyer in his hand.

"I don't know," he replied. "As far as I know, you can't campaign for vice president."

Chapter Eleven

I WAS DASHING OFF the Senate floor, lobbing questions at my closest aides as they trailed me through the Capitol's corridors.

"What's our latest tally on cloture, John? We need to end this filibuster and get to a vote on the bill."

"Four votes shy, Senator."

"Are you counting Scott from Pennsylvania and Williams from New Jersey?"

"Yes, sir."

"Good. If Dirksen comes on board, he'll bring more Republicans with him."

"Dirksen just scheduled a press conference for six o'clock this evening, Senator," said another aide, Bill Connell. "Looks like your lobbying effort with him paid off."

"I hope so. I've been courting him as persistently as I did Muriel."

Everyone laughed. Dan Grant broke in, "But Senator, aren't you a little worried about Dirksen getting the credit?"

Danny was asking the question on all their minds. My staff was looking out for me. If Everett Dirksen, the Republican leader, delivered the last few votes to end the filibuster, he would get the credit; the work I had done to line up most of the votes would fade. But I knew a watchful president would be assessing my role, judging my fitness as his running mate this year.

"No, Danny," I answered. "I'm not worried about that. This is the greatest single congressional enactment since the Fourteenth Amendment. If we pass it, there'll be plenty of credit to go around."

The aides nodded respectfully and took off down the corridor.

Danny followed me into my office, where we were greeted with a chorus of "Happy Birthday" from my three secretaries. It was May 27, my fifty-third birthday. A large cake rested on one of the desks, and one of the secretaries handed me a knife to cut it.

"I'm certain you've put a few too many candles on the cake," I joked, and everyone laughed. I took in an enormous breath and blew out all fifty-three of them.

"Senator," one of the secretaries said, "you received a rather unusual birthday card from a high school in New York."

She propped up a huge poster board on her desk with hundreds of signatures on it.

"Did you say New York?"

She handed me a stack of documents and I passed half to Danny. "Yes," she replied. "A sixteen-year-old boy and his class have taken an active interest in your prospects as President Johnson's running mate this year."

I started sifting through the package. "Sixteen!"

"Yes, his name is Ray Elias."

I motioned for Danny to follow me into my private office. "Danny, look at this. He's got a campaign brochure, fact sheets, strategy analyses, even campaign songs!"

"I know, Senator. From the looks of this stuff, he's become your professional biographer."

"Did you see these bumper stickers? 'Hubert Humphrey for Vice President '64'!"

"Yes, sir, and he plans to contact all the delegates. All two thousand of them. Apparently, he's raised enough money to do it."

"My gosh. Look what he wrote here. 'To the millions of Americans who live on the border of despair, Hubert

Humphrey has brought forth a vision of hope.'"

"Yes, it's an impressive piece, Senator. But Johnson's not going to believe it came from a high school kid."

"I know, I know. I can scarcely believe it myself."

Chapter Twelve

I WAS WALKING to the front of Mr. Francis's social studies class to start reading my biography report when Mr. Francis stopped me. "Mr. Elias. Would I be correct in assuming that your topic is a certain senator from the state of Minnesota?"

The class laughed. For weeks, Hubert Humphrey had been the talk of the school. Classmates came up to me all the time with ideas about how to promote Humphrey for vice president. Even teachers stopped me in the hallway to chat about the civil rights bill making its way through the Senate under Humphrey's stewardship. For once, everyone in social studies class was paying attention.

"I'll tell you what, Mr. Elias," Mr. Francis said. "I'm sure you know your material. So why don't we try something different."

"Okay," I said hesitantly.

How about you put away your notes and just let me ask questions. How does that sound? A kind of interview?"

I nodded cautiously.

Mr. Francis looked around the room. "Wouldn't that be more interesting, class?"

Students nodded tentatively, unsure of what this new approach would yield.

"Great," said Mr. Francis. "Let me start off with this question. What do you find most compelling about Senator Humphrey?"

I launched right in. "It's the way he spots injustice and then tackles it head-on, as if there's no way he could fail."

"Go on," Mr. Francis urged. "Tell us what you mean."

"Well, I have a story that explains it. Can I tell it?"

"Yes, of course."

"Before becoming a senator, Humphrey was mayor of Minneapolis. He ran on a platform of civil rights, an unusual thing in 1945. Well, one day, he paid a visit to Carl Dayton, head of Dayton's Department Store, and said, 'Now, Carl, I want you to start hiring Negroes. Set an example.' Dayton didn't want to do it, so Humphrey said, 'Carl, I understand your position, but I'm advising you that if you don't hire Negroes, we're going to cancel all of Dayton's contracts with the city.' The result was that Dayton's became the first department store in the country to hire Negroes. And Minneapolis became the first city in the country to pass an antidiscrimination ordinance."

Mr. Francis nodded thoughtfully.

"Some might call what Humphrey did coercion," I continued. "But what he was really saying was, 'I'm not going to condemn you for the way you want the world to be. That's up to you. But I'm determined to change the world because Negroes deserve a rightful place in it. And if I have to cancel the city's contracts with you to do it, well, that's what I'm going to do.'"

The class looked at Mr. Francis to see if he agreed with my interpretation. He nodded approvingly.

"You see," I went on, "right now, the battle over the civil rights bill is taking place in the Senate. It's the culmination of the struggle that courageous Negroes and forward-looking white people have been waging against bigotry in this country. It's fitting that Hubert Humphrey is the floor leader of this legislation. Passage of the bill will change the world for both races, and will be the crowning achievement of Humphrey's years in politics."

Suddenly, Ronnie blurted out, "And that's why we're going to elect Hubert Humphrey the next vice president of the United States." The class applauded, and Ronnie led the chant: "Hu-bert, Hu-bert, Hu-bert."

Mr. Francis seemed unsure of whether to encourage this outburst or quell it. He waited for it to die down, then continued his questioning.

"So let me ask you. How did Humphrey gain this understanding of injustice? Can you talk about his upbringing?"

"Yes. You see, things were tough during the Depression. The family had to move twice, and he had to quit college to work at his father's drug store. Humphrey spent five long years filling prescriptions and jerking soda to help support his parents and brother and sisters. It sounds noble, but in the meantime his dreams were shrinking, and his father never let up. Anything Humphrey wanted took a back seat to what his father demanded. Even in his love life!"

Some of the girls giggled.

"I mean literally. When Hubert borrowed the family car to go on dates, his father would invite himself along with them. In the back seat."

The class emitted a collective groan

"It's true," I said. "And when he got married his father made him hold the wedding in the early morning so he could open the store on time."

More groans.

"I just think sometimes parents do things they think are right, but they don't have a clue how they're affecting us. If they just thought about it for a moment, they . . ."

"Yes?"

"They'd realize the faults they find in us are really theirs, and it's for them to solve."

Some of the students nodded vigorously. Others looked around nervously, unsure whether to agree.

"Are you calling that a hardship? I mean, Humphrey eventually got free and became a senator at a very young age, if I remember correctly."

"Yes, that's true, so maybe those hardships made him

stronger. I don't know, but I think it's a very hard thing to overcome when you want something badly and you have a parent who makes you feel guilty for wanting it."

An awkward silence descended on the class. There was nothing more I could say. I'd probably said too much.

Mr. Francis broke the tension. "Very fine job, Ray." The class stared at me respectfully. I shifted shyly and shrugged. "Thanks."

Chapter Thirteen

THAT EVENING, the lead story on the news was the press conference called by Senator Everett Dirksen. An announcement on national TV meant only one thing: he and his liberal Republican colleagues were joining the northern Democrats to end the filibuster of the southern bloc and bring the civil rights bill to the floor for a vote. Humphrey had enough votes to pass the bill—but ending the filibuster was the big problem, and it looked like Dirksen was about to solve it.

Deeply resonant tones streamed from Dirksen's drooping jowls. "We declare, tonight, our support for the Civil Rights Act of 1964. Although it goes too far in certain respects, we have concluded that the rights and aspirations of Negro Americans can no longer be postponed. Accordingly, we will join in the motion for cloture, and end the filibuster so that we may proceed to a vote on this critical bill."

Just then Dad walked in, summoning me to dinner.

"Humphrey did it," I said, beaming. "He got the votes."

"Let's go, son. It's dinnertime."

"Okay, okay, I'm coming." I followed Dad and sat down just as the phone rang.

"Let it ring," Dad puffed.

Mom popped up. "Oh honey, you know I hate that," she said, grabbing the phone off the kitchen wall. "Hello?" she answered brightly.

Dad started serving himself, pretending to ignore the interruption. But Mom's face turned red within seconds. Diane and I looked at Dad, worried. Then Dad turned to look at Mom.

"Why, no, sir," Mom said. "We were just sitting down. It's okay . . . Of course. I'll put him on."

Wide-eyed, as if in a trance, Mom walked the phone over to me. "It's Hubert Humphrey!" she exclaimed.

Diane gasped. Dad looked dumbfounded, and then turned to squint at me as if expecting me to disclose which of my friends was behind this prank.

I walked solemnly to the phone. "Hello?" I said, my voice squeaky. I cleared my throat and tried again. "Hello?"

Diane was too excited to contain herself and blurted out, "Mommy, is that really Hubert?"

Mom shushed her.

Humphrey laughed. "Someone in your family has me on a first-name basis."

"Yes, Senator, I'm sorry. That was my sister. I'm afraid we call you Hubert around the house. Is that okay?"

Mom tried to stifle a laugh and smiled at Dad, who was staring at me with a blend of disbelief and reproach.

Diane whispered to Mom, "I don't get it. Is that really Hubert?"

Mom shushed her again and Diane plopped her head in her hands.

"No, no, no, I like that," Humphrey said. "Tell your sister it's okay."

I glanced at Diane and mouthed the words, "It's okay." She brightened and slid back in her chair. I walked into the kitchen as far as the cord would reach for some privacy.

"Son," he began, "let me first say what an honor it is to have such dedicated and intelligent young men and women in my corner. You see, that says to me that young people are inspired by what we're doing here in Congress."

"Yes, sir."

"Here's the fact, though. I must ask you to suspend your campaign. I admire your commitment, but I'm concerned about President Johnson's reaction. With only three months before the convention, I wouldn't want to do anything that would . . . well, embarrass the president."

"Yes, sir," I repeated.

"Listen, Ray, is there any way you could come down to Washington so we could discuss this further? I'd like to meet you."

My mouth dropped open in disbelief. "Yes, sir, b-but . . ."

"What is it, Ray?"

"Well, you're in the middle of the civil rights bill!"

"That's fine. We'll make time. I want you to call my office and ask for Danny Grant, my assistant. He'll set up a time, and then we'll talk."

"Yes, sir, that would be great."

"Do you want me to talk to your parents?"

I glanced at Mom and Dad, both suspended in looks of amazement. "That's all right. I can talk to them."

"Very well, son. I'll see you soon."

"Thank you, Senator."

I hung up and drifted back to the table. Mom, Dad, and Diane were frozen in place.

"Hubert said I shouldn't send those flyers to the delegates," I announced. "He said it will embarrass President Johnson."

Mom burst out laughing. "Imagine. He's worried that you'll embarrass the president of the United States. Isn't that fantastic?"

Dad shot her a puzzled look.

"I don't mean embarrassing the president is fantastic," Mom backpedaled. "I mean asking Ray not to embarrass him."

"Yes," Dad chortled. "Very nice."

"It's more than just nice," Mom said. "It's wonderful. I'm going to write an article for the paper."

"Maybe you should hold off—" Dad began.

"There's more. He wants me to visit him in Washington."

"What? When?"

"He said right away."

Mom stared at me with a kind of glow. "Why, I can't believe all of this." Her eyes started to mist up. "Isn't this wonderful, Jim?"

"Yes," Dad said, startled. "A very nice gesture on Humphrey's part."

"You'll help Ray get ready for his trip, won't you, dear?"

Dad paused momentarily, then smiled dryly at Mom. "Of course."

And he did.

Chapter Fourteen

DAD WALKED ME TO TRACK 7 at Pennsylvania Station, the Amtrak line to Washington, DC. I was confident about taking the train on my own, but the passengers flying by started making me nervous.

Dad sensed this and rested a reassuring hand on my shoulder. After all, New York City was his world. He took a step back to look at me in my new blue blazer and smiled approvingly. He had come home early from work the day after Humphrey's call and taken me shopping at the local men's shop.

He reached into his pocket, pulled out an envelope, and handed it to me. "A little extra money from your mother and me, just in case."

"Thanks, Dad."

"Just be respectful. This is a big honor."

"Okay, Dad. I will."

He handed me my bag. It was time. "Your first trip, son. You'll do fine."

I walked toward the platform, then glanced back. Dad was standing there, frozen in position, staring at me with a broad smile.

The train rumbled through Newark, Trenton, Philadelphia, Wilmington, and Baltimore before arriving at Washington's Union Station. The whole ride, I kept reviewing my plan. I was determined to prove to everyone, including myself, that I could pull off this trip without mishaps.

The morning after Humphrey called, I had met with the principal to ask permission to take the time off from school. I wasn't sure he would believe I had an appointment with Hubert Humphrey, but he didn't question a thing. I guess he figured it was true after all the fuss I had been making at school.

From Union Station, I took a cab to the home of Mr. and Mrs. Jeffries in Bethesda, Maryland. I had stayed with them during an orchestra exchange trip in ninth grade and they were thrilled to host me again, asking questions about how I wound up with a private meeting with Hubert Humphrey.

The next morning, a hot June day, they drove me to the Capitol and wished me well. It was the grandest building I had ever seen. At its center was a gigantic dome, larger than the one at St. Paul's Cathedral in London, after which it was modeled. Flanking the dome were the two neoclassical buildings that held the Senate and the House of Representatives. President George Washington laid the cornerstone himself in 1793. The basic structure was completed by 1800, long before anyone could possibly know that one day, it would serve the lawmakers of the most powerful nation in the world.

The patriotic rituals I'd practiced in Boy Scouts took on new meaning as I stood in front of this magnificent building. Awed as I was, I realized that patriotism wasn't about buildings; it was about ideals, and it was my responsibility as an American, even a young one, to serve those ideals.

But the more immediate challenge was finding Humphrey's office. I had studied the Capitol floor plan countless times before leaving for Washington, but the Capitol was overwhelming up close. There were four hundred rooms, miles of hallways, and sixteen acres of space to navigate. People were scurrying in all directions, including pages and interns barely older than me. Everyone except me seemed to know where they were going.

I decided to take the first stairway I saw to the third floor and then figure things out from there. Miraculously, I found myself opposite Senate Room 309—Humphrey's office, just off the Senate floor. This bit of luck was a good omen. But before entering, I started wondering if coming here had been a big misunderstanding. I was barging in on Humphrey during an epic struggle of wills in the United States Senate. The vote to end the filibuster had passed by only one vote, and the vote on the bill itself was coming up within days. Its passage was likely, but not certain. How could Humphrey possibly have time to see me?

I felt an urge to run back down the stairs, take a taxi to Union Station, and call Humphrey from New York to apologize for disturbing him with my immature dabbling in politics. But that option seemed even more embarrassing, so I pushed lightly on the huge wooden door and entered.

One of the secretaries jumped up to welcome me. "Hello, Mr. Elias," she said. "The senator is expecting you." She escorted me to a couch near a window overlooking the vast Capitol grounds.

In less than a minute, a trim man in his late twenties approached me. "Hi, I'm Daniel Grant, Senator Humphrey's special assistant. The senator will be right out."

The senator is expecting you? The senator will be right out? Never in my life had I been treated by adults with such respect. *Does Humphrey treat all his guests like this?* I wondered. But what difference did it make? He was treating me this way.

Within minutes, Humphrey bounded into the reception area. He was a large man, taller than he seemed on TV. His arms were spread wide. The smile I had seen a hundred times was even bigger—the widest smile I had ever seen. The hopes of millions of Americans rested on his shoulders, but you would never know it. He lit up the room. Mr. Grant was smiling, too, and so were the secretaries.

He thrust out his hand. "Well, Ray, thank you for coming down. He said the word "well" in three syllables, making it a greeting in itself: "weh-eh-ehl." His voice was gravelly but calming. Gone was the high-pitched tenseness I'd heard in his political speeches.

"Danny!" He turned to his aide sharply. "Let's see some of Ray's flyers."

Danny pulled copies of my mimeographed flyer from a file.

"Pass them out, Danny? Let's sing. You lead us, Ray."

Unbelievably, Humphrey was asking me to sing. So I did. Humphrey, Danny, and the three secretaries joined in, singing Humphrey's 1960 campaign song to the tune of "The Ballad of Davy Crockett." When I got to the last line—*"So vote for Hubert?"*—I paused and waited a second as the cadence required, and the secretaries, right on cue, sang out robustly, "'Hubert Humphrey, the president for you and me." Everyone laughed.

When the merriment subsided, Humphrey guided me to his office. "Let's talk," he said.

I sat down in a large leather chair across from him. On the credenza behind his desk was a photo of a young Humphrey at the foot of Franklin Roosevelt's campaign train. He was reaching out to shake Roosevelt's hand. Humphrey's father was behind him, unsmiling, with his arms outstretched, touching his son as if trying to nudge him closer. Or trying to pull him back? I couldn't tell.

"Ray, there's something I want to know. How does a young man from Long Island take an abiding interest in a senator from Minnesota, let alone promote him for the vice presidency?"

I started confidently; I was ready for this question. "Well, Senator, everything I ever read about you proved to me that you're someone who cares about ordinary people and would never let them down."

"That's right, Ray. I never will. Let me show you something." He motioned for me to come around the desk. He pulled open a desk drawer and grabbed a handful of thin, oblong boxes. "Do you know what these are?"

"Yes, sir. They must be the pens from the presidential bill-signing ceremonies."

Humphrey nodded and pointed to one. "With this one, President Kennedy signed the Nuclear Test Ban Treaty with the Soviets."

He handed me the box. I held it like the priceless memento it was.

"It was the world's first arms control treaty," he added. "I was proud to get him the votes for that."

I recalled the *Life* magazine article about Humphrey's eight-hour debate with Khrushchev on disarmament in 1958 that laid the groundwork for the arms agreement. I could picture President John F. Kennedy sitting behind his desk in the Oval Office, signing the treaty with this pen and handing it to a smiling Humphrey.

Then he handed me another pen. "And this was for my work on the Alliance for Progress, which secures our economic and defense ties to Latin America."

Humphrey was on a roll. Next was the National Defense Education Act, which provided low-interest loans to college students. Then the Peace Corps, another idea that had sprung from his fertile mind. I knew every one of Humphrey's accomplishments, but still, I was spellbound holding these testaments to his amazing efforts.

"Every one of these pens represents an effort that took years," he said solemnly. "And whenever I introduced these bills, people told me they would never pass. But they did pass, Ray, because they had to. The nation needed them. It just took patience. And in a few days, the civil rights bill will pass and become the Civil Rights Act, and next year, Medicare, and the year after that, a voting rights bill to stand alongside the Civil Rights Act to make sure Negroes gain the same rights that white people take for granted."

I was exhilarated. I now saw exactly what the word "integrity" meant. No one could possibly devote himself so long, so generously, and so patiently to difficult causes unless they had the overriding will to serve their countrymen, not themselves. Humphrey was a man who invoked high-minded principles to inspire an entire nation, not to disguise his personal ambitions. That was the dividing line between leaders who deserved trust and those who could never be trusted. And I knew somehow that Humphrey was spending time with me to teach me that distinction.

"Now, look, Ray. Let's talk about your campaign. You raised money, you assembled an army of volunteers, and you have marvelous campaign materials. But here's the problem. I'm afraid you'd cause quite a stir if you continued with your campaign. Now, I'm not saying I wouldn't be honored to be chosen by the president as his running mate, but the last thing I want to do is embarrass him. You see that, don't you?"

"I see it now, sir. I just figured that a campaign run by students couldn't embarrass a president."

"Don't sell yourself short, Ray," Humphrey said, holding up my flyer. "This is a compelling campaign piece. But you don't know the president. He would view this as pressure, and I can tell you, the president doesn't like to be pressured. Look . . . here's what I'd like to do. Come to the convention in August. As a page. You'll be at the center of all the action. Let's see how this unfolds. How does that sound?"

"That sounds great, Senator."

With a huge smile, Humphrey led me back to the reception area. "Danny!" he boomed. "Make sure Ray gets credentials for the convention."

"Yes, Senator," Danny answered, then turned to me. "We'll send them to you in New York, Mr. Elias."

"Weh-eh-ehl, young man, you've made quite an impression. I look forward to seeing you in August." Humphrey shook my hand one last time, and then Danny walked me to the door.

I stood outside the office for a few moments, watching people streaming through the Senate corridors, wondering if any of them ever had an experience like this. Or maybe they all got started in politics this way: with a hero in mind and an inspiring story to motivate them. I merged with the crowd, feeling like I belonged now. I strode down the marble corridors and out the building, got a taxi to Union Station, and boarded the train back to New York.

Chapter Fifteen

THE ONLY THING I KNEW about Atlantic City, New Jersey, was that it had a boardwalk on the Atlantic Ocean and hosted conventions. It was only ninety minutes from New York, but there was no reason for a kid to go there. That is, before the 1964 Democratic National Convention.

When I arrived in late August, the first thing I noticed was the heat. It was sweltering. The second thing was the frenzy on the boardwalk. Throngs of convention delegates ambled along in the hot sun with oversized buttons on their lapels and red, white, and blue streamers flowing from their shirts. Hawkers were everywhere, selling Johnson paraphernalia. The boardwalk was a riot of color.

My hotel was just off the boardwalk, a drab, unwelcoming structure of twelve floors with squat windows in three symmetrical rows running down a brown brick facade. In the lobby, boys and girls my age raced by. I walked over to the reception desk with Danny's letter in hand and showed it to the clerk. He was hardly older than me but looked official in a red, white, and blue blazer with young citizens for johnson emblazoned on the pockets.

"Oh yes, Mr. Elias, we've been expecting you. You've been reassigned."

"Reassigned!" I groaned. Was the convention experience about to be snatched from me at the last minute?

"You see, technically you're a page," the clerk began, "and this *is* the hotel where the pages stay, but you're not a page anymore."

"But the letter—"

"Relax. You're with the Minnesota delegation now, Senator Humphrey's personal party. It's an honor."

He handed me an envelope. "Give this to security at the convention hall and they'll let you in. You'll get your credentials there."

I was trying to process this new twist as the clerk let out a huge laugh. "Don't worry. I know it seems chaotic. It's a political convention. It will all come together—or not."

At the entrance of the convention hall, a group of twenty Negroes, some of them boys and girls younger than me, were marching in a circle chanting, "Freedom! Freedom! Freedom!" Their signs read: The Mississippi Freedom Democratic Party—For All People. I nodded to one of the young picketers. She nodded back with a warm smile.

The convention hall was enormous. The proceedings hadn't officially started, but people were moving around purposefully, parading banners and chatting exuberantly. This was clearly a celebration, a coronation, really. The country admired President Johnson for the way he'd assumed power after Kennedy's assassination. The Republican presidential candidate, Senator Barry Goldwater of Arizona, kept talking about Vietnam, urging escalation, but almost no one wanted that. Goldwater seemed like a grouch, a naysayer, a pessimist, a warmonger. Only die-hard Republicans thought he had any chance.

The only suspense of this convention was who Johnson would pick for vice president, and he was dragging out his decision until the last possible minute. It had to be excruciating for Humphrey and Senator Eugene McCarthy, the other contender, also from Minnesota.

I made my way through the throng to a room off the main floor. I knocked and a tall man answered, eyeing me guardedly.

"I'm here to pick up my credentials," I said boldly and handed him Danny's letter with the envelope the clerk gave me at the hotel. The tall man moved aside and pointed to a door at the back of the room. "They're in there."

I walked to the door, pushed lightly on it, and went in.

A group of men were sitting in a circle around Humphrey. Danny was there, and I figured the men were Humphrey's advisors. One was gesticulating at Humphrey.

"Nothing in the convention rules excludes Negro representation," he said. "Negroes could have been part of the delegation but were just late getting on the ballot. They didn't follow the rules."

"Oh c'mon," another replied. "You'd have to be a Philadelphia lawyer to figure out those rules."

"They slept on their rights," the first one said. "That's what all the Southerners will say, and it's hard to argue with that."

Danny spotted me and whispered to Humphrey. Humphrey looked up, smiled, and motioned me over. I took an empty seat in the circle of men.

The argument continued in full force. "Hubert," another aide said, "a credentials fight over seating the Mississippi Negro delegation will be bruising. And President Johnson will be watching, assessing just how you deal with it."

"It could kill your chances, Senator," someone else added.

"Not to mention Goldwater," another aide chimed in. "He'll tell the country that a rummy delegation of Negroes brought the Democratic Party to its knees. That will play to the South, and you can kiss those states goodbye in November."

I looked at all the men and tried to look serious like them, frowning and knitting my brow.

Then Danny offered a suggestion. "Won't the Negro delegates accept a couple of non-voting seats with the white delegation?"

"We tried that, Danny," someone answered. "The regular Mississippi delegation won't go for it."

"For God's sake," Danny responded. "Who's running this

convention anyway? A lily-white Mississippi delegation or the Democratic National Party?"

Another advisor weighed in. "Hubert, if this isn't settled, we'll have a hell of a civil rights spectacle on national TV, a convention rules fight, a pissed off president, and an ex-vice presidential contender."

The others all nodded in agreement. Humphrey looked around the room gravely. Everyone had spoken.

The tall man who had greeted me appeared in the doorway and announced, "Senator, Dr. King is here."

Humphrey jumped to his feet. "Tell him I'll be right there." Turning to his aides, he said, "Okay, gentlemen, let's tell Dr. King where we are on this."

Everyone except Danny headed for the door, and I got up to follow them out.

"Ray, wait," Humphrey said, freezing me in my tracks. "I want to know what you think."

Astonished, I just stared at him.

"I'm sure you've thought about it, and you heard the arguments. How do you think we should come out on this?"

I swallowed and said, "Senator, I don't think it would be right to deny Negroes a place at the Democratic National Convention."

"A voting place?"

"Yes, sir. Let people say what they want."

Humphrey fixed his eyes on me. I wondered if I'd said something wrong. I was about to explain further when the phone rang. Danny rushed over, grabbed the phone, and handed it to Humphrey. "It's the White House, Senator. The president wants to speak to you."

"Oh, boy." Humphrey laughed. "I'll tell you, that man has big ears."

Danny smiled nervously. Humphrey took the call in a corner of the room as Danny and I waited. The conversation was short.

Humphrey walked over with a distressed look. "C'mon," he said. "Let's talk to Dr. King."

The Reverend Dr. Martin Luther King was surrounded by a half dozen Negro men. They were chatting amiably with Humphrey's aides but came to attention when Humphrey walked in. Humphrey and Dr. King greeted each other warmly.

"Hubert, are we making any progress?" Dr. King asked.

"Martin, I can deliver a solution that would allow two Mississippi Freedom Democrats to be official 'observers' at this convention."

"Are these at-large seats you're offering?"

"Well, no, Martin. Strictly observer status."

Dr. King's retinue shuffled slightly. A stony silence enveloped the room. Humphrey's aides glanced at King apprehensively, waiting to see if the most famous civil rights leader in the nation would support Humphrey's proposal, or balk at it.

"Martin," Humphrey went on. "I know this isn't everything. But I promise you this: no all-white Southern delegation will ever be seated at a Democratic convention again. And if a revolution is necessary to prevent that, I'll be the one leading it."

"I know you will, Hubert," Dr. King said. "I'm assuming this is what the president wants?"

Humphrey nodded.

"Okay. I'll bring it to the delegation."

As Dr. King and his group turned to leave, Danny stepped forward. "Excuse me, Dr. King. I just took a peek out there. It's wall-to-wall reporters. You may want to use the back door."

Dr. King smiled and said to his group, "And here I thought Hubert was promising an end to political back doors for the Negro."

Humphrey launched an uproarious laugh. Dr. King joined him, then both men's aides. Everyone was relieved that this meeting had ended with a laugh. I was spellbound, my eyes darting between these two great men.

"But thank you, Mr. Grant," Dr. King said. "In this case, I will happily bow to discretion."

Dr. King and his group headed for the back door, and Humphrey beamed at his aides. They had gotten through this, and I was part of it. A part of history.

Chapter Sixteen

MURIEL AND I were seated in a private aircraft bound for Washington, summoned by the president. It could mean only one thing: he was ready to tap me as the Democratic vice-presidential nominee.

He had dragged out the decision to add suspense to the convention. As a politician, I could understand that. Still, it was unkind to float one name after another just to keep everyone guessing. I may have been the front runner, but his publicity gambit kept me in perpetual anxiety. It was over now. I had won the prize, but a bad taste lingered.

"Why so pensive, Dad?" Muriel asked.

"I was just thinking. I wanted to offer Dr. King two at-large voting seats in the Mississippi delegation. That is, until Lyndon vetoed the idea. But that young man, Ray Elias, saw right away that it was the right thing to do. I mean, others saw it, but he was the only one to come right out and say we needed to do it."

Muriel's eyebrows tilted ever so slightly in a smile, but her lips compressed with a hint of worry.

"That's nice, Hubert. As Lyndon's vice president, you're going to need someone like that you can trust."

PART THREE
Winter–Spring 1965

Chapter Seventeen

BEFORE MY CAREER at the University of Chicago even started, my mother tried to halt it. Being on my own in a far-away place scared her. Chicago was the Wild West to Mom. She favored New York University, just an hour away in New York City, and begged me to reconsider. What really kept her awake at night was something she'd learned from her friend Mildred. Her nephew had a nervous breakdown his first year at Chicago, dropped out, and never went back.

Dad was against my going for a different reason. He was flipping through channels on TV one night and saw an interview with Harvard professor Dr. Timothy Leary, who was advocating LSD for mind expansion. Leary said that the University of Chicago was a place where students were bold enough to experiment with psychedelic drugs—a compliment from Leary's point of view, but Dad saw it as yet one more peril to which I would surely succumb.

Since I didn't use drugs and presented no immediate risk of mental collapse, my parents suspended their doubts and helped me pack for Chicago. Dad told me to make sure I didn't do anything foolish with girls—but his way of warning me was more colorful: "Don't let your schmuck go to your head."

Mom's advice was loftier; she urged me to find time, as she did, to serve the "less fortunate." She made me promise to find a worthwhile charity and volunteer. I had no idea what I would do, but I promised I'd do something.

The University of Chicago was founded by John D. Rocke-feller, the richest and most ruthless of the nineteenth-century robber barons, yet it was one of the most liberal universities in the country. The Gothic buildings of the quadrangle were modeled after Oxford University but built four hundred years later, an expense so enormous that only Rockefeller could afford it. He endowed it as a Baptist enclave, but the joke at orientation was that the University of Chicago was a Baptist university where atheist professors taught Jewish students. I figured this was just another cliché, but maybe there was some truth to it.

Hubert—by now I had taken to referring to him by his first name—urged me to go. He said the University of Chicago "combined liberal openness of mind with conservative Midwestern values." His recommendation sealed it for me. My father declared that he had no idea what Hubert was talking about, but my mother seemed comforted by the description. It also had a famous political science department, and that was what I planned to study, just like Hubert.

We exchanged letters during the 1964 presidential campaign. I don't know how he had time to write, but he did. In November, he and Johnson were elected in a landslide, defeating the Republican, Barry Goldwater. The only states they lost, other than Goldwater's home state of Arizona, were five Southern states antagonized by Johnson's and Hubert's civil rights record.

The election was a vindication for Lyndon Johnson. Despite his Texas roots, Johnson had made civil rights a priority. He said he did it to honor John F. Kennedy's legacy, and I'm sure he was also nudged by Hubert, but I think his conviction ran deeper. His first job after college was teaching the children of the Mexican farmers of Cotulla, Texas. They had grown up in poverty, just like he did, and I think he empathized with the afflictions of minorities.

Still, he seemed a coarse man. There was that photo of him in *Life* magazine holding up his beagles by the ears. Maybe they did that in Texas, or maybe beagles didn't mind being yanked off the ground by their ears. But it seemed like he was treating Hubert the same way, dressing him up in a Western outfit way too big for him and putting him on a frisky horse. Hubert looked terrified. He had been pulling larger crowds than Johnson during the election campaign, and I wondered if Johnson was showing him up, just as he did at the convention by dragging that nomination process out.

And then there was the war he was escalating. I didn't think much about Vietnam until after high school graduation, when Gerry told me he was enlisting. That was a shock. Gerry wasn't a great student; he was always complaining about school, but he could have gone to college somewhere and received a draft deferment. Instead, he claimed it was his duty to defend America against communist aggression. This didn't make a lot of sense to me. How could fighting a guerilla war in a jungle ten thousand miles away protect the United States against Russia or China?

But the last thing I wanted was to question Gerry's patriotism. Or expose my own lack of it! After all, as long as I stayed in college, I would receive a deferment from military service. I was worried about Gerry—mostly because of the danger of war, but also because he seemed caught up in pro-war propaganda.

After the summer we went our separate ways, him to base camp in Georgia and me to Chicago. But we wrote each other every week. I followed his progress from boot camp to deployment in Vietnam. He was a field artillery man, which sounded safer than infantry, so I worried about him less.

His letters portrayed Vietnam as a kind of summer camp full of pranks and rowdy exploits, including the "filthy liaisons" of his comrades, as he called them, with Vietnamese women in Saigon. It was an intriguing world, but not one I wanted to be part of. Still, I read those letters intently, scanning for hints of danger.

Chapter Eighteen

ONE DAY AFTER my classes in mid-February, a few weeks after Hubert was inaugurated, I walked into the lobby of Woodward Court, my dorm complex, and was greeted by Sam Watson, the attendant.

"Hey, Ray. I have that package from the vice president you've been waitin' on."

"That's fantastic, Sam. Thanks."

"My pleasure, son." He extended his large hand and a smile to match. Sam treated the dorm residents like honored guests.

A picture of his son in Marine uniform sat prominently on the lobby counter. That annoyed some of the residents, but most took it in stride. Everyone loved Sam and, after all, he was just a father showing pride in his son, not promoting the war.

"Sam, if you see my roommate, tell him I'll be at the council office."

"I think he's already over there, Ray."

I charged down the snow-blanketed sidewalk of Woodlawn Avenue to Ida Noyes Hall, a splendid mansion built by inventor La Verne Noyes in honor of his wife, Ida. Originally intended as a woman's gymnasium, Ida Noyes Hall was now the center for public lectures, social events, and student activity offices like my Domestic Youth Policy Council. Hubert encouraged me to set up the council as an auxiliary to the Domestic Policy Council, which President Johnson appointed Hubert to lead as part of the Administration's Great Society agenda.

I ran up the wide staircase two steps at a time, eager to share the package from Hubert with the council volunteers. When I walked in, my roommate, Lew Ross, and the other volunteers were seated at old metal desks, poring over voter lists. Posters of President Johnson and Hubert lined the walls alongside maps of Chicago's Hyde Park voting precincts. Lew was not only my roommate but a supportive friend, like Ronnie in high school. He was shy, like me, but in a different way—a Midwestern way. He didn't talk much, but quietly observed, and understood things intuitively.

Lew spotted the package I was holding and ran over. "Is that what I think it is?"

"Well, let's find out," I said coyly.

I cut open the package and pulled out a thick stack of bound documents on domestic topics: voting rights, labor reform, housing, education, health care for the elderly, and poverty. Everyone stared in amazement at the sheer size of these reports. I passed them around, one to each volunteer, as Lew and I scanned the cover memorandum:

To: Ray Elias
From: The Vice President of the United States
Re: Domestic Youth Policy Council
Date: February 1, 1965

Hubert's memorandum laid out ways that our council could support—on a student level—the work of the Domestic Policy Council he was heading up on the national level.

"Hey, Hubert got Mayor Daley to speak at our fundraiser," Lew shouted.

Absorbed in the merriment, I didn't notice a young woman enter the room until one of the volunteers pointed to the striking figure standing in the doorway. She had rich dark hair flowing down her back, almost to her waist, a sharp, straight nose, and green eyes set in deep black eyebrows, but there was an overall softness to her face. She wore a long black skirt, a man's white dress shirt, and a gray vest, creating an almost conservative look but for the beaded necklaces dangling in successively long rings around her neck, and a scarlet-red headband. It was a jarring mix of purposeful contrasts.

To say she startled us was an understatement, not because she stood motionless, statue-like, at the door, but because she was beautiful. Every boy in that room noticed it.

"Which one of you is Ray Elias?" she asked casually as she strode in.

"I am," I said, stepping forward. "And who——"

"Ruth," she said, thrusting her hand out. "Ruth Torricelli." I took her hand.

"From Students for a Democratic Society," she added.

"SDS!" I exclaimed, and pulled back my hand.

"What? Too radical for you boys?" She chuckled and walked over to the wall, scanning the maps hung on it. All eyes were trailing her. "This is amazing," she murmured. "The entire student population broken down by home state, voter affiliation, and local address. What are you guys planning, a military uprising?"

"No," I said stiffly, "a campaign to enlist student support for President Johnson's Great Society."

"The Great Society, huh?"

"That's right," I countered, deflecting her sarcasm. "We're not just focused on the war like SDS."

She shot me a look, then turned her eyes back to the maps. "But how did you get all this stuff?"

I said nothing. No one else did, either. She eyed each one of us, then caught sight of a framed photo of Hubert on my desk. "Oh. I get it. Friends in high places." She walked over to my desk, picked up the photo, and read the inscription aloud: "'To Ray Elias, my campaign manager and good friend. Hubert Humphrey.'"

She stared at me for a minute, took a deep breath, and

started singing. *"Humphrey is a senator, a neighbor, a friend. We're gonna stick with him all the way to the end. He used to come over just to help us out . . ."* She stopped and shrugged. "That's all I remember."

I looked at her in utter amazement. "How do you know that song?"

"I'm from Wisconsin. My dad worked for Humphrey in 1960, so I heard that song a lot."

I kept shaking my head. She actually knew that song, the song I sang with Hubert in his office last year. This brash girl was fascinating. But I didn't want to show it. The others were watching me, waiting for cues on how to treat her.

"When they say, *He used to come over*," she continued lightly, "they mean he used to come over from Minnesota to help us in Wisconsin. You knew that, right?"

"Of course," I said, more brusquely than I intended.

She threw her head back with a laugh. "Of course you did." Then a sad look came over her. "But now it's the Democrats who are waging the war."

"President Eisenhower started this war in the fifties," Lew blurted out.

"That's right." She turned and stared at me. "But it's Johnson and your good friend Humphrey who are escalating it."

"Is there something I can help you with, Miss . . . ?"

"Torricelli. Ruth Torricelli."

She gave Hubert's photo a last look and carefully placed it back on my desk. "Can I talk to you privately?"

The others took their cue to retreat to their desks, and I motioned to a seat beside my desk. She sat down and wasted no time getting to the point. "I'd like to borrow your lists."

"What? I don't think so."

"What's the matter? Afraid of a little healthy competition?"

"I don't think we have the same objectives in mind."

"What do you know about SDS? It's not really that far

from Humphrey's progressive ideals."

"*Progressive?* That's not a word I would use to describe it."

"What word would you use, then?"

"Angry, confrontational, and radical."

"Well, I'll just have to educate you," she said, grinning. Then she got up abruptly and extended her hand. "I hope I haven't taken up too much of your time."

I rose and shook her hand. "Not at all, Miss Torricelli," I responded stiffly. "Very nice to meet you."

My eyes were fixed on her as she walked to the door. She turned and said, "Hey, Elias, how come you don't have any women working here?"

I glanced at Lew. She was right. There weren't any, and we never noticed. We both looked at her guiltily. She nodded sharply with pouted lips and walked out.

Chapter Nineteen

"THE POLICY COUNCIL will take the lead on all domestic policies," I announced to my aides at our first meeting in my West Wing office. "Your memos look good, but I've made a few changes. Take a look and get back to me. They need to be just right for the president." Turning to Danny, I said, "You sent all these to Ray?"

"Yes, sir, but . . ." Danny pointed to his watch.

"Oh my, Lyndon will have my head."

I hastily took leave of my aides and charged out of my office through the narrow West Wing corridors to the Cabinet Room, Danny keeping up behind me. We stopped at the oak doors to catch our breath, then walked in.

The president sat at the center of a long oval table, his six-foot-four frame slouched across his chair and his chin resting glumly on his fist. It was a look that might be mistaken for boredom but for the deep furrows slashed across his forehead and the creases framing his mouth. His eyes were fixed on Secretary of Defense McNamara, who was pointing to colored dots on a map.

"Three waves of X-15 fighters will bomb known supply routes here and here, Mr. President, with follow-up missions in waves every ninety minutes."

McNamara was in full throttle. Odds were good that I could take my seat opposite the president without comment. "The bombing will slow movement of men and materiel into South Vietnam," McNamara droned on. "We've named the operation Rolling Thunder."

"Hubert." The president's voice rang out, freezing me

before I could sit. "I can see the duties of vice president have done little to improve your punctuality." He chuckled and the others followed suit. Then his grin dissolved as he turned to the secretary of state. "Dean?"

I slipped into my seat as Dean Rusk mimicked McNamara's breezy tone.

"Mr. President, Rolling Thunder has the enthusiastic support of the South Vietnamese. Our European allies, while not enthusiastic, are not objecting."

Johnson turned to the air force chief of staff. "General McConnell?"

"Commanders are fully briefed, Mr. President. Aircraft are operational. We recommend immediate initiation."

"I have a question, sir, about the timing," I broke in. "With the Russian premier visiting the capital of North Vietnam, don't we run a risk of provoking the Russians?"

Ignoring me, Johnson turned to McGeorge Bundy. "Mac?"

"Actually, Mr. President, the vice president is correct. We have reports that Premier Kosygin is still in Hanoi. He extended his stay."

Johnson pounded his fist on the table and roared, "Who said anything about bombing Hanoi?"

"Yes, Mr. President," Bundy said meekly.

"Sir," I interjected.

"Yes, Hubert," the president sneered.

"If Kosygin is anywhere in North Vietnam, don't we risk antagonizing the Russians?"

"Since when are you afraid of the Russians, Hubert?" The president turned to the others. "Doesn't everyone remember when Hubert led the Americans for Democratic Action? A rowdy bunch of anticommunists if there ever was one."

Everyone obliged the president's remark with somber nods. It was true that I fought communists in the Democratic Party and the Minnesota labor unions, too, but this was vastly different: we risked antagonizing a superpower.

"But then again," the president continued, "maybe he's grown timid now that he's the second-highest elected official in the land."

"I'm only saying, sir, that this may create an unnecessary complication. We may need the Russians to help us get out of this thing."

"Get out of this thing? What the hell do you think I'm trying to do, Hubert? My God, sometimes . . ." He shook his head and rolled his eyes.

No one was looking at me, only at Johnson. The room was a cauldron of tension. I glanced around the table, looking for allies. But there were none. Not this time. As a senator I had worked with these men, all seasoned and sensible diplomats, but the president had turned them into sharks with an appetite for blood.

"In bombing known supply routes, we may well be saving American lives," Secretary Rusk chirped, "an objective a little more important than not offending Mr. Kosygin's sensibilities."

That's right, Dean," the president snarled, glancing at me. "Thank you for reminding us."

"With all due respect, Mr. Secretary," I countered, "what will save lives will be finding an opening for settlement, not hitting back and escalating this conflict." I turned to the president. "Sir, our long-term strategy must be negotiation, not escalation. That's what will save lives."

The president slowly turned to me. His tone was low and menacing, gradually increasing in intensity, like the war itself. "I'm not the one who escalated this thing. They ambushed our men at Pleiku and Qui Nhon, slaughtering American troops in their quarters, for Christ's sake. As long as I'm president, America will retaliate, and hard, for such acts."

The president stared at me with the icy disfavor I had seen a hundred times when we were senators, but never directed at me. Everyone in the room lowered their eyes. I could take on every one of these men in a debate one-on-one, even the president. But this wasn't a debate chamber. It was the Cabinet Room at the White House, the president was my boss demanding submission, and everyone was expecting me to give in. I would have to find another way to get through.

Chapter Twenty

ON SATURDAY MORNING, I strode across the quad toward Mandel Hall for orchestra practice with my bass perched on my shoulder. It was February but it was mild, an unexpected reprieve from the bitter cold and fierce wind that earned Chicago its nickname, the Windy City. Still, it was gray. Always gray. The steely-gray buildings were enshrouded in gray light, and winter-weary students shuffled through the gray slush of trodden snow.

Orchestra practice was an escape from the demands of school and politics; I looked forward to the break on Saturday mornings. But the one thing I couldn't escape was the growing discontent over the Vietnam War. In front of the Administration Building, a student in jeans and a frayed army jacket exhorted a small crowd to join the upcoming protest against military recruiting on campus. Ruth was sitting at a table nearby with a stack of anti-war flyers. When she spotted me, she got up and intercepted me. "Hey, Elias, what are you hiding there? A tactical nuclear weapon?"

"Very funny," I said, turning around and accidentally launching the long neck of the bass in her direction.

"Hey, watch out," she said, ducking. "That thing is lethal."

I resumed walking, but she followed. "So, how's your youth council going? Making progress?"

"Yes, thank you," I said and kept walking.

She touched my arm. I stopped and turned again, slowly this time to control the neck of the bass.

"You know, you're on the right track," she said. "With your council, I mean. Our country has a pressing social agenda."

I nodded indifferently.

"But none of it is possible with a war going on," she continued. "I'm sure Hubert Humphrey knows that."

I turned and started walking away, but again she trailed after me. "So where does Humphrey stand on the war?" she persisted.

"He stands with the president, of course," I replied sharply without turning, but as soon as the words left my mouth, I realized I had no idea where Humphrey stood on the war.

"I'm sorry to hear that. Why don't you write to him? Let him know that a casualty of this war is his beloved domestic agenda."

I stopped and glared at her. "Look, I'm sure the president and vice president have a plan to deal with this war." *Another idle boast*, I thought. I had no idea if Johnson had a plan.

"Don't move," she said abruptly. "I'll be right back." She turned and ran to her table.

"I've gotta go," I yelled after her. I took a few steps toward Mandel Hall, second-guessed myself, and then stopped and waited for her.

Ruth dashed back and handed me a book. I looked down at the title. *The Two Vietnams: A Political and Military Analysis.*

I shrugged. "I can't take this."

"Oh," she said, retreating a step.

"I mean, my hands are full," I added, softening.

"Oh. No problem." Without missing a beat, she unsnapped the music pouch on the underside of the bass cover. "I'll just put it in here."

"Hey, get out of there!" I yelled as sheets of music spilled out of the pouch and onto the ground.

"Hmm . . . Brahms, Beethoven, Mozart," she said. "Just as I thought."

"Put my stuff back."

"Okay. Stay still. I'll just leave the book here along with the other great masters." She patted me gently on the shoulder.

I couldn't help smiling. There was a playfulness about her that countered her radicalism. I pretended to be annoyed. But I liked her.

Onstage at Mandel Hall, I unwrapped my bass. The act of pulling off the huge cloth cover was a calming one, a familiar routine I'd been doing since fifth grade. For eight years, the string bass had been my solace, the one thing I could rely on when the world seemed confounding and my options for dealing with it felt inadequate.

The bass had also been a rare source of closeness with Dad before things got so tense between us. Every Saturday morning in junior high, he drove me to my lesson with Mr. Peterson and sat without complaint. There was even a smile waiting for me when I finished. He paid Mr. Petersen, then expertly maneuvered the bass into the car. He never said anything, but I felt he was proud of my playing.

I don't remember making an effort to become a good bass player, as I did to become a better soccer player. It just happened naturally over time. In ninth grade I made the all-county orchestra—not as a regular, but as an alternate. I had no idea how regulars and alternates were chosen, but I was disappointed because alternates rarely made it to the concert orchestra. Then one of the "regular" bass players dropped out unexpectedly and I got the nod to take his place.

At the audition for "seating" within the bass section, I played well and was selected first chair. In theory, that meant I was the best student string bass player in the county. At the time, I thought maybe that was the way things worked in the world: even if you could just make the cut, with a chance to prove yourself, you could wind up first. That lesson was proved again when I made the starting soccer team after practicing with Gerry.

But I was nervous that it could easily work in reverse: you could think you were the best, then suddenly find yourself displaced by someone better. And that's what happened that Saturday. I was first chair in the University of Chicago Symphony Orchestra, but I knew that the player standing to my right, Brian, the second chair, was better. Brian was not a student, but a talented young Negro bass player from Woodlawn, the community that bordered the university. He'd won a scholarship to study with Joseph Guastafeste, principal bassist in the Chicago Symphony Orchestra. Brian was good and improving rapidly; I could hear it in his rich vibrato, which I had never learned from Mr. Peterson.

The orchestra leader could hear it, too. Without warning, he suggested that Brian and I compete for the first chair by playing a passage of Brahms's *Symphony No. 2 in D Major*. Brian and I took turns playing before the entire orchestra; that's the way auditions worked when a first chair was challenged for position, even in student orchestras.

The competition was close—at least, that's what friends told me later. But I knew the truth: Brian was better. My playing was crisp and precise, but his was full and melodious.

The conductor awarded Brian the first chair. I tried not to feel disappointed. *I have other things in my life,* I told myself. I didn't have to be the best, because clearly, I wasn't. Still, it hurt. I kept thinking of those lessons with Mr. Peterson and Dad's pride in my progress. I decided I wouldn't tell my parents about my demotion. I doubted Dad would be sympathetic. His verdict would be that I didn't work hard enough, that I wasn't focused.

So, as fifty-five fellow musicians looked on uneasily, I shook hands with Brian, picked up my bass, and shuffled over to the second position behind him in the row of bass players.

"Hey, Ray, planning on going sailing on Lake Michigan today with that thing? Better bundle up. It's cold out there."

After losing my position in the orchestra and returning to my dorm, I was in no mood to field jokes about the string bass perched on my shoulder, not even from Sam.

"Very funny, Sam."

Sam dipped below the reception desk and pulled out a box. "Hey, this might cheer you up."

"The leaflets!" I exclaimed. I put the bass down, tore open the box, and examined one thousand crisp and beautifully printed announcements. This was no high school mimeograph job.

> *Young Democrats of the University of Chicago*
> *And the Domestic Youth Policy Council*
> *Present*
> *The Honorable Richard J. Daley,*
> *Mayor of Chicago*
> *Thursday, June 8, 7:00 pm*
> *Mandell Hall*

I showed Sam an invitation.

"Yes, sir," he said. "Mighty handsome, I say. Gotta stick with Mr. Daley—the president, too! Not with the likes of them." He gestured toward a young soldier in uniform speaking to a group of students in a corner of the lobby. The soldier looked out of place among the casually dressed, long-haired university students. I spotted Lew, listening intently.

"It's some guy back from Vietnam, stirring up the kids," Sam continued. "You know, tellin' stories. My boy's doin' the fighting while guys like that doin' the talking." Then he switched gears. "Say, Ray, how come we don't hear nothin' from Mr. Humphrey about Vietnam? He's behind the president, ain't he?"

"Of course, Sam. I'm sure he is."

Then it hit me. For the second time within hours, I realized I had no idea where Hubert stood on Vietnam, but I was acting as if I did. I stole another glance at the soldier.

"Sam, can you keep an eye on my bass for a second? I want to tell Lew the announcements are in."

"Sure thing, Ray."

I approached Lew but he brushed me off, motioning to the speaker. "You gotta listen to this."

The soldier spoke in an eerie monotone. "The same thing happened at Ben Suc. We were circling an open field in choppers and these people—you know, peasants—were working in the rice field. You could see the huts nearby and everything, just a small country village. So we came down lower, to hover over them. They still didn't move. Hell, they were scared. You could see that, but they just kept working . . .

"So we turned on the sirens. That scared the shit out of 'em and they started for the huts, not too fast, even, just moving back, casual-like. But the army called that evasion. So the captain shouted out, 'Fire!' But no one fired. We just couldn't do it. The captain knew what we were thinking. He yelled, 'Fire' again, but louder. And someone fired. Then we all did. In less than ninety seconds, every one of those peasants lay dead or wounded in the field."

The group let out a gasp.

"Four old men, three women, one of them holding a baby. All dead."

Everyone stared at each other, frozen in disbelief.

The soldier stepped back, almost shrinking into himself, his face contracting in shame. He seemed about to cry. Then he spoke again, haltingly, breaking up. "I have only one thing to say to the people of Vietnam: God I'm sorry."

This couldn't be right. It was too devastating to contemplate. Cold-blooded murder of civilians? I looked at Lew pleadingly, hoping he'd smile and say this was just a rehearsal for an anti-war skit or something, anything other than an account of war crimes committed by Americans. But President Johnson wasn't even acknowledging that Vietnam was a war, and the generals weren't, either. They called it a "conflict," "engagement," or "action." It was as if by refusing to acknowledge what it was, they could close their eyes to its horrors and ignore its crimes.

Something made me look back at Sam. He was eyeing me. His face, normally so good-natured, was twisted in a blaze of suspicion. Was he waiting for me to do something, to neutralize this soldier? To convince the students that he was telling them lies? Did Sam think that, just by listening to this soldier, I was against his son the Marine?

Then I had an idea. I'd call Hubert. He would reassure me that atrocities were not occurring. But would he tell me? Would he even know? No. I would call Gerry. He'd know. Word traveled fast among the troops. All I had to do was get him to call me. Mom could talk to Mrs. Moretti. It would be only a matter of days. Then I'd know.

I rushed past Sam's desk to the phone booth and began the painfully slow process of calling home: dialing "0," asking for a long-distance operator, then waiting for her to place the call and get permission from whoever answered to reverse the charges. That was the procedure. Long distance calls were expensive, and I never had enough coins. Through the glass doors of the phone booth, I could see Sam still scrutinizing me.

Diane answered and gleefully accepted the charges. I asked her to put Mom on, but she ignored me and started reciting verse as if she were performing at a poetry recital.

'Twas brillig, and the slithy toves
Did gyre and gimble in the wabe:
All mimsy were the borogoves,
And the mome raths outgrabe.

I recognized these words to Lewis Carroll's poem, "Jab-berwocky." As a seventh grader, she probably had to memorize the poem, just as I did, and was showing off. Crazy what teachers think of. I waited, despite my impatience. She was almost done when Dad snatched the phone.

"Hey, Daddy!" Diane protested. "I was reciting a poem to Ray."

"Ray, what's this about?" Dad hissed. "You're supposed to call Sunday afternoon."

"Dad, I need to talk to Gerry."

"What are you talking about? Gerry's in Vietnam."

"I know that. Could you put Mom on, please?"

As he handed the phone to Mom, I heard him say, "It's something about the Moretti boy."

"What's wrong, Ray?" Mom asked, alarmed. "What's this about Gerry?"

"Mom, nothing's wrong. I just need to talk to Gerry. Can you call Mrs. Moretti and ask her to have Gerry call me?"

"Call you? From Vietnam? Are you sure everything's all right?"

"Yes, Mom. Fine."

"Okay. I'll call her."

"Thanks. But look, I gotta go now. I'll call you tomorrow. Sunday. You know, the usual time. Cheaper rates."

"Ray, are you sure everything's okay?"

"Sure, Mom. I gotta go. Just ask Gerry's mother to have him call me as soon as he can. At the dorm."

Chapter Twenty-One

WHEN I WAS SUMMONED to the Oval Office after the cabinet meeting on Operation Rolling Thunder, I knew I was in for some thunder of my own, Texas style.

"Come on in, Hubert. Let's talk."

The president motioned me to a seat across from his desk, rather than the couch. This was no informal occasion. There was no small talk. Just whole minutes of silence as I sat and he fidgeted aimlessly at his desk.

"When I was John Kennedy's vice president," he began wistfully, as if he were reciting a fairy tale to a child, "we had an understanding. It wasn't spoken, I just knew. The president's job was to run the country, and the vice president's job was to back him up."

"Well, sir—"

"No matter what."

His face tightened, his eyes narrowed, and his voice dropped three registers to a menacing monotone. "You're not at the University of Minnesota debating political theories, you know."

"Yes, sir."

He placed two fists on the desk and catapulted himself from his chair and toward me like a guided missile. He plopped his huge hands on my shoulders and leaned his giant frame over me, so close that his glasses almost touched my forehead. I had seen the "Johnson treatment" many times, directed at others. I never knew it could make you feel so small. The president was a perfect instrument of intimidation: every sinew of his body was disciplined to subjugate, every gesture calculated to dominate.

"Ubert!" That's the way he said my name when he was agitated—short, clipped, and cutting. "You know what every man in that room was thinking?"

"No, sir."

"That I'm a damn fool for letting my vice president sound off like that."

"With all due respect, sir, someone had to make those arguments."

"Well then, tell them to me privately, goddamn it."

"All right, sir. I can do that."

The president straightened up and walked back to his desk. "And by the way, that goes for your wife, too."

"My wife, sir?"

"At dinner last week with the O'Briens and Valentis, Muriel challenged me right there about why I didn't send you to Churchill's funeral."

"Challenged you, sir? She was just asking."

"Bullshit."

"Really, Mr. President, I know a little something about my wife."

"Not enough to tell her when to shut up. But of course, you haven't learned that yourself."

"Now Lyndon, wait a minute—"

"Forget it. Muriel's a great gal. I know that. But who I send to funerals is my business. You got it?"

"Of course."

"Now, let's forget it and have a drink. Scotch and soda, right?"

Before I could answer, he rang for the butler. I did not want to drink with this man. I felt I was suffocating, gasping for air like a salmon swimming upstream on a Minnesota river, trying to spawn before dying.

Chapter Twenty-Two

FAITHFUL TO THE PROMISE I'd made to my mother before leaving for college, I found a charity to volunteer for. Not exactly a charity, but a brand-new government program aimed at breaking the cycle of inner-city poverty: Project Head Start. Alberta Watson was the volunteer coordinator who recruited me. She said I would be a role model for young Negro boys from the projects, even though I was a white university student and definitely not from the projects.

That's how I met Philip, a withdrawn four-and-a-half-year-old who had a hard time looking me in the eye. I protested to Alberta, "There's no way I can be a role model for a young Negro boy with psychological issues."

She just shrugged and said, "Be yourself." *What could she possibly mean?* I hardly knew what "being myself" meant. I figured that was something people just said when they wanted you to calm down and didn't know what else to say.

But Philip and I got along right way. *A miracle*, I thought. I quickly learned that just because he didn't look at me, it didn't mean he wasn't listening. His eyes were alert and his expression was expectant, so I blathered my way through as many memories as I could recall from kindergarten and then started talking about my Domestic Youth Policy Council. Trying to describe the council's mission in simple terms re-inspired me. Somehow, I think my excitement put Philip at ease.

Alberta picked me up every Sunday morning, and this Sunday I was grateful for the break. The words of that soldier had hit me like a grenade, still reverberating. Later that night,

Lew announced that he was quitting the council, saying that "stopping the war was the only thing that mattered now." I'd lost my loyal lieutenant right before the campus-wide petition drive we had planned for weeks.

Also, I couldn't get that strange girl out of my mind. I had talked with Ruth twice, and both times it was more of a confrontation than a conversation. An encounter with her was like an attack of vertigo: one moment everything appeared perfectly normal, and the next the world was spinning uncontrollably.

Absorbed in these thoughts, I barely listened to Alberta rambling through changes in the schedule. The next thing I knew, we were pulling up to an elementary school on Chicago's South Side, not Philip's apartment in the projects. Inside the school's gym, dozens of kids, volunteers, and coordinators were taking their places. I scanned the room for Philip, but he spotted me first, charged over, took my hand, and led me to his place on the floor among the other kids.

The children were sitting in a semicircle, with volunteers sitting behind them and the coordinators standing in the back. Two Chicago police officers were standing off to the side chatting, but looking a little nervous. One of the coordinators quieted the kids and introduced the officers. They were from a division called "Community Relations." One of them stepped forward with a broad smile. I could just smell propaganda being cooked up and served to the kids. Anything a white police officer had to say to Negro children required more sensitivity than I imagined these officers had.

I didn't like Chicago police officers. For one thing, they looked mean. I never noticed that about policemen until I got to Chicago. New York cops didn't look mean, or so I thought. I wondered if I was just more accustomed to New York police because I saw them so often on family trips to the city. This police officer was smiling, so I paused to check myself. Here I was, a white person in a room of Negroes, freely indulging my prejudices. The irony put me on edge, and I felt ashamed.

The officer started with an explanation of the police motto, "We serve and protect." The kids listened respectfully, then got excited when the officer started explaining all the paraphernalia attached to his belt. He didn't carry a gun but had a billy club that he called a baton.

He asked the kids if they knew what the baton was for. Spontaneously, every boy and girl lifted their arm and brought it down in a crushing motion, over and over again. The officer's face turned red. He shouted, "No, no, no, children—that's not it! The baton is used for many important things. Like carrying an injured person."

He frantically summoned the other police officer and began demonstrating how an injured person could be cradled on the baton. But it was useless. Bedlam had broken loose. Many of the kids were imitating a bashing gesture so violently that they had to be restrained.

How could a white cop convince Negro boys and girls that a billy club was used for anything other than violence? If there were a benign purpose to a "baton," these Negro children would hardly know about it. How out of step could a person be, how blind to reality?

I couldn't help but wonder whether the war was also a lie hidden within President Johnson's lofty claim about "making the world safe for democracy." Fighting a war in a place nobody had ever heard of, against an enemy no one had ever thought of, seemed ridiculous on its face—like the cop's myth about the baton.

In that moment, I felt proud of Philip and the rest of those boys and girls. In their simplicity, they were staring down a lie. A smile of satisfaction broke across my face just as Philip turned to look at me. He slid over on his knees and threw his arms around me. I hugged him tightly, and as I looked out, I saw the other volunteers and Alberta looking on with soft, consoling smiles.

Chapter Twenty-Three

TWO WEEKS HAD PASSED since I'd tried to reach Gerry. He could be anywhere: in the field on a mission, reassigned with no time to call, or raising hell somewhere on leave with his buddies. Still, it seemed odd not to hear from him after my urgent message. All I could do was wait and busy myself with last-minute preparations for the campus-wide "canvass."

Hubert suggested we do the petition drive, or "canvass," to show student support for President Johnson's Great Society, a bundle of social legislation that included a voting rights act for Negroes, Medicare for the elderly, and a War on Poverty to close the gap between the rich and poor in America. Hubert said the canvass would show Johnson that students were concerned about social policy, not just the war.

Canvassing was hard work, and there were no shortcuts. It was time-intensive, bone-wearying, and ego-deflating. A battalion of volunteers was required to invade the dorms, knock on doors, and engage students in dialogue about the intricacies of policy change—that is, if you found them willing to talk about anything other than the war. Then you needed to get them to sign a petition supporting the domestic programs of a president they detested for his foreign policy. It was an uphill battle.

Despite the swirl of animosity toward Johnson about the war, I managed to enlist twenty volunteers for the canvass. We gathered on the quad on a brisk day in late March. It was still cold, but the hint of spring had lured a few winter-weary students onto the brown stubble that passed for grass. A cadre of uniformed men from the various military branches assembled in front of the Administration Building to recruit students for the Reserve Officers' Training Corps.

"Now remember," I began my pep talk, "young people can be the driving force for social change . . ."

Chants started drifting in from University Avenue, and I tried to speak over them. "We have to emphasize the role of civil debate, respectful dialogue, and trust in our institutions . . ."

Protesters were marching into view, yelling slogans in a raw, pulsating rhythm. As they neared the recruiting table, the students lounging on the grass scattered. I exhorted my contingent to follow me out to begin the canvass, but no one moved. All eyes were fixed on the unfolding confrontation.

Suddenly, Ruth emerged from the phalanx of protesters and approached the officer in charge. I couldn't hear anything, but their exchange looked peaceful. Then she slipped from view, swallowed up in the crowd of protesters.

The scene suddenly became eerily quiet, and then a cloud of ROTC leaflets filled the air. A table was upended, protesters fell to the ground, and I heard the screeching of police squad cars on Ellis Avenue. I stood horrified and helpless, like a bystander witnessing a fatal accident.

As the protesters dispersed, I spotted Ruth running toward the middle of the quad, taking refuge in Bond Chapel with a few others. I felt rage welling up inside me. She was running away? What kind of conviction was that? Create chaos and run? She had turned a protest into a riot—and for what? To bring attention to the war everyone was already paying attention to? For all her breezy charm, she was a coward, running away. I felt ashamed that I was ever attracted to her.

Several hours later, my depleted band of volunteers limped back to the council office in Ida Noyes Hall. We collapsed into our seats. I clung to a batch of unused leaflets, a testament to the futility of our day's effort.

Suddenly, Sam appeared in the doorway. He had never come to the council office. I had never seen him anywhere except behind his desk in the dorm lobby. He had an urgent, agitated look.

"Ray, there's a problem," he said.

"You mean the ROTC riot on campus? We were there—"

"No. I mean at home."

Everyone glanced at me, then silently slipped out of the room.

"What is it, Sam?"

"Your mom called. She said not to worry, but to call home right away."

"When did she call?"

"She called three times. Last time, maybe an hour ago."

For an instant, Sam struck me as cartoon-like. Why was he working himself up about Mom calling to tell me when Gerry would call? I grinned at him stupidly. Then it hit me. *Mom called three times.* Oh my God. It wasn't about Gerry; it was about Dad. Something terrible had happened to Dad.

I charged down the wide staircase to the phone booth on the second floor and began the agonizing process of making a long-distance call. "Please hurry," I begged, as if the operator could alter the unnerving slowness of the process. "Just one minute, sir," she snapped. In the next thirty seconds, my mind traveled around the world of imagined horrors befalling Dad. I'd catch the first plane out tomorrow morning—

"Go ahead, sir," the operator finally intoned.

"Ray?" said my father.

"Dad? You sound fine."

"Yes, son, I'm fine. Why wouldn't I be? It's just that . . ."

"What? What's going on, Dad?"

"Let me put your mother on. She knows more about it. She's right here."

"Ray?" Mom said solemnly. "It's Gerry . . ."

"What about Gerry? Did you hear from Mrs. Moretti?"

"Gerry was killed in Vietnam."

I went into shocked silence. Everything went black, and I stopped breathing.

"We just found out," Mom continued. "It happened two days ago."

My knees buckled. I dropped the phone and jammed my palms into the walls of the phone booth to steady myself. I could hear patches of Mom's voice floating from the dangling receiver.

"Ray, are you there? Ray? Please."

I managed to grab the phone. "I'm here."

"It was in the paper today," Mom continued, crying. "Oh Ray, he died in a place called Quang Tin. Whoever heard of such a terrible thing? American boys dying in far-off places like that. For what?"

A flood of boyhood memories with Gerry raced across my mind, like a fading newsreel with spotty images of people in motion but no sound: playing stickball until dark, perilous rock fights with neighborhood boys, scrambling high into the trees lining our street, endless debates about whether Catholic or Jewish girls were prettier, and countless Saturdays at the mailing house. And soccer!

Mom was barely intelligible, choking with tears. "Ray, did you know . . . that you and Gerry were born four days apart?"

I don't remember hanging up. I stumbled out of the phone booth and drifted down the corridor. Ida Noyes Hall felt dark and ominous, shrouded in an eerie quiet punctuated by faint voices coming from the far end. The voices led to the open door of the SDS office.

An air of breezy satisfaction pervaded the room; people were laughing. The room was a colossal mess. Every desk was jammed with papers spilling out of folders. Wasted mimeograph stencils were strewn around, mingling with half-eaten fruit. Mail lay unopened on the floor, imprinted with the marks of trampling feet. The merriment in the room was weirdly incongruous with the grim posters of war atrocities on the walls.

A smiling SDS member came up to me. "Can I help you?"

I marched past him to Ruth, who was talking casually with the others.

"Why are you celebrating?" I asked flatly.

"Ray!" she said, taking a step back. "What are you doing here?" The conversations in the room came to a halt. I looked around at each face, my rage building. I started to shake but my voice was low, steady, and threatening. "What are you people so happy about?"

Ruth tilted her head to the side and narrowed her eyes.

"Because if it has anything to do with that pathetic spectacle you put on today," I continued, "you should be shutting down this stupid office and personally apologizing to every student in the university."

"What are you talking about?"

I suddenly realized that I was still holding unused leaflets from the canvass, clutching them like a schoolboy with his late homework. I hurled them to the floor by her feet. She jumped out of the way and the SDS workers took steps toward me. With clenched fists, I stared them down, then glared at Ruth.

"Men are dying," I said. "Good men. And all you do is make petty rants, start riots, then run for cover. You're a bunch of cowards."

I turned and headed for the door. Everyone stepped aside to let me pass. At the door, I turned for a parting shot. "And look at this place. A pigsty."

Ruth rushed after me. "Ray, wait," she said, grabbing my arm. "Look, we didn't want that to happen today."

I pulled my arm away and stared her down. "What are you talking about? You caused it."

"No. *They* caused it."

"You're crazy. I saw the whole thing."

"You didn't see anything. I was just talking to the officer in charge, but one of his men started calling us names, then put his hand on his holster. We thought he was drawing his gun, so we turned the table over and pushed it toward them to protect ourselves. We didn't go there to create a disturbance, but to create awareness. Those soldiers—"

"Create awareness? Are you insane? What did you expect them to do? Surrender on the spot, admit that their lives were a lie? I can just imagine them saying, 'Oh, wait one minute, Miss, let's get rid of these uniforms and join your little band of anarchists.'"

"Ray, you're living in a dream world. The soldiers you call good men are committing atrocities against the people of Vietnam."

"Don't say that. You don't know that. American soldiers are not killers."

I had no idea whether our troops were killers or not. Again, I was saying things I couldn't prove. After listening to that soldier two weeks ago, I couldn't be sure of anything. All I could express was rage, and all I could feel was grief. Gerry was dead. My heart was broken.

I began to falter. I couldn't argue anymore. I turned and started to walk away. But Ruth wasn't done.

"Time to put away childish things, Ray," she yelled after me. "Your council, your rules of civility, your idealistic talk about democratic process, dialogue, and reform. It all means nothing as long as this war goes on."

She was right. It didn't matter what I said, what she said, or what anyone said. These protests would go on, men would die, Americans would clutch at each other's throats, and the president's demonic obstinacy would fuel the flames of division. What was the point of arguing when we were all being scorched?

I staggered out of the SDS office and down the corridor to my office. Inside the darkened room, a faint light from the hallway seeped under the door, just enough to shed an eerie half-light on Hubert's photo. I closed my eyes, trying to block the surging feeling that my attachment to Hubert *was* childish, as Ruth said. Or that it was an "affectation," as Dad had once called it. Hubert's mementos seemed distant and irrelevant now, like photos in a family album that revive memories but no emotion. I sat motionless in the dark for thirty minutes, then went back downstairs to the phone booth and dialed the operator. I wondered what Hubert would think of me calling him on a Saturday night and forcing him to pay for it. But I didn't care.

Chapter Twenty-Four

WHEN I GOT HOME Saturday night, Muriel was waiting with a ham and cheese sandwich and a jar of ketchup at the ready.

"I fixed you a snack," she said. "But honestly, Hubert . . . wasn't there food at the reception?"

"Well, yes, but I was too busy meeting folks," I replied. "Anyway, ham and cheese relaxes me. With plenty of ketchup!"

Muriel shook her head in mock dismay and we both laughed.

"So where did he send you this time?" she asked.

"Opening of the Gambian embassy."

"Gambia? Where's Gambia?"

"West Africa, next to Senegal. Got its independence last month and Lyndon wanted me there."

"My gosh, why is he sending you to these things?"

"Penance, Muriel."

"For what?"

"For speaking out against the bombing at the cabinet meeting."

"I thought you talked it over with him."

"We did. I think he wants to be sure I remember the conversation."

I dug into my sandwich. Muriel bit her lip, same as I did when thoughts lingered. But there was nothing more to be said.

She was about to retreat to the kitchen when the phone rang, and she grabbed it. There was a long pause. I thought it was Lyndon wanting to quiz me about the Gambian event.

"Yes, operator, put him through," Muriel said. "Well,

hello, Ray. That's perfectly fine, we don't mind paying the charges." She handed me the receiver. "It's Ray."

I took the phone from Muriel. "Hi Ray. How was your canvass today?"

"Not so great." Ray's voice was quivering.

"What's wrong?"

"It's the war, sir. It's the only thing students care about."

"I know, Ray—"

"Mr. Vice President . . . Vietnam is drowning out everything. No one cares about social policy."

"I care, Ray, and I know you care, too. We need to stay with it. Remember what we talked about in my office last year? About being patient?"

"Yes, I remember. But I can't stop thinking that it just isn't right what we're doing. Too many boys are dying and there's no purpose."

"I know this war must seem—"

"No, sir. Please let me get this out. It's personal now. My next-door neighbor was killed two days ago."

"Oh, goodness. I'm sorry."

"In Quang Tin, some stupid place in a jungle that no one ever heard of—"

"Ray, calm down for a minute. What's his name?"

"Gerry. Gerry Moretti."

"Gerry Moretti?"

"Yes. I grew up with him. My next-door neighbor. He was a good guy. A good man, I mean. The kind of man who should be building America instead of dying in Vietnam. I just can't stop thinking about what his parents are feeling . . . and the families of all the men killed."

"Look, Ray. Let me confide in you. I'm also troubled by what we're doing in Vietnam. Very troubled. I tried to get through to the president, and . . . well, let's just say I felt like a lone wolf howling in a wilderness."

"Mr. Vice President, are you saying you're against the

war?"

"I wouldn't say that exactly. I just think we're getting into a situation we can neither predict nor control. That's not a great position for the United States to be in. And the cost? Far too great. Young Americans like Gerry are losing their lives every day."

"Honestly, sir, that's what I think. That's what all the students think."

"I know, Ray. But I couldn't get through to the president. He thinks the only way we can get out with honor is to win. Otherwise, those boys will have died in vain."

"In vain, sir? I don't think any of those soldiers want more bloodshed just to save face."

"I tried to make those arguments to the president."

"Sir, maybe there's another way to reach him."

"Another way?"

"I have an idea."

"Okay, Ray, what is it?"

"A memo to the president. But instead of focusing on all the military and strategic points, explain the effect on America's youth and how this war is robbing us of our faith in our country."

"I don't know, Ray. This might not be the best time."

"I can help, sir. You know, bring the student perspective. We talked about that in Washington, remember?"

"Yes, I remember."

"Don't you owe it to Gerry and all the boys to give it a try?"

I looked up at Muriel staring at me. Ray's voice was so sincere, his argument so urgent. He was driving past my defenses like a tank through a brick wall. I was hesitant, but it felt more like timidity than caution. What right did I have to be timid standing up to the president when men like Ray's friend Gerry were dying?"

"Okay, Ray, send me your ideas. I'll start working up a

memo to the president. But keep working on your council. That Daley event is coming up. Stay focused on domestic issues. If we can end this war, the nation will start talking about them again. All right?"

I heard a whoosh of air on the other end of the line as Ray exhaled in relief. "Yes sir," he said.

"One last thing. It's important to keep this between us, okay? The president is concerned about leaks, and I've got to be careful. Like we were about your campaign."

When I hung up the phone, Muriel's eyes met mine. "Are you really going to challenge Lyndon on Vietnam?"

"I'll probably catch holy hell, but I have to give it a try."

"All, right, Dad," she said, walking over and kissing me on the forehead. "I'm with you. Just be careful."

Chapter Twenty-Five

IN THE CAVERNOUS reading room of the University's Harper Library, I hunched over a pile of books just as I had at the Rockville Centre Public Library a year ago. This time, the stakes were higher: I was helping Hubert end the war in Vietnam. I'd boasted to him that I had a special perspective, and now I had to deliver.

As I was poring over the volumes, Ruth walked in with a few friends, spotted me, and strolled over.

"Hi, Ray," she said softly.

Her voice carried no hostility from the other night, and no hesitancy, either. She was direct and disarming. Not a hint of defensiveness. True, she'd been tough on me Saturday night, but she wasn't abusive, which was more than I could say for myself.

"About the other night," I began. "I was out of line throwing the leaflet at you—"

"No. You were right."

"What?

"It was wrong to run away from the ROTC protest. I should have stood my ground, come what may. I acted like a coward."

I nodded with measured slowness, letting her contrition sink in.

She bent slightly toward me and cocked her head to scan the books on the table. "What are you doing?"

"I'm studying Vietnam," I said, forcing myself to sound casual.

"Oh. How come?"

I couldn't answer. I was too embarrassed to tell the truth: that I was helping the vice president of the United States convince the president of the United States to get out of Vietnam? It would sound outlandish.

"If you want to know about Vietnam, I can help."

"Well . . ."

"You're not going to find anything in this old place," she said, raising her arms to the ceiling in a gesture of helplessness. "Come with me."

"What? Wait. I don't know—"

"Trust me, Ray."

Trust her? How could I trust her? We'd just had a big fight.

"C'mon," she said, tugging gently at my arm.

I got up cautiously and followed her out. I had no idea where she was taking me. If I had, I surely would have found some reason to object. But not knowing, well . . . I didn't know what to object to. I just had to trust her.

She led me through the brisk winter night. I trailed behind, still hesitant. She turned slightly, winked, and took a step back, putting her arm through mine. My hesitation dissolved. This was the fourth time she had touched me; I remembered each time vividly, including ten minutes ago in the library. But those gestures had been offhand and ambiguous, or so I thought. Not like this. We were arm in arm.

We arrived at the bookstore on 57th Street at Woodlawn and walked down four short, narrow steps. I had to duck to avoid hitting the head jamb. The place was cramped; books were stuffed on warped shelves that pitched precariously on buckled floors. A good shove, and the entire store would come tumbling down. The cashier, an old man, sat imperiously on a raised platform, fingering a newspaper sprawled in front of him. He seemed to take no notice of Ruth tugging my arm and leading me to a section in the far corner of the store.

"Now, Ray," she said gravely, "those tomes in the library

are ancient. You need to focus on the last decade—what's happened since the French defeat in Vietnam."

"Yes," I said obligingly. "I've been reading about that. Dien Bien Phu, right?"

Ruth nodded mechanically. She pulled a book from the shelf and held it out to me. "The people of South Vietnam are not communists. They just want to be rid of foreign domination. Americans don't see that because they believe all the crap Johnson is feeding them."

The cashier lifted his head from his newspaper, then raised his eyes over his glasses to stare at us. What a picture we made: an impetuous and exuberant young woman coaching her ignorant and reluctant charge.

She handed me another book. "Can you imagine? We're actually driving the Vietnamese people to the communists, the very thing we say we want to avoid. It's insane." She shook her head, then scanned the stacks for more books. She pulled out another and plopped it on top of the first two. I wondered how many more of these she was going to make me read.

Suddenly, she turned sharply. "C'mon, Ray, I want to show you something else."

I trailed her to the American history section, where she searched the shelves excitedly and pulled down *Common Sense* by Thomas Paine. She turned immediately to a passage and read it aloud. "'The laying of a country desolate with fire and sword, declaring war against the natural rights of all mankind, is the concern of every man to whom nature hath given the power of feeling.'" She looked up at me and recited the next sentence by heart, her eyes blazing. "'The cause of America is in great measure, the cause of all mankind.' You see, Ray, if our cause is mankind, then we must ensure that our cause is just."

Of course. It was so simple, confoundingly simple. Not the truth about the war, but about Ruth herself. I felt as if a curtain was suddenly drawn on a stage and the woman playing

Ruth was finally revealed. Ruth was a patriot. Just like me. I smiled.

"What?" she asked.

"Nothing. It's just that . . . I didn't expect you to have such feelings. You know, about America."

"Ray, this may come as a shock to you, but I love America. I just want her to stay faithful to her ideals."

"I can see that, Ruth. These will help a lot." I lifted the pile of books in a gesture of gratitude.

"You know, that's the first time you've called me by my first name."

"Oh, well—"

"But what do you mean that the books will help a lot?"

I hesitated

"Come clean, Ray. Help with what?"

"I can help . . . help Humphrey."

Ruth's eyes tightened into narrow slits. She pulled her head back as if trying to focus on some alien being that had just appeared.

"He's trying to convince Johnson to rethink American policy in Vietnam," I added, sounding apologetic.

"What are you talking about?"

I blushed. I couldn't believe I'd said "rethinking American policy." I sounded like some policy wonk reviving a dead cliché. But that *was* what Hubert was trying to do, and I *was* helping him.

"Hubert—I mean Humphrey—is trying to get Johnson to reconsider his position on the war."

Ruth stared at me, shaking her head. "Oh, Ray." I expected her to tell me again to put away my childish things.

"Look, maybe I can get through to him. Isn't that the way things work in a democracy?"

She kept shaking her head. She was pitying me.

"Wait a minute," I said. "That's what you told me to do. To write to him. Don't you remember? On my way to orchestra practice?"

"I remember. I did say that . . ."

"But?"

"But Humphrey is part of the structure now. He's been bludgeoned by Johnson to toe the line."

"That's not true. Hubert Humphrey can't be bludgeoned."

She hung her head. "If you say so, Ray."

"You don't believe me, do you?"

"Ray, there are forces at play that one person can't stop. Not even Johnson. It's the momentum of the Cold War. One big lie after another. That if we lose one stupid country on the tip of Southeast Asia, the rest of the world will fall to communism like dominoes."

"You don't know Humphrey. A good fight is his stock-in-trade. He can stop it."

I knew I sounded corny, but I didn't care. I knew what I was saying was true. I trusted Hubert to come through. Ruth stared at me with a gauzy, indulgent smile. "Okay, Ray. We'll see. We'll see."

Chapter Twenty-Six

I WORKED ON MY LETTER to Hubert for three days straight. On the last day, I pulled an all-nighter. I crammed every historical fact, political point, and moral argument I could think of into a five-page memorandum, single-spaced, in the same formal style Hubert used when he wrote to me.

To: Hon. Hubert H. Humphrey,
        Vice President of the United States
From: Ray Elias, Chairman,
        Domestic Youth Policy Council
Re: Why America's Youth Can't Support
        the Vietnam War.
Date: May 7, 1965

I reviewed the letter one last time before placing it in a large envelope and ceremoniously depositing it in the mailbox. It was Friday morning, and dawn was breaking. It suddenly hit me that Gerry's funeral was scheduled for the next day in Rockville Centre. When Mom first told me about it, I'd thought of going, and then put it out of my mind. My parents made it clear that they didn't expect me to come. Besides, I'd had a letter to write to Hubert. But now that was done, and it wasn't even 7:00 am; I could actually make it to Long Island by late afternoon.

I ran back upstairs to my room and packed a few things, then took the train downtown and the bus to O'Hare. I had no trouble catching a flight to New York, and the price was right for students going standby. Twenty-five bucks! At

LaGuardia Airport, I reversed the process, taking a bus to Manhattan and a train to Rockville Centre.

I decided not to tell my parents I was coming. I couldn't figure out how to break it to them. They didn't want me to leave school, even for a weekend. They viewed college as a kind of tightrope: one slight diversion, one breach of focus, could throw me off balance and cause a fatal fall. Mom was always thinking about her friend Mildred and her nephew with the nervous breakdown. I'm sure they also worried that Gerry's funeral would set off an emotional land mine in me. I understood their fears, but I just couldn't see how a weekend off to honor a friend would threaten anything. It was something I would regret not doing. So, rather than argue, I decided to simply show up and deal with the consequences.

When I walked into the house, my sister was lying on the living room floor studying, ankles crossed and legs swaying rhythmically in the air. Even though I hadn't told anyone I was coming, Diane greeted my arrival as the most natural thing in the world and immediately started jabbering away. Pepi barked with delight. It was so comforting to enter my accustomed life merely by turning a key and walking back into it—that is, until my mother came down the stairs and gasped.

"What?" she stammered. "Why . . . ?"

"I'm home for Gerry's funeral," I blurted out.

She frowned but said nothing.

"Anyway, I wanted to surprise you." A stupid lie, of course, but I ran to her and kissed her. She hugged me tightly.

"Cars have been coming and going all day," she said, sobbing softly.

"I know. I saw them."

"What are you going to tell your father?" she asked.

Just then, Dad walked in. "What are you doing here?" he asked sharply. "In some kind of trouble?"

"No trouble," I replied.

"Gerry's funeral," Mom said, leaping to my defense.

"You didn't say anything about coming," he said. "Who drove you from the airport?"

What difference could it possibly make who drove me from the airport? I thought. Why did his questions always sound like accusations?

"I took a bus," I said flatly. "Gerry would have wanted me here."

Dad bit his lip and looked down at the floor. I think he was upset about Gerry's death, too, but he always defaulted to a belligerent mode. "Maybe he'd want you to stay put in Chicago, study hard, and outlast this terrible thing like he can't do." With that, he stomped off. I'd been home barely ten minutes and was already in a fight with Dad.

"You should go let the Morettis know you're here," Mom said gently.

I walked out the door and down the street to Gerry's house. I knocked on the front door, even though I had never entered that way; Gerry and I always went through the kitchen in the back, like we did at my house. Going through the front entryway felt strange, like I was visiting a different house.

In a way, it was a different house that day. The living room was overflowing, but I knew no one except Gerry's parents. There were a few kids my age. They may have been Gerry's friends from St. Agnes, or relatives. I felt like an intruder from another world: the world of college boys with draft deferments who would never get killed in Vietnam.

Mrs. Moretti spotted me right away. "I'm glad you came, Ray," she said, giving me a hug. She motioned for me to follow her as she led the way to Gerry's room. She opened his closet door and pulled his soccer coat off the hanger, the one with the St. Agnes insignia emblazoned on the front.

"Take this," she said unceremoniously.

"Mrs. Moretti, no. I couldn't."

"It's not doing any good sitting in this closet."

"Mrs. Moretti, I don't know. It was Gerry's."

"Ray, please. Gerry would want you to have it. I want you to take it." She started to cry.

"Of course," I said, fighting back my own tears. "I promise I'll wear it."

She gave me a gentle hug. "You boys were good friends. It meant a lot to him. You'll come to the funeral tomorrow?"

"Yes, ma'am. Of course."

I walked back home, shaken. How would my mother react if I died on a battlefield? She would be devastated, of course. I couldn't bear to think about it, yet boys like Gerry were dying every day, and families were suffering in countless homes throughout America.

I was barely through the door when my father accosted me. "What are you doing with that coat?"

"Mrs. Moretti gave it to me. She said Gerry—"

"You shouldn't be wearing it."

"She said Gerry would want me to have it."

"You can't wear it."

"Why not?"

"It's morbid, that's why. And you're not Catholic, for God's sake."

"Jim!" my mother shouted. She took a deep breath, then shifted to a low threatening tone I had never heard. "That coat is Ray's way of remembering Gerry. Leave him alone."

Dad stopped dead in his tracks. Maybe he was shamed by Mom's anger more than he was persuaded by her logic. Either way, the matter was settled.

The next day was cold and rainy on Long Island. As the priest at the funeral invoked the injustice of Gerry's death, I felt a kinship with everyone there, even though I didn't know anyone and nobody was Jewish. The priest transcended religion and evoked a consoling image of Gerry's life. No matter how brief his life or how senseless his death, he had now been called home to God. It was beautiful.

But my mood darkened as I recalled my father's reaction to Gerry's coat. Stupidly, I had expected Dad to change while I was away, but there seemed to be no way to reach him. I decided I would wear Gerry's coat all the time. I would be faithful to Gerry's memory, in spite of my father and small-minded people like him.

After the funeral, I sat alone in my room, staring at the big oak tree. On Sunday, I just waited for time to pass until my mother drove me to the airport. Although the trip passed in silence, I was grateful to be with her. I expected some words of wisdom, the way she had consoled me the day after my fight with Dad on current events night. But she said nothing, just hugged me tightly and said goodbye. I hadn't said goodbye to my father. It had been the most unsettling weekend of my life.

Chapter Twenty-Seven

OUR LIMOUSINE PULLED UP to the west portico of the White House for a dinner honoring the United States space program. Surprisingly, Lyndon himself was there to greet Muriel and me. He kissed Muriel warmly. He flirted with all the ladies no matter who they were, even Jackie Kennedy, or so I was told.

He put his huge arm around me. "Hubert, can I have a word?" He guided me into a corridor. Then it began.

"What in the world were you thinking?" he hissed.

I stared at him, puzzled.

"That damn memo you sent me on Vietnam."

"Mr. President. You said we should talk privately—"

"That's right. I said *talk*. The last thing I need is another one of your rambling memos."

"With all due respect, sir, you need objective advice."

"Not from someone who leaks everything to the press. And not in a goddamn memo!"

"Lyndon, someone has to talk to you without hiding behind charts and maps."

He leaned into me, towering over me, forcing me against the wall. "I don't want it getting out that my vice president is soft on the war. Do you understand?"

He pushed me against the wall like a bulldozer ramming a pile of dirt. "Another stunt like this, Ubert, and I'm putting your vice presidency in mothballs. Permanently."

I felt his ferocious power draining mine, the oxygen in my body flowing into his. Hatred welled up in me like a blaze spiraling skyward. I was engulfed in it.

My fists clenched against the wall. Could I throw a punch at the president of the United States? My God, I wanted to. Maybe just a good shove to reclaim my ground . . . but I imagined the lurid headlines that would come of it: vice president brawls with the president at white house dinner. Johnson would probably like it. He might even leak it. The thought doused my anger, and the fire burned out. I retreated into the confines of gentlemanly composure.

Johnson sensed it all. He was an animal with an instinct for weakness and a penchant for terror. What would he take from this incident? Respect for challenging him or contempt for backing down? He leaned back, shoulders slackening, now fully composed and erect.

He walked back toward Muriel. I followed slowly, and he waited for me to catch up. "Don't be surprised if I acknowledge your boy tonight," he said to her, his lips twisted in a half smile. Then he rushed off.

"Hubert. What is it?" Muriel grabbed my arm and ran her hand across my clammy palms. "You're covered in sweat!" She loosened my collar, pulled the handkerchief from my lapel, and started dabbing my forehead.

"Good God, Hubert. What on earth went on between you and Lyndon?"

"Let's talk about it later," I said, still breathing heavily.

At the center table in the State Dining Room of the White House, Johnson was chatting amiably with America's leading space scientists, Wernher von Braun among them. As Hitler's chief scientist during the war, von Braun did his best to destroy England with his V-2 rocket, but after Germany's defeat, he was hustled off to the United States, repatriated and put in charge of America's space program.

"We welcome you tonight to honor the men and women of our space program," Johnson began. "But before I introduce our special guests, I'd like to mention what a great job the vice president is doing overseeing the program."

Amid applause, Johnson scanned the room, pretending not to know where Muriel and I were sitting. "C'mon, Hubert. I know you're out there." Johnson let out a huge belly laugh. "Somewhere in outer space."

I rose slowly, glancing tensely at Muriel and forcing a smile.

"Now, sometimes Hubert and I don't see eye to eye on things. So I came up with this idea to send him on the next manned mission."

The crowd laughed nervously.

Johnson turned to von Braun. "You see, Doctor, I realized we wouldn't miss him . . ." Johnson paused, drawing every ounce of pleasure from the suspense. "Because even from outer space, you can still hear Hubert."

The crowd laughed heartily. I clutched the table. I felt the tablecloth moving, about to pull my plate over the side. Muriel thrust her hand on mine, preventing disaster. I sank back into my seat.

Muriel and I sat in the back of the limousine, gliding through the grand boulevards of Washington, DC. The silence was saturated with foreboding.

"What is it, Bucky?" I asked.

"I was thinking of the Depression. Those years working for your father."

"The wilderness years," I quipped, vainly hoping to derail Muriel's reverie.

"We would go to bed dreaming of a different life, but wake up to just another day of filling prescriptions and jerking soda." Tears started to flow from her eyes. "I remember that look of desperation as you watched your dreams evaporate."

"Muriel."

"Never standing up to your father . . . it was the same

look I saw on your face tonight, and every time you meet with Lyndon. It's like going back in time, stranded at the drugstore, serving out our sentence. And I know you've been hiding those stomach pains. Just like you did then."

I stared vacantly out the window into the dark streets. Dad's voice drifted in on me like a random tune I couldn't get out of my head: "Hubert, If I'm going to make it as a pharmacist, I'm going to need you to learn the business and work with me." With those words, my fate was sealed. I stared at Dad like he was a judge pronouncing a sentence. Soon I'd be off to pharmacy school, preparing for a life behind the counter in a small town, not as a public man making his mark in the Twin Cities. I felt robbed of my destiny; and my father, who would never turn his back on a needy customer, even as the debts piled up, was the thief. I couldn't say a thing.

"Why are you always trying to please him, Hubert?" Muriel asked, sobbing. "The American people elected you, too."

"I have to be loyal to the president," I said feebly. "I just can't do this any other way."

I knew I had to make the break with Lyndon. But I would have to do it my own way and in my own time, just as I did with Dad. I wasn't sure Muriel could believe that, but she'd have to trust me.

Chapter Twenty-Eight

I HAD NEVER BEEN much of a drinker. College kids at the University of Chicago didn't drink; they smoked. I tried marijuana, of course, but my mind always descended into a swirl of anxiety, making it that much harder to regain stability. What was the point of escaping reality if regaining it was more difficult after you escaped?

Jimmy's was an old-time Chicago bar, out of place among the mansions in the Gothic precincts of the university. But the bar itself was pure U of C. The walls were filled with artifacts of University of Chicago life: the golden age of football, when the "Monsters of the Midway," led by coach Alonzo Stagg and Jay Berwanger, the first Heisman trophy winner, ruled the sport. But portraits of philosophers also filled the walls, mirroring the peculiar weirdness that marked the University of Chicago.

I took a seat at the bar, looking around to see if anyone recognized me. I caught snatches of conversation at a nearby table: "imperialist conspiracy," "authoritarian elite," "nationalist struggle," and "proletariat dialectic." I felt repulsed by the impenetrable vernacular of the anti-war movement, which was exactly what I came to the bar to get away from. What was the point of this anymore? The president was implacable. Only his vice president had the status, the conviction, and the eloquence to move him. But I had heard nothing from Hubert, so I waited. And drank.

"You've been coming around a lot lately," the bartender said, a bit too familiarly. "So what is it? Sex, drugs, or both?"

"Just a beer, please."

He slinked away to fetch the drink, and I gazed up at the soundless TV displaying the nightly montage of footage from Vietnam. From an adjoining room I heard the strains of folk music, and I thought that might relax me. When the beer came, I got up and followed the music.

A solo guitarist was introducing a tune. "Now, I'd like to sing something written by my fellow troubadour, Tom Lehrer. It's about a man we used to know who disappeared, lost in time and forgotten. Perhaps you've heard of him. If you know the words, join in."

Whatever happened to poor Hubert.
Has anyone heard a thing?
He once shone on his own,
now he sits home alone,
and waits for the phone to ring.

Ripples of laughter spread throughout the room. I couldn't believe it. Hubert had become a joke. These cold-hearted people were laughing at a man carrying the hopes of millions on his shoulders. No one knew that, of course, or cared that Hubert was trying to end the war. It was easier to ridicule someone than to trust them.

I threw a dollar down on the counter, left my beer at the table, and headed back to the dorm. When I entered the lobby, Lew and a few of the volunteers were waiting for me.

"Read this," Lew demanded, thrusting the *Chicago Daily News* in my face. I barely got through two sentences when Lew blurted, "You said Hubert was against the bombing."

Lew grabbed the paper from me and read Hubert's statement. "'While I support the bombing, the war has to be won on the ground, by ground forces.'"

I snatched the paper back. "I can read, for God's sake."

But I didn't have to. The meaning was clear. Hubert had come out in favor of the bombing. And a ground war! Had

Johnson rejected his memo? Obviously he had. Even so, why was Hubert now endorsing the bombing?

A blurb followed the article, announcing Hubert's appearance at Michigan State University the following evening. *I can make that,* I thought. *I'll talk to him. Lansing was only three hours by car.*

"Lew, loan me your car," I said.

"What?"

"Or come with me. I want to go to Lansing. Let's go talk to Hubert."

"Are you crazy? I don't think I could stomach it."

"Well then, give me the damn keys! I'm going."

Lew thrust the keys in my hand. "If anything happens to that car, you're paying."

"Okay. Okay. I promise. Nothing will happen."

In Lew's beat-up Volkswagen, I made my way through Chicago's South Side, into northern Indiana, and past the Gary Works of United States Steel sprawled along seven miles of Lake Michigan's shore. This conglomerate of giant smokestacks belching smoke represented the hegemony of American industry: rough, relentless, and prodigious. Within these ghostly structures, tens of thousands of men and women labored their way to the middle class and upward mobility for their children. Yet in the flush of war, this dark landscape stood as dismal testimony to America's withered dreams and the grim penance of young men dying in Vietnam.

But then there was the freshness of America's heartland, the rolling fields of corn wavering in the June breeze. Michigan was the northern edge of America's corn belt, a limitless bounty as enviable as our industrial might. I felt the pulse of our nation's greatness. This was Hubert's patrimony, the source of his inspiration and mine, too. I prayed he could tap into it tonight and generate hope for others, as he had with me. Sure, he had made those bombing remarks, but I still had faith in him as the conscience of our country trying to resist the tide of war.

I parked Lew's car as a troupe of students scampered by. Spotting the license plate, a pretty girl said, "Illinois, huh? Come for the fun?"

"I guess so," I said pliantly.

Maybe entertainment was what Hubert was to these students. But I was hoping for something I could bring back to Chicago: to prove to myself, to Ruth, and to my council that the original Hubert Humphrey was alive and well, his old self fighting for what he believed. I felt a burst of optimism.

Inside the gymnasium, Hubert strode up to the podium smiling. He assumed the posture I had seen so many times: his brow rode high above his eyebrows, arched sharply like the limbs of a delicate tree. His lips were pressed together with proud purpose.

"It is refreshing to return to the atmosphere of excitement, of expectation and love of learning that is characteristic of a great university."

Light applause, more respectful than approving, greeted his words.

"The subject which I am about to discuss with you pertains to war and peace. No group should be more interested in war and peace than those who will be expected to bear the brunt of the fighting if war should come."

Amid tepid applause, ripples of protest rolled through the crowd. Hubert forged ahead. This was his wheelhouse: students he loved and minds that his oratory could reach. He seemed to shift into high gear, but it sounded shrill, defensive, unsteady.

"Vietnam offers a classic example of what can be accomplished by militant communist forces intent on deliberate subversion of a country from within."

Now the rumble of opposition took hold. Security personnel eyed the crowd uneasily. The anti-war placards that had been tucked away when Hubert started speaking reappeared.

"Our action in Vietnam is a part of the continuing struggle that the American people must be prepared to wage if we are to preserve free civilization as we know it and resist the expansion of communist power."

Anti-war chants and catcalls spread like a chain reaction through the crowd and exploded in a cloud of anger that enveloped the room.

Hubert paused, his jaw jutting out defiantly, his fists clenched around the podium as if he were gripping the helm of a ship in a listing tide. He bravely resumed. "We must continue to pursue the goal of peace and freedom—acknowledging both the prospects of success and the consequences of failure. If we act with vision and wisdom, we shall not fail."

But no one was with him. His speech was filled with shallow phrases and hollow testaments. His imagery was abstract. He was invoking someone else's voice and pressing someone else's cause: Johnson's? There were taunts now, placards thrust upward. He had lost everyone. I could feel their anger. Not because he was the face of the government dragging them into unwanted conflict, but because he was distorting what was at stake in Vietnam. He was playing these students for fools. He was lying.

As the speech ended, I fell in with a crowd tagging after him, but his security detail whisked him away. I doubled my pace, cutting through a dense weave of protesters. *Just call out his name and he'll see you,* I commanded to myself. "Hubert, it's Ray," I shouted. But it was half-hearted and drowned out in the tumult. I was not the insistent and confident boy invited to Washington, DC for a ceremonious encounter with a great man. I was an interloper; hesitant, doubtful, and distrusting. I stopped abruptly and was jostled to the floor by the crowd surging after Hubert with jeers, taunts, and derisive slogans.

Chapter Twenty-Nine

I WAS SITTING IN AIR FORCE TWO, lost in thought, as Danny handed me a drink. I nodded appreciatively at my trusted aide, who never spared any effort to fortify me.

"It was a fine speech, Mr. Vice President. And a valiant effort."

"'Valiant' was not the word I was thinking of, Danny. More like 'vain.'"

"Mr. Vice President, the cause is just."

"Danny, please. They didn't believe a word . . . how could they? I had trouble believing it myself."

Danny looked at me numbly.

A stewardess appeared, holding a giant black box containing a phone. She attached it to a console by my seat. Only one person had access to me like that. Danny moved a few seats over to give me privacy while I spoke to the president.

"Hubert?" Johnson's voice boomed through the receiver. "I heard you did a fine job in Lansing. Real fine. Senator Hart called and told me."

"Thank you, sir," I answered blankly.

"I just want you to know how much I appreciate that, Hubert. You need to keep up the good work. We need that old populism of yours out there. You're one of America's finest speechmakers, and I'm happy to have you on my team."

"Mr. President. I was just wondering, sir . . ."

"What's that, Hubert?"

"The Domestic Policy Council. There's work we need to do there, especially on civil—"

"Now Hubert, yes, we'll get to all of that. But right now, I need you to focus on Vietnam."

"Yes, sir, but—"

"You need to get off the Domestic Policy Council."

"Mr. President, I'm the chairman!"

"And that kid you've got working for you in Chicago, get him off, too."

"Ray Elias?"

"Whatever. I heard about him from Dick Daley. I need you to work on Vietnam. Nothing else. No offense, Hubert, but I'm calling in Joe Califano."

"Califano? For what?"

"To take over your council. He'll dither on all that policy shit like those Harvard types."

"Mr. President, with all due respect, domestic policy is the lifeblood of—"

"Ubert, not another word. There'll be time for your domestic agenda. But right now, I want you out on the hustings, drumming up support. And keep your bags packed. I may be sending you to Vietnam."

"Vietnam, sir?"

"Relax, Hubert. Not permanently."

Johnson laughed and hung up. I gulped down my drink.

"Changes with the council, sir?" Danny asked as he got up to fetch another drink.

"Johnson's disbanding it."

"What? Why?"

"Listen, I've got to break it to Ray. When's that Benton dinner in Chicago?"

"In two weeks, at the University of Chicago."

"That's perfect. Make sure Ray gets invited."

"Sure thing. I'll call the president of the university first thing."

"Good. Thanks. He was there tonight, you know. Ray was."

"Not one of the protesters?"

"I don't know. I just don't know."

Chapter Thirty

THE MORNING AFTER I returned form Lansing, there was an urgent knock on my door. I had a call from the office of Richard J. Daley, mayor of Chicago.

I rushed downstairs, thinking that mayors or their secretaries were not used to being kept waiting. But the secretary was pleasant. She asked me if I could come downtown; the mayor wanted to see me.

"Of course," I said. "When?"

"Will tomorrow be all right?"

I panicked. *Oh my God. The Daley event.* Hearing nothing from Hubert for weeks, I let it drift. But now Daley's office was calling. The event must be on.

When I arrived downtown, I expected to meet with Daley's staff. Instead, I was led into a waiting room to see the mayor himself.

Daley was a legend, not just in Chicago but throughout America. He was a relic of a bygone era, the last of the big-city bosses. His power wasn't in money, but in votes. With each person he put to work, each family he fed, each charity he fostered, and each scholarship he underwrote for working-class boys and girls, he solidified his hold on the electorate of America's great second city.

The tale that Daley had stolen the 1960 election for John Kennedy made its way around the country and gained credence in the telling and retelling: Daley had withheld voting returns from Chicago precincts until late into the night, assessing how many were needed to win Illinois. In the end, the Chicago tally yielded a Kennedy plurality of 450,000, a suspiciously high number, winning the state by a slim 9,000 votes, and the presidency. If true, this made Daley unimaginably evil; subverting a national election? But the story could not be proved, and that made it just a mischievous rumor by the disgruntled loser, Richard Nixon.

To me, Daley was frightening for a different reason. He had a reputation as gruff, hot-tempered, and tyrannical. I was content not to deal with him. It was Hubert's idea to have him speak at my council's event, and Hubert made the arrangements personally.

Daley's office was the largest I had ever seen. It was gigantic, at least fifty-by-fifty feet, with a twelve-foot-high ceiling. Daley sat behind a huge desk, empty except for a telephone. He was squat and so wide that he fit the desk perfectly. A contingent of Chicago cops were arrayed in the back of the room, standing motionless. As I walked the distance from the doorway to the mayor's desk, I felt less and less confident, as if with each step I was being sucked into the domain of some all-powerful alien being.

The mayor didn't get up to greet me. His searing eyes roved up and down my body, then he commanded me to sit down. "Humphrey says you're a good kid, not one of those radicals at the university."

"Thank you, Mr. Mayor, for inviting me to discuss our event."

Daley moved right past my overture and launched into a reflection about the University of Chicago. "I can never figure out why the best colleges in the country end up with some of the weirdest students. Don't get me wrong. The University of Chicago is a drawing card for the city, a great university. All those Nobel prizes and everything. It's a distinction, but I doubt a single person in Hyde Park votes for me."

I had no idea what he expected me to say, and he caught me staring at him. He stared back. Daley's inscrutability was a carefully cultivated talent to intimidate and keep you off balance. It was working. He sensed it and kept up with his disarming non sequiturs. "For instance, take Leon Despres. Do you know him?"

"No, sir. Only by reputation."

"Well, I just don't get it. I give him more money than all the other aldermen combined. Why? Because he yells so loud about government reform and my autocratic style, whatever the hell that means. Autocrat or not, he still takes my money. Hyde Park gets more than the other wards because of that goddamn university."

"I don't know about that, sir. I'm not involved in ward politics."

"What do you mean? Humphrey says you're an astute young politician."

I nodded feebly.

"So did you vote for him?"

"Who, sir?"

"Despres, your alderman."

"No, sir. I can't vote. I'm not twenty-one."

"Oh, that's right. Listen . . . what's your name again?"

"Elias, sir. Ray Elias."

"Elias. Is that Irish?"

"No, sir. Jewish, but I'm part Irish."

"Good combination. Leon Despres is an okay guy. A pain in the ass, but a decent sort. He's Jewish. A hundred percent. Why didn't you invite him to speak?"

"Well, sir, honestly, the vice president suggested you, and I was thrilled with that."

"Well, that's why I called you down. You see, there's been a change."

"A change, sir?"

"The event is off. I spoke to the president."

"Excuse me, Mr. Mayor? You spoke to President Johnson about our event?"

"Yes, Humphrey's domestic group has been transferred

to someone else. That Italian kid from Harvard. Califano. Johnson wants your leadership committee, or whatever I'm supposed to speak at, disbanded too."

"I don't understand. Why did he call you?"

Immediately, I knew that was the wrong question to ask. Daley gave me a "what kind of queer question is that?" look.

"Look, kid. Johnson's got Humphrey on a short leash. Don't you get that?"

I did get it. Anyone watching Hubert in Lansing two days ago could see that. But why would Johnson pull the council? Hubert was supporting the war now. Anyway, why didn't Hubert just pick up the phone and tell me? None of this made sense. I just wanted to get out of there.

"Mr. Mayor, whose idea was it to bring me down here?"

"What are you talking about?"

"I mean why didn't you just have someone call me?"

A time-release smile spread across Daley's face, giving way to a convulsive laugh that made his body shake. Then, in a slow, measured, and menacing tone, he said, "I just wanted to see what Hubert saw in you. You know, for future reference. We need smart young men in my operation."

I stood up abruptly, wondering if the policemen would run over and throw me back in the chair. "Well, Mr. Mayor, I'm afraid your time was wasted, then." With that, I strode toward the door.

Daley waited until I'd completed the long walk to the door, then bellowed, "Hey, kid!"

I stopped and turned.

"Don't get too broken up over this. It's just politics."

In an emotional free fall, I spilled out of City Hall into the Civic Center Plaza across the street. I didn't care about the event being canceled. In a way, it was a relief. But disbanding the council? That was my connection with Hubert, and it was cut off without a word from him. Instead, I had to hear it from this sadistic tyrant. What happened to Hubert? Would I ever find out?

Not if he was too busy, scared, or embarrassed to call me.

Chapter Thirty-One

NO SOONER HAD I arrived back at the dorm after my meeting with Daley than I received another call. For the second time in as many days, Sam sent someone to my room to summon me to the lobby for an urgent call. *What now?* I wondered. *More bad news?*

This time it was the secretary to the president of the university. She wasn't as polite as Daley's secretary; she sounded peeved about having to wait, even though she knew students didn't have phones in their rooms and had to go to the lobby to take calls. This put me in a foul mood—even more foul, I mean.

The secretary told me I was invited to a banquet in honor of William Benton.

"Who's William Benton?" I asked.

"He's the chairman of the *Encyclopedia Britannica*, and a senator from Connecticut," she said gruffly. "Most students know that. He's a benefactor of the university."

"Why me?"

"I don't know. You're on the list and I'm making the calls."

Why would I be on such a list? I was trying to figure it out.

"Are you there?" she asked impatiently.

"Yes, ma'am."

"Well, anyway, a ticket will be waiting for you at the president's office. We're open from nine to five. Have a nice day."

I sat by the phone, trying to figure out why I would be invited to a dinner sponsored by the university president, a person I'd never met, in honor of a man I'd never heard of.

I concluded that it must have been a mistake, so I didn't pick up the ticket.

Days later, rumors started to circulate that Hubert was coming to campus. This made even less sense. Surely, he would have told me . . . or would he? After all, if he'd left it to Daley to disband my council, he might also leave it to a secretary to invite me to the banquet. But the secretary never said a word about Hubert. I decided it was all too complicated to think about.

The day of the banquet, I noticed increased security on campus. It was clear that Hubert was coming, but I still hadn't heard from him. Without an invitation from him, I wasn't going to walk into a fancy banquet—maybe the only kid there, possibly the only person without a tuxedo, and with no idea where to sit. It was just too weird.

Out of curiosity, I drifted over to Hutchinson Commons that night, hiding in the shadows across the street. About fifty demonstrators were crammed into the entrance, holding signs with caricatures of Hubert. Guests pulled up in limousines and were whisked inside by security. Chicago police were working barricades to keep the crowd at bay, billy clubs stretched between them. I scanned the protesters for Ruth. Was she among them? I was grateful I didn't see her, and then wondered why it mattered to me.

Another limousine drove up. Even in the dark, I could make out Hubert's profile: chin jutting out, sharp nose, eyes lodged deep in his high forehead. The crowd also spotted him and cranked up the chants and epithets. Surrounded by Secret Service agents, Hubert made his way through the gauntlet of protesters into the banquet hall. The crowd began to disperse, and I drifted back to my room.

I was lying in bed, thinking about the strange events that had conspired to separate me from Hubert that night, when I heard a loud knock.

Lew got to the door first. "Who is it?" he called out.

"Secret Service," a voice answered brusquely.

My heart started pounding.

Lew thought it was a joke and jousted with the agent. "You've got the wrong address. The person you're looking for is at Hutchinson Commons, at a banquet for some fat cat."

The reply was ominously calm. "Open the door, son. Vice President Humphrey is here to see Ray Elias."

I bolted out of my bedroom, shoved Lew aside, and opened the door. Standing between the two Secret Service agents was the vice president of the United States. The agents moved to the side, and Hubert stepped forward.

"May I come in?" he asked.

"Of course. I'm sorry about that." Lew was making a hasty retreat to his bedroom.

Hubert waved off my apology. I led him into my tiny room, barely big enough for a bed, a desk, and a chair, plus my bass stuffed in the corner. He took off his hat and looked for a place to sit.

"Please take my chair," I said, embarrassed.

"No, I'm fine, Ray," he said, smiling broadly. "I'll just sit here on the bed."

I watched nervously as he took stock of my room, viewing the large poster of himself. He chuckled. "You know, Ray, I can't help but think of my old room at the University of Minnesota. It was just like this, both a palace and a cell."

I knew what he meant. He was trying to break the ice, but I was still too flabbergasted to speak.

He spotted the string bass in the corner, paused for a second, and then nodded to himself, remembering that I played the bass. "I was hoping you'd come tonight," he said. "The president of the university reserved a seat for you."

"I didn't know you were coming."

"What? Didn't the university president call you?"

"No, his secretary called about a dinner for Senator Benton but said nothing about you being there."

"Good Lord. I'm sorry, Ray. Danny called the university president personally."

"No one mentioned it, sir. He must have sloughed it off to the secretary. Kind of like you did with Daley."

Hubert gave me a startled look. I knew my sarcasm was childish, but I stood my ground. I needed to get this out.

"What do you mean?" he asked.

"Daley hauled me downtown, toyed with me like one of his ward lackeys, then gleefully announced that your council was disbanded."

"Wait. Slow down, Ray. You saw Daley?"

"And my council, too."

"Oh my. The president must have called Daley."

"The president?" I said. "Johnson called Daley about me?"

"This is not about you, Ray. It's about me. I was waiting until tonight to tell you."

I was trembling. I felt entangled in a world of adult cruelty, tossed around by powerful men engaged in a contest of wills I could not understand. I had to get to the bottom of it. "Are you on a short leash, sir?" I asked.

"What?"

"That's what Daley said."

Hubert loosened his tie and shifted nervously on the bed. He began to perspire. "Ray, you should know that I made every argument to the president. Every one I could think of, and yours, too. The man cannot be moved. I am duty-bound to support him. Can you understand that?"

I shook my head.

"For better or worse," he continued, "the president's policy is the country's policy."

"But that policy is wrong. You don't believe in it."

"What I believe is no longer important."

"How could what you believe not be important?"

"I made the case, Ray. Now it's my job to support the president. I owe my allegiance to the office of the presidency itself."

"Sir," I began, almost shrieking. I took a deep breath, downshifting into an almost pleading tone. "I was in Lansing. I heard your speech. You didn't just explain Johnson's policy, or even simply endorse it. You spoke like a zealot and a crusader. If you had toned it down, people would know you were just going along with it . . . that you *had* to go along with it. I would know."

"Oh, no," he said. "You don't understand. Lyndon would never go for that."

He got up and took three steps to the window. He stood there quietly for a while, staring out in that same far-off way my father did, with a wistful look and vacant eyes, as if he were trying to recall a familiar voice. I waited for him to come out of it.

"It's tough taking on the president of the United States day after day," he said finally. "He never lets me forget that he made me vice president, and that he can break me. Anything less than blind loyalty is betrayal to that man. He gives you no room to breathe . . . Can you understand that, Ray?"

I looked at him with wide-eyed amazement. "Loyalty?" I barked. "What loyalty has Johnson shown you? Mocking you at White House dinners, forcing you to cut programs you've worked for all your life, handing your Domestic Policy Council to Califano. How can you stand for that?"

"You're not getting what I'm saying, Ray."

"No, sir, I'm not."

Hubert turned again and stared out the window, his jaw cocked defiantly, his lips compressed, his eyes reposed in sadness.

"Truth is, Ray, I don't have the stomach to fight him."

Was Hubert telling me he was giving up? It made no sense. Not Hubert. He never gave up a fight. I wanted to probe deeper, but I scarcely knew how to ask a question. I knew, though, that if I let it go, I would be giving up, too. "What about Gerry?" I asked.

Hubert whirled around. "What?"

"You said you'd never give up on the boys—"

"I know," he sighed. "Not now. There'll be another time to fight. I just have to do it in my own time and in my own way."

I looked away. For the first time, I felt sorry for Hubert Humphrey. Who would follow him after his capitulation to Johnson? *How could I ever follow him?* "What if it's too late, sir?"

Hubert looked at me sadly.

"I mean, how are you going to ask people to trust you someday if . . ."

"Say it, Ray. If what?"

"If you can't be truthful with them now?"

Hubert walked over to my desk. He picked up one of the photographs he had inscribed to me and lingered over it with a melancholy smile. "I have my flaws, Ray. I fall short of my intentions. I'm not making excuses for shrinking from this fight."

He put the photo down and gave me a final penetrating look. "I know you're angry right now. But don't let bitterness overtake you. Keep your heart open. Try to trust me."

He turned slowly and walked out the door, smashing into Lew, who was eavesdropping.

I threw on Gerry's St. Agnes coat, made my way across the quad to Drexel Avenue, pushed open the huge glass door of the brownstone at 5626, and started looking for Ruth's name on the mailboxes. The names were strewn about like graffiti on a city street corner. I couldn't find anything that looked remotely like Ruth Torricelli, especially in the faint light at night.

I wasn't even sure if Ruth lived there. I remembered seeing an address on an envelope she was carrying the day she intercepted me on the way to orchestra practice. Not much to go on, and that was months ago. But I'd made a mental note of it.

I was about to start ringing bells randomly when a bearded student my age came through the main door.

"I'm looking for Ruth Torricelli," I said. "Do you know which apartment she's in?"

"Yes. She's my roommate. I'm Mitch. Who are you?"

"I'm Ray, a friend," I said, then added for good measure, "I run the Domestic Youth Policy Council office down the hall from SDS in Ida Noyes."

"I guess it's okay, then." He pushed the door open. "Here you go, man. It's 2A, upstairs on your left."

I walked up the stairs, collected myself, and then knocked on her door. Another bearded guy opened the door and stared at me. I supposed he was wondering how I got in without ringing.

"I'm looking for Ruth," I said.

He opened the door and then disappeared into one of the rooms, leaving me standing there, taking in the scene. A pretty girl in a loose tie-dyed shirt with rings of beads around her neck was lounging on a beat-up couch in the center of the living room. She was startled by my sudden appearance, but smiled. "Hi, I'm Julie."

The living room was cluttered with leaflets, posters, and laundry. A hookah sat on an old coffee table. A giant poster of the Buddha stared down from the ceiling. A movie poster for François Truffaut's *The 400 Blows* and a giant photo of Janis Joplin, bejeweled and bellowing, decorated the wall.

Ruth walked in from the kitchen. "Why, Ray. What—"

"Maybe we could talk?" I said stiffly.

"You look like you've seen a ghost."

"Well, actually, you're not far off," I said dryly.

Ruth led me through the living room into the kitchen, where she motioned for me to sit at the table: three planks of wood on top of two sawhorses. There were no cabinets, just shelves jammed with jars of nuts, grains, and boxes of tea.

"Did this ghost have a name?" she asked coyly as she poured some tea. She held up the pot, offering me some, but I shook my head.

"Yes. Hubert Humphrey. He came to see me."

"What? Humphrey?"

"In my dorm room tonight."

"I don't believe it. The vice president of the United States came to your dorm?"

"He wanted to talk."

"Okay, I gotta hear this. But wait." She reached for a jug of wine on one of the shelves. "You look like you could use some of this."

She poured a glass for me and I took a sip. It was so awful, I could barely avoid wincing. I smiled faintly and muttered, "Thanks."

"So tell me. What was the vice president of the United States doing in your dorm room?"

"Well, I was invited to the Benton dinner—"

"That event at Hutchinson Commons? Why were you invited?"

"I was invited by the president—"

"What president?"

"Of the university."

"I'm not following you."

"Ruth, please let me get this out?"

"Sorry," she said, plopping her head in both hands.

"I was invited because Hubert was the guest of honor, but for some weird reason no one told me that, so I didn't bother going. After the event, he came looking for me."

"Wow!" she said, her green eyes pools of wonder. She poured some wine for herself and raised her glass. "I could use some of this, too."

"He told me he tried to get Johnson to stop bombing and begin negotiations."

"Humphrey really *is* against the war?"

"I told you that in the bookstore."

"I know, but . . . maybe I didn't really believe you." She gulped some wine.

"Anyway, Johnson wasn't thrilled about the fact that his vice president was against the war, so he disbanded Hubert's Domestic Policy Council, and mine along with it."

"Oh Ray, I'm sorry. Wait a minute." She shook her head abruptly. "If Humphrey is against the war, what's he doing running around the country cheerleading for it?"

"I don't know, Ruth. I swear I don't know." I took a swig of the awful wine, then drew my hand across my lips to erase the taste. "I mean, he gave reasons, but they don't make sense. He seemed . . . I don't know . . . broken. There was such sadness in him."

I got up from the table and started pacing around the kitchen, clasping my hands over my head and looking skyward.

"Ray, what is it?" she asked.

"Ruth," I said quietly. "Do you think I'm bitter?"

"What! No."

"Then why am I so angry?"

"Ray. Come here. Sit down."

I walked slowly back to my seat. Ruth walked around behind me and, without a word, began massaging my neck and shoulders. No one had ever done that. I started to loosen up, breathing softly, opening and closing my eyes in rhythm with her ministrations. My emotions were breaking free from weeks of ceaseless mental toil. For the first time, I was aware of my body.

"Ruth? I just need to know something."

She kept massaging, saying nothing.

"What do you do when someone you . . . someone you trust lets you down?"

"You have to try to find a way to keep trusting them," she said softly.

"What? What did you say?" I tried to turn my head to look at her, but she nudged it forward and kept massaging. This was the most improbable thing I had ever heard. There was depth I couldn't grasp. She was urging me not to withdraw trust in the face of disappointment, but to redouble it. That path seemed beyond empathy. It was pure fantasy.

"Ruth, I don't know how to do that."

"I know you don't, Ray."

"Will you show me?"

Ruth stopped massaging and walked around to stand in front of me. She took my face in her hands and softly kissed me. A rush of wind swirled up my spine so fiercely, I thought I must be shaking, but my body was perfectly still.

Until that moment, I had assumed trust was a byproduct of sentiments like accountability, reliability, consistency, and mutuality. But now I saw that these were attitudes generated by the mind disguised as expressions of the heart, without true depth of feeling. A kind of emotional balance sheet. But Ruth was talking about something different. And so was Humphrey. It was pure heart, a world beyond the realm of thought and impervious to pretense: a world of vulnerability and risk, surrender and daring.

That's what Ruth awakened in me. *This must be what love is,* I thought.

PART FOUR
Summer 1965–Spring 1966

Chapter Thirty-Two

BY MID-JUNE, the Gray City had turned green. And yellow and blue and purple. The campus gardeners, conditioned to the long arc of winter, planted early bloomers like crocuses, irises, and tulips to enliven the few short weeks before summer break. But students had precious little time to appreciate the gesture. We were stuck in our dorms studying for finals.

It was the end of my third quarter—the University of Chicago did not have two semesters like most universities, but three ten-week quarters—and I was cramming. I had approached all three quarters of my academic year that way: I fell behind because I was tending to my political activities, and then, in one mad dash, I made up for lost time.

I returned to Rockville Centre for the summer and went to work at the mailing house. There was a somber air about the place; the Vietnam spring had yielded a bitter harvest. Not just Gerry's death in Quin Tin, but another—the brother of one of the stencil makers, a helicopter pilot, was killed in an attack on his barracks at Pleiku. There was little laughter, just halfhearted smiles and no arguments about the war. Tex, the confirmed cynic, was silenced by the deaths. For him and all of us, the senseless killing of young men placed the war beyond the bounds of debate. Blame seemed pointless, even to Tex.

Hubert had moved into high gear, defending the war. Every outburst of enthusiasm confirmed his imprisonment by Johnson. In my dorm room, he said he would fight in his own time and in his own way. But what did he mean? Was he biding his time to run for the presidency? Was his loyalty simply disguised ambition?

I kept thinking of the frightful sadness in his face that night, as if this vibrant man were watching his vital force ebb away in front of his eyes. I knew there was more to Hubert's story. Still, I found myself silently praying that it wouldn't happen to me.

Around the house, my father and I followed an unspoken rule to not discuss anything which might lead to an argument. That meant anything. But at least Dad was trying. We resumed our Sunday morning fix-it sessions. One day, we were lubricating the creaking joints of the old metal porch chairs when, out of the blue, he said, "Looks like Congress will finally push through that voting rights bill."

A moment passed. I said nothing.

"It's a good bill," Dad continued. "It's right for the country." He set the oil can on the table and looked at me. "You've got to admire Humphrey, staying with a fight like that."

I nodded, then changed the subject. "What's next on our fix-it list, Dad?"

I had told Mom about my dorm room fight with Hubert, but not Dad. He would be appalled. He was finally placing his stamp of approval on Humphrey, just as I was moving away from him.

Ruth and I wrote each other throughout the summer. One day, Diane retrieved the mail and noticed the handwriting on one of Ruth's letters. She started running around the house yelling, "Ray's got a girlfriend in Wisconsin."

Dad assumed that things with Ruth would follow their natural course, but mercifully, he spared me his colorful cautions about the pitfalls of sex. Mom took an interest in Ruth. When we were alone, she said, "So, tell me about this girl."

"No, it's not like that, Mom," I said. And it wasn't. Like *that*, I mean. Not yet, anyway. "She . . . well, we talk a lot. She helps me see things. Politically, and in other ways."

"Other ways?" Mom giggled. "I see."

The summer flew by. As I got ready for my second year in Chicago, I thought about new ways to make a difference in politics, but without Humphrey and without inflamed protest. What we needed was a student organization that was opposed to the war but also opposed to violent action. I had the skills to build a movement the old-fashioned way: getting signatures one by one, door to door, and reaching out to campuses nationally, gaining momentum around principles of nonviolence the way Martin Luther King Jr. was doing in the South.

I hinted at the project to Ruth in a letter, and she asked for details: Did I have a name yet? When would I get started? Who did I plan to enlist? I told her I was still working it all out but hoped I could see her as soon as I got back. I knew I was destined to clash with Humphrey. It was time to stop calling him Hubert.

Chapter Thirty-Three

WHEN I RETURNED to Chicago, my council office was a wreck. Over the summer the space was occupied by a karate class, and their homework must have been to destroy the place. There were gouges in the walls, broken tiles, holes in the ceiling, chipped paint, and torn molding. Even the bookcases were broken into distinct pieces, no doubt the result of karate blows. The maps I had painstakingly created and all my photos were shoved into boxes and stuffed in the corner.

I felt a flash of indifference. I didn't need those things now. Suddenly I found myself on the floor tearing through the boxes, hunting for my favorite autographed photo, the one Ruth had picked up and read: *To Ray Elias, my campaign manager and good friend.* At last I found it, still intact. I leaned back, listening to my heart pounding and startled by the eruption of sentiment. I hurriedly placed it back in the box and closed it up.

I pasted a temporary sign on the door, written in Magic Marker: Student Mobilization to End the War. I was sifting through the wreckage when Lew appeared in the doorway, grinning. "Heard you were back and had something new in mind," he said.

"Maybe," I said coyly. "Come on in and I'll tell you about it."

"Well, I brought a few old friends, if that's okay." A gang of old council volunteers strolled in after him, carrying planks of wood, carpentry tools, and paint. "We heard about what happened to the office, so we rustled up some supplies." He surveyed the hapless state of the office. "Man, these guys were animals. Probably SDS guerillas."

Ruth suddenly burst in. "The only gorilla in this room is you, Lew."

"Oops. Sorry, Ruth."

"Never mind," she said, shaking her head. She walked over to me, kissed me hurriedly, and started to walk back to the door. I touched her arm, the gentle way she always did, and she stopped, walked back, and kissed me again. She smiled and said softly, "I brought some friends, too."

She turned again to the door and whistled loudly, a skill I never knew she had. "Okay, guys. Coast is clear. Come on in." Ruth's roommates walked in, hauling the sawhorses they used for their kitchen table.

"Ruth!" I exclaimed. "What . . . how . . ."

"You can't saw wood without sawhorses," she said, winking. "Let's get started."

Tasks were assigned, and Ruth and I worked as a team to build new bookshelves. I starting laying out measurements with a framing square.

"Looks like you know something about carpentry, Ray."

"My father taught me. I wasn't very patient, but I guess I learned a few things."

Ruth raised her eyebrows and cocked her head, waiting for more of the story, then changed the subject. "Ray, I'm not sure about the name of your organization."

"Why? What's wrong with it?"

"Well, the acronym of Student Mobilization to End the War is SMEW. I mean, really! Isn't that a rodent of some kind? Or maybe the pig slop we used on my grandparents' farm in Wisconsin."

"Hmm," I muttered.

"Why not just shorten it to Student Mobilization Committee? SMC."

"Better," I said.

"Then, if we ever get past this stupid war, you could keep

the name and work on the domestic things. You know, that you and Humphrey used to—"

"I doubt that."

"You never know. Things change."

Suddenly, Ruth caught a whiff of something in a corner of the office. She spotted one of the volunteers smoking a joint and rushed over, pulled it out of his mouth, and stomped on it.

"Hey, what are you doing?" he shouted.

"If you want to smoke, do it on your own time."

"This *is* my own time!"

"No, not here. This is serious."

Everyone stared at Ruth as she walked back to the sawhorses. She nodded tight-lipped to the group, tossed her long hair back with a flick of her wrist, and picked up a saw. "Maybe I should tell you a few things about myself," she said.

I put down the framing square and listened.

"My father was the eldest of eight kids from Milwaukee's East Side," she began. "When he was sixteen he started working for Schlitz Brewing Company to support the family. He never finished high school. After twenty-seven years, he's still there, little more than a laborer. He's a proud union member, that's true, and says he would never be a boss. But still, he should've been something more. And he could've been, too. But he's an alcoholic. I think it was before he met my mother. Maybe he hid it from her, or maybe she thought she could change him. I don't know. But she watched—and my brother and I watched—the alcohol sap his spirit. He drifted into bitterness, and Mom sank into resignation."

Ruth glanced at the guy she just scolded as he eyed her uneasily. "People think marijuana is a harmless way to escape. Maybe it is, to a point, but it separates you from who you are, and what your contribution is meant to be. It's like pushing a pause button on facing the truth about yourself. You become a bystander to your own crumbling dreams."

I watched her intently as she dove deeper into the emotional congestion of her life.

"My dad was against me applying here," she went on. "He couldn't understand why I wasn't content with the University of Wisconsin-Milwaukee. To him, that was as high as any daughter of his should reach. He insisted I apply there, and only there." She laughed softly to herself. "He actually forbade me from applying to Chicago. But Mom intervened. She isn't an educated woman, but she went to the library, got help from the librarian, and learned about the University of Chicago. She declared that if I were accepted, she would get a job to pay for my tuition. My father was dumbfounded—in his mind, it was mutiny. But Mom fought for me and set me free and, in a way, I think she set herself free, too. So I applied, got accepted, and got a scholarship, too."

Ruth picked up a saw and started cutting the plank I had measured. She looked up, catching me staring at her. "What?"

"Nothing."

"No, what?"

"I was just thinking. Why SDS?"

"What do you mean?"

"I mean, you don't seem—"

"The radical type? I'm not radical, Ray. I'm a working-class Italian Catholic girl with the brains to see the gap between the haves and the have-nots. And for the have-nots, there's no crack at the American dream unless they get lucky like me, getting a scholarship to the University of Chicago. For them, America is a nightmare of worry: worry about getting an education for their kids, worry about paying doctor bills on a laborer's salary, and worry about whether their sons will be killed fighting a war that middle-class kids are spared because they go to college. That's why SDS."

"Then why are you helping me? I mean, what about your own work?"

Ruth stopped sawing to ponder my question. "I admire

the way you care about people. There's nothing preachy about it with you. You just work hard."

"Thanks."

"Besides," she said, unveiling a seditious smile, "you're really cute when you try to hide the fact that you like me."

Chapter Thirty-Four

IN JANUARY OF 1966, President Johnson finally called upon me for a mission to Vietnam. He had just met with the president and vice president of South Vietnam in Honolulu. I was summoned to meet them and then fly to Vietnam for two days of "fact-finding." Nominally, I was the head of the mission, but the president also sent along three top advisors—Harriman, Valenti, and Bundy—to guide my every step. Or, more precisely, to prevent missteps.

We were scarcely in the air when Vice President Ky started twirling two pearl-handled pistols in the air as the president of Vietnam, Nguyen Van Thieu, looked on impassively. When I asked Thieu if the pistols were loaded, he shrugged. Ky's wife, a Vietnamese beauty queen, asked if I might advise her on a personal matter and led me to the rear of the plane for privacy. In hushed tones, she asked me if she should have her eyes westernized. The thought of this stunning beauty forfeiting her natural gifts to chase some imaginary benefit struck me as a bizarre metaphor of our effort in Vietnam.

The futility of our mission became more striking when we landed. I kept stressing to Thieu and Ky our intent to transfer principal responsibility for the war to them, but they just kept asking for more troops. The commander of our forces, General William Westmoreland, echoed their sentiments, voicing the need for more American troops and making a mockery of Johnson's objective to Vietnamize the war. As for Ambassador Lodge? His grasp of the military situation seemed as limp as his handshake. He took off every afternoon for a nap.

The briefings I received reminded me of that awful day

in the Cabinet Room with McNamara's maps and charts: an elaborate ruse to obscure the truth. In a private briefing, Edward Lansdale, a counter-insurgency expert, approached me privately. "Have no illusions Mr. Vice President," he said. "Hundreds of thousands of men cannot win this war. It cannot be won militarily, only politically."

My god, I thought. *If we can't win this war militarily, how in the world can we force a political settlement?*

I bridled at the orchestrated futility of the war, but what could I do? How could I question it? Where would I start? With Westmoreland? He was a decorated World War II hero and a four-star general. What weaponry did I have to counter his artillery of lies? Maybe he and the other generals had some plan I did not understand or was not privileged to see. And who was I to trifle with the security of the United States? I didn't even have a staff of my own to advise on the war. Bill Moyers, the president's special assistant, showed great courage helping me behind the scenes. Jim Rowe did, too, but even if I did raise questions with the president, I would be back in his doghouse. No. The president alone bore the pressures and responsibilities of this war, and I had sworn loyalty to him. I had to fall in line with that. And wait.

Chapter Thirty-Five

THE STUDENT MOBILIZATION COMMITTEE was quickly taking shape. Within our ranks, many suggested we hold a big event with a well-known speaker to punctuate our success. Ruth and I went through the biggest names in the anti-war movement, and one stood out for her: Tom Hayden. It was true that he founded SDS, but he had moved on, organizing Negroes in Newark to take on the slumlords. Hayden was not just a famous anti-war activist, but someone who advocated broad social change. So Ruth reached out. At first he declined, but she wouldn't take no for an answer. He finally yielded, agreeing to squeeze in a visit between other commitments.

On Sunday night, two weeks before the Hayden event, Ruth and I settled into one of the battered sofas in my dorm lobby to watch television, a rare treat. We needed a break, and *Bonanza* was on. It was one of NBC's most popular shows, and my favorite in high school. As it was about to start, an impetuous dorm resident barged in and flipped to a different channel, announcing, "You have to see this."

A special report on Vietnam was airing. A phalanx of Secret Service were moving Humphrey through a throng of jeering students. He stared helplessly at the contorted faces shouting insults at him: "murderer," "baby killer," "fascist." The students splattered him with rotten eggs, and spittle drained from his forehead.

The Secret Service pushed the crowd back, clearing a path. Humphrey made it past the screaming protesters into the teeth of another crowd surrounding his car. A reporter shoved a microphone into Humphrey's face. "Mr. Vice President, what's your reaction to your reception here today?"

"These bearded, unwashed communists. Our nation went to war twice in this century to stop fascists like these Hitler youths."

I stared at the screen, horrified. I started to tremble. I felt tears welling up. My God, how could they treat this man like that? Then I stiffened with anger. How could he say things like that? Ruth rushed to the TV, turned the station back to *Bonanza*, and stared down the student who'd barged in. She walked back to the couch and extended her hand. "C'mon. Let's get out of here."

On the morning of Hayden's appearance, SMC volunteers gathered on the Mandel Hall stage to begin final preparation. The stage lights were on and the microphone was working, but the hall was blanketed in darkness. Lew stood at the podium muttering, "Testing, one, two, three." Ruth's roommates, Mitch and Steve, pinned a huge SMC banner on the curtain behind the podium. I sat twenty rows back, in the dark, monitoring the activity on stage.

One of the SMC volunteers, Jack Gould, shouted from the stage, "Ray, wherever you are, I can't figure out how to turn on the damn house lights."

"Just behind you," I shouted back. "There's a row of eight levers. Hit the ones in blue." I knew this because the bass section of the orchestra stood in front of those levers, and during breaks, I . . . well . . . I experimented.

Suddenly, Ruth charged onto the stage, agitated. "Where are you, Ray? I have bad news. Why is this place dark?"

"I'm over here, Ruth," I called out.

As the house lights came on, Ruth raced over to me. Lew and the others rushed off the stage after her. "Ray, there's a problem," she said. "Tom Hayden can't make it."

"That's impossible," Lew exclaimed. "Last minute like this? Why?"

"What difference does it make?" Ruth said. "Something about a mission to North Vietnam. I just got the call."

"Can we get someone else?" Mitch offered. "What about Dellinger? I heard he's in town."

"He left yesterday," Steve grumbled.

"How about Aptheker?" Lew suggested. "She lives in Chicago."

"She's a communist, for God's sake," Jack replied.

"Then we'll have to cancel," Lew said sullenly. "We'll never find a substitute this late." Everyone looked at me, nodding.

"No," I said. "It's too late to cancel. I'll give the speech."

"What?" Lew said. "No. It's too much, you can't—"

"I'll do it if Ruth gives it with me."

Ruth looked at me as if I had lost my mind.

"Two people giving a speech!" Mitch said. "It's weird."

"Besides," Lew added, "Ruth is SDS. No offense, Ruth, but this is an SMC event."

"No, really, it would be cool," Jack countered. "SDS meets SMC on the same stage—that kind of thing."

Everyone groaned.

"Seriously, it could work," Jack protested.

Ruth put her hand on my arm. "I'll do it. It's just crazy enough to work."

"Okay, let's get started," I said, jumping up. "We don't have much time."

Ruth and I raced to a lounge area off Hutchinson Commons and started writing. By 7:00 pm, we were ready with our speech.

Mandel Hall filled rapidly. Lew and a squad of SMC volunteers wove through the audience, passing out leaflets. A contingent of reporters and cameramen, expecting Hayden, set up at the front of the hall.

From backstage, Ruth and I peeked out at the incoming crowd. It was the largest group either of us had ever faced. She made a mock horrified gesture, grabbing her cheeks with both hands and widening her eyes. It broke the tension.

A chant emerged from the crowd: "No more war! No more war!"

Ruth nodded at me. "It's time."

"Ruth. We can't tell this crowd that Hayden left for Hanoi."

"Why not?"

"It's wrong what he's doing. We're trying to stop an unjust war, but that doesn't give Hayden the right to negotiate on his own."

Ruth stared at me, trying to grasp what I said. "You're right, but that's what he *is* doing."

"We can't go up there and condone that."

"Okay. Then how are you going to explain why he isn't here?"

"I don't know."

We walked to the podium together, and the chants trailed off.

"Fellow students and friends," I began, nodding to a group of Negro residents from neighboring Woodlawn, "and members of the community. Welcome. My name is Ray Elias, chairman of the Student Mobilization Committee. And this is Ruth Torricelli, vice chairwoman of Students for a Democratic Society. We've joined forces to speak to you tonight because Tom Hayden cannot be with us."

The crowd stirred.

"He left Kennedy International Airport an hour ago for Southeast Asia with other anti-war leaders," I continued. "We hope he'll return with the real facts about what's going on in Vietnam."

A few cries of "Right on!" and "All right!" pierced the

packed hall. I glanced at Ruth.

"I think we can agree to give him up this evening so he can pursue that work," I added.

Murmurs of assent rippled through the hall.

"At least some Americans are moving to bring us the truth about the war, not the lies that Johnson has been spinning."

That struck a chord, and cheers went up throughout the hall. Ruth shot me an approving glance. I nodded for her to take over.

"From the men who call themselves our nation's leaders," Ruth said, "there are no such gestures of truth. Instead, we hear hollow lies about war. A war that has claimed the lives of thousands, earned the contempt of the world, and sustained a dictatorship despised by its own people. All in the name of freedom."

The audience emitted a round of boos.

"We must say to our nation's leaders that the cause of freedom is not served by the perversions of this war, but in denouncing the senselessness of it."

The crowd applauded vigorously.

I stood next to Ruth, marveling at her. *We're making headway*, I thought.

I picked up where she'd left off. "My friends, it falls to us, the young people of America, to wage this struggle for the nation's soul. We must say to our leaders: 'You are blind, deaf, and dumb to what's true and right about America. Yours is a hollow patriotism, and your lofty sentiments are a disguise for cynicism.' It is we, America's youth, who represent America's noble traditions and ideas. It is we who carry the torch of freedom. It is we who will guide our nation back to its ideals. Let us stand up and cry out in a thunderous chorus, 'Take America back.'"

The crowd began to chant. "Take America back! Take America back!"

Then Ruth took up the argument. "My friends, let's send

a message to Johnson and Humphrey: 'You don't speak for America, and you don't own the symbols of its greatness either.' Join us now in honoring our country, our land, our America. Join us in singing 'America the Beautiful.'"

The crowd exchanged puzzled glances. They hadn't come here to sing, but a few in the crowd took up the challenge and began singing.

Ruth pointed to the reporters lining the hall. "The press is here tonight, ready to tell this city and the nation what we said and did here. Let America know how we honor our country, our America—the true America."

I took Ruth's hand and we raised our arms, urging the crowd on. Our two voices rang out: *"Oh beautiful for spacious skies, for amber waves of grain."*

More people started singing.

"For purple mountain majesties, above the fruited plain!"

The hall began to fill with song. Everyone knew the words. We were making this beautiful but neglected melody our anthem, a patriotic tribute from the youth of America.

"America! America! God shed his grace on thee. And crown thy good with brotherhood, from sea to shining sea."

Ruth exhorted the crowd, "Show them that we're taking our country back."

Four hundred voices merged into one giant resounding, unrehearsed homage to America. The reporters were writing furiously, and the photographers were clicking their cameras. I stood at the podium, my arm around Ruth, singing fiercely and proudly.

Chapter Thirty-Six

OVER THE YEARS, Muriel and I had dined with Lyndon and Lady Bird, but never as president and vice president at our home. When Muriel and I moved into a new apartment on the Potomac, Johnson started chiding me for not inviting him. I dismissed the comments as routine Johnson hazing, but he became insistent; not just suggesting, but commanding. And so, a date was set, and tonight was the night.

When the doorbell rang, Muriel rushed from the kitchen to join me at the door. Johnson kissed Muriel and I kissed Lady Bird, who spoke first.

"Very nice, Muriel," she said, looking around at the apartment.

"Yes, sir, Hubert," Johnson echoed. "Real comfy-looking."

I asked if he wanted a drink.

"Yep. Why not? It's a special occasion. Scotch?"

I charged off to the liquor cabinet while Muriel led Lady Bird to the kitchen. Johnson wandered over to the couch and plopped down. "Say, Hubert, I want you to know what a great job you're doing on the hustings. I don't know what I'd do without you."

"Thank you, Mr. President."

He fingered the fabric of the couch absent-mindedly. "Yep, I hear your speeches are eloquent. Real barn burners. Like the old days, huh, Hubert?"

I walked over with his drink, then headed back to make my own.

"Problem is," Johnson continued, "I'm so busy in Washington, I never get to see any of them."

I splashed some Scotch into a glass for myself and headed for the armchair opposite the president.

"So I was thinking . . . why don't you let me hear one of them?"

"Hear what, Mr. President? A speech?" I offered a twisted smile.

"That's right. I want to hear one." Johnson stretched out on the couch. "Right now."

I glanced toward the kitchen, hoping for a rescue, but Muriel was chatting with Lady Bird; dinner was nowhere near ready. I turned back toward Johnson. "Well, sir, it's really nothing special."

"Now, don't be modest, Hubert."

"Just the usual things."

Johnson leveled a cold, hard stare at me. "Hubert, do the speech!"

I swallowed hard, trying to summon oratorical passion in my own living room with a drink in my hand for an audience of one. "Historians will say about this war," I began, "that it was the proving ground of America's commitment to freedom for all people—white, black, brown, and yellow—a place where we illuminated the world with the light of liberty."

Johnson suddenly got up, pointing toward the hallway. "Bathroom this way?"

I nodded.

"Fine." Johnson walked down the hall. "Keep going, Hubert."

Johnson entered the bathroom, turned on the light, and started to relieve himself.

"I'm listening, Hubert. Keep going. Tell me what you said at Stanford."

I cocked my head upward, defiantly, mouthing the words he wanted to hear. As the president of the United States was urinating, I plodded on. "The struggle of our forefathers was not achieved in one war, or even in one century. It is the duty and honor of every American to undertake that struggle in every generation. So it falls to each generation to take up the challenge of our beloved president, John Fitzgerald Kennedy."

As Johnson flushed the toilet, I delivered President Kennedy's most famous line: "'Ask not what your country can do for you—ask what you can do for your country.'"

Johnson strolled back into the room and flopped onto the couch. "That's great. I love the Kennedy bit." He started applauding. "Go on."

Mercifully, Muriel peeked into the room, saw me heaving with sweat, and rushed in with plates, trailed by the first lady.

"Steaks are ready, Mr. President," she said. "I know you like yours raw."

Chapter Thirty-Seven

AS WINTER LOOSENED its fierce grip on the city, Ruth and I walked to the quad to celebrate our joint speech—by playing soccer. She had teased me all winter about wanting to see my moves on the field. Wisconsin wasn't big on soccer. Football was king there, so she had never seen a soccer match.

I began by juggling the ball between my legs. Showing off, really. "Bet you can't get by me," she said facing off with me. Then *whoosh*, I was past her.

"Hey, no fair."

"Don't watch my feet," I said. "By then it's too late."

"Okay," she said intently, looking into my eyes with gritty determination.

I was still too quick. I dribbled past her, just as Gerry had done to me hundreds of times. Ruth laughed as she ran after me, then lunged and tackled me.

"Uh-uh, no hands," I said.

"*I'll* make the rules," she howled as we rolled on the ground. Then she asked, "Where did you learn to do that?"

"Gerry."

"Gerry?"

"He was a friend. He taught me. My coach thought it was hopeless, and I believed him. But Gerry saw that I could play. You remember that night I barged into the SDS office?"

"How could I forget?"

"I had just learned that Gerry was killed in Vietnam."

"Oh my God. I'm so sorry, Ray."

"I couldn't tell you at the time."

Ruth embraced me and lay with me silently on the fresh

spring grass as I drifted through remembrances of Gerry. She slowly got up and extended her hand to nudge me up, too. "We need to get ready."

"I wish I could stay here with you."

"It'll be okay, Ray."

"How selfish of me. I should be consoling you! I'm not the one facing my parents."

Ruth and I had been to the Little Corporal Restaurant on East Wacker before. It was reasonably priced, with an ample menu and lavish desserts in a pastry case that rotated dreamily in the center of the room. But the real attraction was the decor, created with the little corporal in mind—the little corporal being Napoleon. I'd asked our waiter if Napoleon was a corporal before he was emperor. He gave me a quizzical look and said, "I'll ask."

Ruth chided me about sending the waiter on a useless errand, but I did want to know. And I loved the way Ruth would rein me in when I acted silly. A few days later, I checked for myself at the library. Napoleon had never been a corporal, but he got the nickname because he liked to lay the sights of his artillery guns himself, which was usually a corporal's job.

As soon as we walked in, I spotted my parents sitting at a table in the middle of the room near the dessert tower, just as they saw me. Mom rushed over to hug me, then turned to Ruth, beaming. "Hello, Ruth, I'm Sarah Elias. So nice to finally meet you."

They hugged each other, both beaming. Mom gently took hold of Ruth's arm, walked her back to the table, and introduced her to Dad. Ruth held out her hand and Dad shook it with a forced smile, then turned to me with a pained expression. "What made you pick this place, son?"

Out of habit, I got defensive. I started to answer, but Mom

put a stop to it. "Shush, Jim. We don't need to hear about the silly restaurant. We have a lot to catch up on." Turning to Ruth, she said, "Now, dear, tell us a little about yourself. How did you two meet?"

A warm feeling welled up in me. I loved Mom. She knew the story of how we met all too well, but that was Mom, going out of her way to make Ruth feel comfortable.

Ruth responded with equal enthusiasm. "Well," she said, "one day I walked into Ray's office, and he had all those Hubert Humphrey photos, so I started singing."

Mom smiled. Dad had a puzzled look on his face and crossed his arms, so Ruth turned to him. "You see, Mr. Elias, I'm from Wisconsin, and those Humphrey songs that Ray used to sing around the house in Rockville Centre were used by Humphrey in the Wisconsin presidential primary of 1960."

Dad brightened. "But how did you know them?"

"Well, my father was a volunteer for Humphrey. His union supported Humphrey. And that song was everywhere." Then, turning to Mom, she said, "So you see, Mrs. Elias, I learned that song four years before Ray even heard it."

Mom exploded with laughter. "Isn't that marvelous, Jim?"

Dad nodded tentatively. "Are you an admirer of the vice president like Ray?" he probed Ruth.

"Well, not exactly. But I certainly remember him when he did things that were . . . admirable."

Dad eyed her suspiciously. Mom started to change the subject, but Dad cut her off, turning to me. "So what do you hear from the vice president?" he asked.

"Actually, not much, Dad."

"What do you mean? I thought you were always writing to each other."

"He kind of stopped writing."

"Stopped? Well, sure—he's busy. You have to keep up the initiative."

"I was doing that, but then I didn't hear back, so I stopped.

To be honest, we don't see eye to eye on the war."

Dad flinched. Mom put her hand on his arm, trying to derail any further cross-examination. Ruth tried to calm me with the same gesture.

"That's an odd thing to say," Dad said. "What does Vietnam have to do with anything? Humphrey's going to be the next president of the United States."

I looked at my father, trying to find something to say in response, but Dad beat me to it. "Staying close to Humphrey is a golden opportunity. Why jeopardize that?"

Mom and Ruth retired their good-natured smiles and hung their heads.

"Dad," I said, "I don't want to stay close to a person when I don't believe in what they stand for."

Dad looked at me blankly, thunderstruck. "What? I thought he represents everything you believe in! That's what you told us." He turned to Ruth, waving his arms in the air. "You should have seen it, Miss, everything in the house was Hubert, Hubert, Hubert. There were times we thought we'd go out of our minds with nonstop Hubert."

"Now honey, no need to exaggerate," Mom interrupted, trying to slow him down.

"I don't understand," Dad continued. "How do you discard someone because of a disagreement . . . over the stupid war? The war will end." He turned to my mother. "My God, why in the world did we send him to this fancy school?"

"You didn't send me here," I snapped. "I applied and got in."

"James, Ray—enough!" Mom cried.

Dad stood up. "I'm getting a drink. The service around here stinks. Does anybody want anything?" But he was off before anyone could answer.

The three of us watched Dad disappear into the bar. I gave Mom an apologetic look and shrugged.

Ruth started to get up. "Mrs. Elias, maybe I should leave

you two alone."

"No, dear. Please stay. I can see that you care for Ray, so you should hear this."

Ruth looked at me nervously and sat back down.

"Ray," Mom began gravely. "When you applied to the University of Chicago, we were skeptical, as I'm sure you remember. But you were determined to go, so we were happy we could make it possible for you."

"I know, Mom. I appreciate that."

"I don't know if you do, Ray."

I was taken aback at this rare reproach from my mother.

"Did you ever wonder how we could afford to pay for this school, what with the downturn in your father's business?"

I looked down at the table, embarrassed that I'd never really thought about it. "I knew you'd saved a little. And I worked."

Mom breezed past my lame response. "When you were born, back when times were good, your father talked to my father, your Grandpa Jack, and said, 'Let's make sure Ray never has to worry about going to college.' They each put twenty-five hundred dollars in an account. That made a total of five thousand dollars. And it grew, of course—enough to pay for four years at any college in America. No matter how bad things were, no matter how much we needed the money, your father never touched a dime."

I looked at Mom in awe. I couldn't imagine my parents making such a staggering investment right after the war and sticking with it, even when they badly needed the money. Ruth stared at Mom with wide-eyed amazement.

"And whenever I asked your dad about it, even when you two were fighting, he would say, 'We were blessed with a smart boy; let's make sure he has every opportunity.' I know he can be rough, but he only has love for you. And there's nothing he wouldn't do for you."

I stared at Mom. What she was saying made no sense.

How could all that torment, criticism, and harshness come from someone who loved me? A feeling of shame welled up in me. Mom was saying that Dad never used our fights as an excuse to stop loving me. But I did. That's what Humphrey seemed to say that night in my dorm room. And that's what Ruth tried to make me see that same night. I sat there, thinking how unworthy I was of anyone's love when I was so dense and unforgiving.

"I brought something for you," Mom continued, shifting the mood.

She pulled out the little blue-and-white coin box I kept on my closet desk at home. "Remember this?"

"My pushke box!" I gushed.

Ruth looked at us, puzzled. She had no idea what the box was, but she smiled.

"Remember how you would fill it up then send the money to Israel to plant trees?"

I turned to Ruth. "I used to change my dollars for coins so I could fill it up faster."

Ruth put her hand on mine.

"Try to grow a tree at home," Mom added. "Plant the seeds of empathy around you. That's how love grows, like a tree . . . from empathy and trust."

I shifted my gaze between Mom and Ruth, realizing they were the two people in the world I loved, and the only two I trusted. I fought to hold back tears. But how could they love me with my rigidity, my lack of empathy, and my defensiveness?

Dad walked back with his drink and stood by the table, not sitting down, not saying anything, just watching us, another reverie of Dad's. Then he began to bow ever so slightly, as if in prayer. But he looked straight at the three of us, as if struggling to read in our faces what intimacy was taking place.

There was pain in Dad's eyes, but also hints of content-ment, as if the two emotions were locked in conflict within his soul. I felt a surge of compassion for him, but still resentment for the turmoil he had caused me. The resentment seemed stronger, but I thought I could contain it. I didn't want bitterness to have the upper hand. That was my internal battle. I was fighting battles, just like Dad. But the two women at my side placed empathy above everything. They knew what love was. And maybe in that moment, Dad was hoping I saw it, too.

PART FIVE
Spring 1968

Chapter Thirty-Eight

I WAS NEVER EXACTLY SURE what people meant when they said, "Do the right thing." Was it what *they* thought you should do? Or was it the thing *you* knew you should do?

Until that fateful night in my dorm room three years ago, I always thought of Humphrey as someone who did the right thing. But that night, my trust in him unraveled—not because I knew what the right thing was, exactly, but because I could see that he had stopped trying to find it himself.

The emotional break took time. There were memories to contend with, and the pain of disconnecting from someone so inspiring, hopeful, and special was hard. Just as I would reach a plateau of detachment, he would utter another outlandish statement about the war. He compared America's effort in Vietnam to George Washington's stand at Valley Forge, and our support for the puppet regime in South Vietnam to our alliance with Great Britain. When he called the war a "great adventure," the nation's media erupted, calling him "predictable, dogmatic, and out of touch." I tried to ignore Humphrey's descent into triviality and irrelevance, but it always stung.

As the new year broke seven days after my twentieth birthday, SMC was thriving at the University of Chicago and in other places where I helped launch satellite chapters. Now it was time to move on. I had tired of politics. I turned the Chicago chapter over to Lew.

Ruth also felt ground down by her work at SDS. Our romance had been borne out of the turmoil of war, and that made us uneasy. We needed to cool the temperature down and look at life outside of war and politics.

I became Alberta's assistant at Head Start and helped train volunteers. Philip tagged along with me, and we became inseparable. Every other Sunday, I would go to his home for lunch with his parents and older sister. He still had trouble looking directly at me, but he sat in my lap while I talked to his parents. Ruth occasionally joined us and bonded with the family as well.

Ruth reconnected to her Wisconsin farming roots and created a nonprofit company to deliver fresh produce from Wisconsin farms to the tables of Chicago's inner-city residents. She called it Farm to Fork. We stayed up at night, planning the company launch. I promised to join her after graduation in June, roving the Wisconsin countryside and enlisting farmers to join.

We often went to concerts at Orchestra Hall to enjoy the phenomenal transformation of the orchestra under Georg Solti. I rejoined the university orchestra and happily took my second place beside Brian. He had become a great bass player, and I was learning more from him than I had from Mr. Petersen.

One night, Brian handed me two tickets to a post-concert reception of the orchestra. "I'd like you and Ruth to come," he said. "I'll introduce you to Joe."

Joe was Joseph Guastafeste, Brian's teacher and the principal bassist in the Chicago Symphony. I was so excited to meet him, I could barely focus on the concert. Ruth kept elbowing me to calm down. Backstage at the reception, Brian waved me over and introduced us.

"I was looking forward to meeting you," the great bass player said.

"Me, sir?"

"Yes. To thank you for helping Brian."

"Mr. Guastafeste, I think it was the other way around. I taught Brian nothing."

"That's not what he said. He told me you are a gentle-man. You made him feel comfortable in the bass section, and were gracious in giving up the first chair."

Brian nodded and slapped me on the shoulder. Guastaf-este shook my hand again, and the two of them moved off to greet other guests.

"You see?" Ruth said, beaming.

"What?"

"I keep telling you that you have an instinct for doing the right thing, but you always doubt yourself." Then she lunged at me right there in the middle of the reception, kissing me with such force that I fell backward. When we came out of it—I don't know how many seconds or minutes later—we had attracted onlookers. We smiled at them and started giggling.

At school, we studied hard. For my first two years at Chicago, I hung on by the seat of my pants. But when I jettisoned politics, I began to study in earnest, and a vast world of inexhaustible inspiration opened up. In my third and fourth years, I studied mostly philosophy. I fell under the spell of the ancient philosophers—Plato and his student, Aristotle, and their idealization of the human soul as perfectible. According to Aristotle, virtue is attained by the practice of moderation, resisting expedient beliefs, self-serving actions, and fits of temper. I recognized that I had been seeking such an ideal in Humphrey. The gifts of the university had become clear and the rewards of scholarship were reassuring, but deep down, I knew I was destined to be a public man, not a scholar.

The year 1968 opened ominously for America. On January 31, the combined communist forces of the North Vietnamese and their allies in the south, the Vietcong, launched a massive campaign of surprise attacks throughout South Vietnam. The offensive, named Tet after the Vietnamese Lunar New Year, penetrated so deeply into the military and civilian centers of the country that it sent shock waves throughout Washington and the nation.

Two United States senators rose up to challenge Johnson's aspirations for a second term. Eugene McCarthy was the first to step forward with a purely anti-war agenda. I admired McCarthy but felt the pull of the charismatic Robert Kennedy, brother of the slain president, and my senator. I was, after all, a New Yorker.

Still, I had drifted too far from politics to clamber back into the fray. I shifted my attention to Dr. Martin Luther King Jr. I marveled at his patience, his wisdom, and his spellbinding oratory. No group in America had more to be angry about than Negroes. Yet Dr. King had tamed that anger and transformed the repressed ambitions of millions of Negroes into effective non-violent protests. He seemed to be the embodiment of Aristotle's ideal of moderation, and was amazingly successful.

In February, Dr. King assumed the leadership of the sanitation workers' strike in Memphis.

Chapter Thirty-Nine

ON MARCH 31, 1968, a Sunday night, neither the Tet Offensive nor Dr. King's campaign in support of the Memphis sanitation workers were on our minds as Ruth and I prepared for a party at her apartment. The winter quarter finals were behind us. We were thriving in the fresh optimism of the spring quarter, our last as undergraduates.

Ruth's roommates moved the sawhorses and oak slabs from the kitchen and set them up in the living room along with folding tables, crates, and boxes to make room for twelve of our friends. Julie was frantically combing the apartment for more place settings.

The party coincided with a hastily scheduled address to the nation by President Johnson. We assumed it was another dismal update on the war and saw no reason to ruin dinner by paying attention to him. Mitch couldn't stand the suspense and announced that he would take dinner in his bedroom and watch the broadcast.

In the kitchen, Ruth stirred a large steaming pot of pasta sauce, then offered me a taste. "Whoa, that's incredible," I gawked. Oohs and ahhs followed as others tasted Ruth's creation, then she sampled it herself. "Oh yes!" she exclaimed. "You know, after God created the Italian landscape and populated it with the gentlest souls on earth, He blessed it all with Italian cuisine."

Everyone nodded reverently at Ruth's unabashed tribute to her heritage.

At dinner, the conversation drifted to the Democratic presidential primary shaping up between McCarthy,

Kennedy, and Johnson.

"So, Ray," Steve asked, "when are you going to join Mc-Carthy's campaign?"

Lew chimed in. "I'm working on him."

"Seriously, Ray," Julie said. "Join us. McCarthy's the only true anti-war candidate."

"Yeah," another said. "Bobby's a Johnny-come-lately to the campaign. He's not even really against the war."

Ruth jumped in to fend off my interrogators. "Ray is taking his time. Besides, I don't think he likes Gene," she added with a stealthy grin.

Mitch suddenly burst into the living room. "Hey, you guys. You're not going to believe this."

"Not now—we're having dinner," Ruth protested, followed by a chorus of jeers from the group.

"No, seriously. Johnson's on TV. He's not running."

We bolted from the table to Mitch's bedroom. Walter Cronkite was reading the pivotal words of Johnson's speech:

"'With America's sons in the field far away and America's future under challenge right here at home, and with our hopes and the world's hope for peace in the balance every day, I don't believe I should devote an hour or a day of my time to any personal partisan causes or any duties other than the awesome duties of this office, the presidency of your country. Accordingly, I shall not seek, and I will not accept, the nomination of my party for another term as your president.'"

"That's one down," someone said. "We still have to dump the Hump."

Ruth glanced at me. Cheap shots at Humphrey still stung.

Chapter Forty

ON SUNDAY, MARCH 31, I was in Mexico City hosting a dinner for the president of Mexico at the U.S. Embassy. It was the first time a Mexican president had set foot in the American embassy since the Mexican revolution in 1910, so I wanted everything to go smoothly.

The Mexican president was lecturing me on the harm of American wheat tariffs when Danny suddenly burst into the room.

I stood up and pulled him aside. "My goodness, Danny. What's so important? President Ordos is—"

"Johnson's not running."

I stared at Danny in disbelief, then laughed. "Well, I'll be damned."

Danny smiled, too. "You know, Hubert, if we don't move fast, Bobby will lock this thing up."

"Okay. Get everyone together. Let's kick this around. Of course, I've got to talk to the president before we make an announcement."

Danny gasped. "Why do we have to do that?"

"He's still the president. Just start calling everyone. Jay and Orville, Max, Bill Connell, Walsh, Stewart. You know . . . Norm Sherman, of course, Freddie Gates, and Fritz. Right away. And Dwayne to figure out the money. Don't miss anyone."

Danny nodded. "I'd better get going. It takes ten minutes to get a dial tone down here."

"I'll break free as soon as I can. And Danny? Call Ray, too."

"Okay."

Four days later, I was seated on the dais of the Democratic Congressional Campaign Committee. I was about to speak when I was again pulled away with momentous news, this time by my friend Max Kampelman.

"Hubert, terrible news," he said. "The worst news."

"For God's sake, Max what is it?"

"It's Dr. King. He was murdered in Memphis today. The news just came in."

"Oh my god, not Martin. How?"

"He was shot on the balcony of his motel by a man in the rooming house across the street."

I tried to conjure up that awful scene, but my mind went blank. I just saw darkness, and then red . . . Martin's life force flowing out of him. Then the stomach pains came, and I tilted forward. Max grabbed my arm and steadied me.

"Hubert, are you okay?"

"Yes, Max. I'm okay. Listen, I've got to go back in there and tell everyone. But stand by, please."

"Of course, Hubert."

"Where's Bobby? Does he know?"

"He's scheduled to speak in Indianapolis, but he hasn't canceled."

"If he goes on, see if you can get me the feed."

"Okay, Hubert. I'll call our guys in Indiana."

After dinner, I retreated to my hotel room and played the recording of the speech Bobby Kennedy made earlier that night in Indianapolis.

"Ladies and gentlemen," Bobby began in a timid and

squeaky voice. "I'm only going to talk to you for a minute or so this evening, because I have some very sad news for all of you and, I think, sad news for all of our fellow citizens, and people who love peace all over the world. And that is that Martin Luther King was shot and was killed tonight in Memphis, Tennessee."

A shock wave of disbelief and terror ran through the crowd. I realized that they had been standing there for hours waiting for Bobby, and would not have known that Dr. King had been killed.

The crowd went silent as Kennedy continued: "Martin Luther King dedicated his life to love and to justice between fellow human beings. He died in the cause of that effort. In this difficult day, in this difficult time for the United States, it's perhaps well to ask what kind of a nation we are and what direction we want to move in. For those of you who are black, considering the evidence that there were white people who were responsible, you can be filled with bitterness, and with hatred, and a desire for revenge."

Murmurs could be heard in the crowd, but all were as riveted as I was to hear the solemn passion of this quiet man delivering an unrehearsed tribute not only to Dr. King, but also to the virtues that our nation would require to bear his loss.

"We can move in that direction as a country, in greater polarization—black people against whites, and white against black, filled with hatred toward one another. Or we can make an effort, as Martin Luther King did, to understand, and to comprehend, and replace that violence, that stain of bloodshed that has spread across our land, with an effort to understand, compassion, and love."

I sat on the edge of the bed in awe of the man Lyndon hated and I was told to fear. But right now, I saw only the decency of his heartfelt tribute. He had captured the moment far better than my tepid remarks earlier that evening.

"Let us dedicate ourselves," he concluded, "to what the

Greeks wrote so many years ago: 'To tame the savageness of man and make gentle the life of this world.'"

My God. He was quoting Aeschylus. A white American politician reciting poetry to a crowd of grieving blacks. He dared to do it, and it was beautiful. *How in the world can I compete with a man with such daring?*

Chapter Forty-One

THE NIGHT OF Dr. King's assassination, hundreds of young Negro men marched through Hyde Park. Strangely, their ominous presence bore no violence. It was as if these men—like the nation—were lost, seeking a way out of this dreadful setback.

After they receded into Woodlawn, Ruth and I sat by the window, staring at empty streets. In the eerie quiet of the night, I told Ruth the story of how I'd met Dr. King at the 1964 Democratic National Convention; how Humphrey wanted to seat a racially mixed Mississippi delegation, not an all-white one, but Johnson crushed the idea. I tried to explain the chemistry between Dr. King and Humphrey: the warmth and affection of two people with a deep common purpose.

"Ray, your eyes are sparkling," Ruth said. "Do you think this may bring Humphrey to his senses?"

Ruth would bring up Humphrey's name every so often, a little test to stoke the embers of affection to see if they would ignite.

I gave a quick shake of my head.

"Shouldn't you talk to him, at least?" she asked.

"Ruth, the Kennedy people have been calling me."

"Oh?"

"About helping in Indiana."

"You're going with Bobby?"

"No. I'm just going down to hear him out."

"I see." I understood that she was acknowledging my decision, but didn't quite agree with it.

On a cold April morning, I walked the half mile to the Illinois Central Railroad, and caught the train to South Bend, Indiana. At Kennedy's headquarters, the boyish-looking twenty-nine-year-old campaign chairman, Matt Regan, greeted me enthusiastically. "Hello, Mr. Elias. Glad you could make it down here."

"It was no problem. Pretty quick train ride from Chicago."

"Let's talk a little bit before the senator joins us. I've heard that your strength is organizing, especially young people."

I just nodded, not sure if that was a question.

"McCarthy is getting the young people," Regan continued. "I'm sure you're aware of that. But Senator Kennedy is a better choice. He's not just an anti-war candidate, but supports broad domestic change. I'm sure you appreciate that because of your connection with Hubert Humphrey.

The words "your connection with Hubert Humphrey" passed through me like a pressure wave. There was no connection, only shards of memories, a catalog of severed hopes and dashed expectations. *What was I doing here?* I wondered. *Setting myself up for another round?* I shifted in my seat, about to deliver an excuse to leave when Robert Kennedy walked in.

He didn't bound in like Humphrey had four years ago, with a huge smile and open arms to welcome me into his family of secretaries and aides. Instead, he seemed diffident, almost bashful. No outstretched arms, no exuberant greetings, no singing. He wore a smile—more of a sheepish grin. With shy politeness, Kennedy shook my hand.

Regan brought Kennedy up to speed. "Mr. Elias has a long history of political involvement, rather unusual in such a young man. He started with Hubert Humphrey."

Kennedy nodded. "Hubert is a good man," he said. "When my brother won the West Virginia primary and knocked him out of the 1960 presidential race, Hubert pledged his support right away. No hedges, no conditions. They were good friends. You know, they served in the Senate for eight years together."

Then his voice trailed off into a reverie of his own. I had learned that even presidential contenders could not resist the tug of reminiscence when it rolled in like the tide. At that moment, both Kennedy, at forty-two, and I, at twenty, were in the clutches of confining memories.

Then Kennedy drew himself back to the present. "Matt thinks you would be great for our campaign. Young people seem to favor Senator McCarthy, and we could use support in marshaling them to our campaign. President Kennedy was a magnet for young people, and they were a tremendous help to him in the campaign. I would appreciate your support. Can you help us?"

I collected myself, measuring my words. "Senator McCarthy got into this a long time ago," I began. "He's the rallying point on Vietnam. You've been moderate on the war. That's a good thing in some ways, but young people are looking for an anti-war leader and your position has been, I think, ambiguous. A lot of people see it that way."

Kennedy nodded. He wasn't offended, and I was impressed. "Ray, I see the problems of this country. The war is just one of them. The war itself is an outgrowth of deeper divisions: black and white, management and labor, rich and poor. I don't want to be president on one issue."

I nodded.

"Hubert was a strong voice for those things before he was, um . . . co-opted by Johnson," Kennedy said.

I looked away.

Kennedy waited respectfully for a minute. "So let me ask you, Ray. Why haven't you joined up with McCarthy?"

"The truth is, sir, I'm not sure. People ask me that all the time. They've all moved to McCarthy. He's a symbol of the anti-war movement. But his campaign is limited to that. I don't think I see in him the substance of . . . a president."

Kennedy seemed to grasp my implication: that he might be a man of such substance.

"Sir," I continued, "you need to be stronger on Vietnam."

"Then join me. Help me move toward that. I need young voices to remind me how divisive this war is."

"Yes, sir, and how it jeopardizes your goal to expand Negro rights, labor protections, and aid to the poor. Because the war makes those programs impossible."

"Exactly!" He glanced at Regan. "You see what I mean? That's what I need to hear, not cold, hard political calculations." He turned back to me. "Join me, Ray."

I hesitated. Again, memories crowded in. Wasn't this what Humphrey had asked of me, to write arguments against the war? I winced as I thought of it. My long, labored memorandum had been futile. What if Kennedy ignored me, too? But I trusted him somehow and decided to take a chance. I felt I could live with the disappointment this time, if it came.

"Maybe I can get some people organized in Chicago to help out here," I said. It sounded like more of a commitment than I'd intended. But that was okay. I liked this man.

Kennedy quickly agreed. "Fine. The primary here in Indiana is less than a month away, with Nebraska following close behind. We need young people. Let's get through this together." Then, turning to Regan, he said, "Give Ray everything he needs. And Matt, anything that Ray sends on Vietnam, make sure I see it personally."

Regan nodded. Kennedy stood up, and I did, too. We shook hands. He smiled broadly, and so did I.

I walked back to the train, content to be back in the game, ready to help someone I believed in—but as a realistic man, not an infatuated boy. It felt good. I was eager to get back to Chicago and tell Ruth.

Chapter Forty-Two

"HUBERT, we're not saying you won't get labor's endorsement." The gravelly voice of George Meany, the cigar-chomping head of the AFL-CIO pulsed through the giant conference room. "We're glad you're in it. I told the president that. You've had no greater ally than labor. What I'm saying is, we just can't control the rank and file this time."

I sat stiffly at a conference table listening to him, surrounded by a group of stocky old white men. These were the nation's labor leaders. Etched in these hard-bitten faces were the scars of brutal battles with management and against rivals within their own unions. The careers of these men were different from the captains of industry. Both had the cunning to navigate their way to the top, but labor leaders never cultivated the genial subterfuge of boardroom courtesies; they depended instead on blunt language and physical intimidation. And now I was getting a dose of it.

"You see, Hubert, it's not about what you've done. We understand that. But people say Kennedy has a fresh vision. Millions of our members are Catholic, and they loved President Kennedy. Some had sons killed in Vietnam. Shit, half of them will probably vote for George Wallace because they're scared of Negroes taking their jobs. We're just not sure we can deliver for you as we have in the past."

I got up silently, nodding to the men, and walked out to join Danny outside the conference room.

"How did it go?" he asked.

"The nomination won't mean a damn thing without labor's rank and file. I've got to turn them around . . . and young people, too. Have you had any luck reaching Ray?"

"Nope."

"Well, keep trying."

"Hubert, it won't do any good."

"Why not?"

Danny handed me a clipping with a picture of Ray and a headline: university of chicago organizer takes post with kennedy.

I shoved the newspaper back at Danny. I had lost Ray. How in the world was I going to win young people if I'd lost Ray? *I'm glad the voting age is twenty-one*, I caught myself thinking. *Ray is too young to vote against me!*

Chapter Forty-Three

RUTH AND I were sitting in the front of a rented school bus early on a Saturday morning in May, heading for Indiana. As we bounced along, she patted my hand. "I don't know how you do it, Ray," she said. "Getting students to trek to Indiana for Kennedy on a spring weekend. In fact, I'm not exactly sure what I'm doing here."

"I was hoping for more," I countered, "but twenty-five is pretty good."

"Twenty-eight."

"Next weekend we'll have more."

"Ray, I think you're happiest doing this. All those lists you used to make, charts on the walls, position papers. What really moves you is bodies on a bus heading to Indiana."

"When you put it that way, it doesn't sound like much fun."

"That's true. If the bus were headed to Wisconsin, it would be more fun."

"Actually, I didn't mean it that way. I meant—"

"I know what you meant," she said with a playful shove. "I just couldn't resist the plug for Wisconsin."

Ruth loved ribbing me when I was too serious. I could always count on her to bring me down to earth. I couldn't help grinning after she did it.

"But you're right," I said. "This is the way change is made, one vote at a time. One precinct, one county, and one state at a time."

"But you know, Ray, you still have unfinished business with Humphrey."

Kennedy won the Indiana primary on May 7, 1968, and beat McCarthy again in Nebraska one week later. Humphrey wasn't on the ballot in either place. When he joined the race after Johnson's withdrawal, it was too late to enter the primaries; the filing deadline had passed. His fate would be in the hands of the bosses. The California primary on June 4 was the next big test for Kennedy. He'd lost to McCarthy in Oregon. If he couldn't regain momentum in California, the campaign might be over.

The California primary on June 4 was the same day as our last final in our last year as college students, so going downtown to watch the returns come in was a celebration for Ruth and me. The ballroom of the Bismarck Hotel was packed. Even the balconies were overflowing.

A serious-looking volunteer in his thirties pushed a rolling blackboard to the front of the room, causing a momentary flutter in the hall. He took a piece of chalk from a box and placed in on the shelf. It was too early for results. He was just getting ready.

Around midnight, Chicago time, someone ran up to the volunteer with a sheet of long yellow paper, and he began writing numbers on the board. Kennedy was leading McCarthy, but not by much. The trend continued, though, and in the early hours of June 5, it held. Kennedy won the California primary and hundreds of delegates.

Two hotel porters wheeled in a large television screen, and the image of Robert Kennedy appeared. People shouted, "Quiet!" and the chatter came to a halt.

On-screen, Kennedy made his way to the podium before a wildly cheering crowd at the Ambassador Hotel in Los Angeles. With his wife, Ethel, standing beside him, he grinned shyly and began to speak.

"Thank you. Thank you very much. I want to first . . .

let me first thank Don Drysdale, the Los Angeles Dodger, for pitching a shutout and predicting our win here tonight."

Ruth nudged me good-naturedly, stoking my distaste for the Dodgers as a diehard Yankee fan.

"Tonight," I said, "I'll forgive him."

"No matter who we are," Kennedy continued, "black or white, poor or more affluent—or where we stand on the war—we can work together. Work together to solve the great problems facing us."

Kennedy seemed totally at ease, turning often to smile at Ethel. Ruth and I dwelled in easy comfort with each other and in the pride of knowing we'd helped him reach this victory.

"If I could just take a minute or two more of your time," Kennedy continued modestly. "What all of these primaries have indicated is that the people of the Democratic Party and the people of the United States want change. The country wants to move in a different direction. We want change in our own country, and we want peace in Vietnam."

The crowd responded with the loudest applause of the night.

"I would hope now that we can concentrate on having a dialogue between the vice president and myself about what direction we want to go in the United States."

Ruth turned to me at the reference to Humphrey. "You see, things *can* come together."

For a moment, I felt a surge of optimism. What could Humphrey possibly have to fear from Johnson now? Could he join Kennedy in such a dialogue?

"So I thank all of you who made this possible and did all the work at the precinct level, who got out the vote," Kennedy said. "I know the difference that can make. Now it's on to Chicago, and let's win there."

Kennedy left the podium and the television switched to the monotone duo of NBC's Huntley and Brinkley, who dryly proclaimed the end of McCarthy's bid for the nomination. Ruth and I congratulated the other volunteers, then made a hasty retreat to the Illinois Central Railroad for the 2:38 am train back to Hyde Park.

As the train rattled along, Ruth asked, "What's your role in the campaign after graduation? Have you decided?"

"I think I'll head home to New York for two weeks. Then I'll see. Maybe Dad and I can work on the backyard again. It's been a while. I'm thinking I've changed, and maybe he has, too."

"Maybe he's a Kennedy supporter now?"

"No, I don't think so. Strictly Humphrey."

"See, you changed him," she said playfully.

"It does feel weird being at odds with my own father because he supports Humphrey."

Ruth shook her head. "Crazy."

We arrived at her apartment shortly after 3:00 am. With Kennedy's victory I felt like a giant weight had been lifted—not just that the country was coming to its senses over the war, but that I was, too. I had taken a chance on Kennedy. It was not a fling of youthful idealism. It was the melding of youthful enthusiasm with the sober calculation of a mature politician, even if I was still only twenty. I touched Ruth softly on the arm and she paused before walking in.

"Thanks for not giving up on me," I said.

"Give up on you? Never. We're just getting rolling. Like the nation."

Ruth gave me a look more intimate than an embrace, then glided softly into my arms. The apartment door swung open, and Ruth's three roommates stared at us with panicked faces.

"What?" Ruth said, giggling. "We were just making out."

"You didn't hear?" Julie said.

"Hear what?"

"Bobby."

"Yes. Of course we heard. We were downtown—"

"No. Bobby was shot."

"What do you mean? That's impossible. He was just on TV." Ruth glanced at me with a twisted smile. "We saw him." Then turning toward Julie, "Didn't you see him on TV?"

"Ruth. He was shot in the kitchen as he was leaving the hotel."

"What kitchen?" Ruth screamed. Then she staggered for an instant, grabbed my arm, and fell to the floor, sobbing.

I felt a swirl of dark energy rushing through my chest, whisking me into the shadowy world of mangled fate, failed hopes, and betrayals. I kneeled beside Ruth as she looked up at me in total helplessness.

"What do we do now?" she murmured.

I shuddered. "There's nothing we can do anymore."

She closed her eyes. I lay down beside her and clutched her tightly, as if by sheer will I might patch up yet another shattered dream.

Chapter Forty-Four

I WAS STARING OUT at the rugged Colorado hills when I heard an urgent rapping at the door. I opened it, unshaven and still in boxer shorts. It was Danny with Harold Brown, the Secretary of Defense.

"Mr. Vice President," Brown began calmly, "your people tell me you're not going ahead with the commencement speech today."

I gave Brown a blank stare, turned, and walked back toward the window.

"I've got a hundred and fifty air force pilots out there," Brown protested. "The finest young men in America. They deserve to hear from you, even—"

"Bobby's dead."

"Yes, of course, but I spoke to the president. He still wants you to make the speech."

"Harold, you can tell the president to go to hell."

Brown glared at me for an instant, then whirled around and stormed out of the room. Danny gave me a nod of satisfaction.

"Danny, tell Bobby's people we're putting his Vietnam plank in the platform."

PART SIX
Summer 1968

Chapter Forty-Five

RUTH AND I graduated on June 7, one day after Robert Kennedy died, so there was no joy in it. How could we feel pleasure in personal accomplishment with our country in shambles? How could we pretend that America's turmoil had nothing to do with us? If one sick human being could plunge a nation into chaos, what hope did young people have to achieve change? "Life goes on," my father said when President Kennedy was assassinated. But just "going on" seemed hardly a worthwhile reason for doing anything.

I canceled my plans to go home. In my pessimistic state, it seemed inevitable that Dad and I would clash. I used my work with Head Start as an excuse to stay in Chicago for the summer.

Dodging my own home, I was only too willing to accompany Ruth to hers. I had met her parents a few times when they came down from Milwaukee for some union event her father was attending. That summer, we made the ninety-minute trip most weekends to spend time with her family.

Ruth's mother, Grace, seemed timid and reserved. Her hair was gray, except for a shock of black that drooped across her face. She was constantly sweeping it back with a flick of her wrist, the same endearing motion I had seen Ruth make countless times.

Grace was the rock of the household. I knew of her steely resolve from the way she defended Ruth's decision to apply to the University of Chicago. Then, one night, I witnessed it. She announced at dinner that Ruth and I would be given our own bedroom. Ruth's father seethed, yet glumly accepted his wife's edict. Ruth's brother, Anthony, whose bedroom we'd inherited, was good-natured about his eviction.

Anthony was twelve and a diehard Braves fan, even though the team had deserted Milwaukee for Atlanta two years earlier. Thanks to the robust rivalry between the old Milwaukee Braves and the New York Yankees, Anthony and I never ran out of statistics to trade or arguments to have.

Ruth was content to enjoy my camaraderie with her brother from the sidelines; the only baseball player she could name was Hank Aaron. Her father took part in the sparring between Anthony and me. He was also a baseball fan, but there was a derisive strain to his comments that was out of step with the playful banter between Anthony and me.

Mr. Torricelli was a mirror of my own father, but I could observe him almost clinically, without emotional entanglement. He harbored the same apprehension that the world was a hostile place that rarely yielded benevolence. Both men came to their suspicions in their own way, but there was a common thread of fear, blame, and resentment.

Ruth endured her father's discontent with a practiced calmness. Her patience was remarkable; she loved him despite his flaws. I thought about the look my father gave us at the Little Corporal that night. I wondered if I could do better with Dad, like Ruth did with her father, and share genuine affection. I decided I would go home at summer's end to try.

Every third weekend or so, we would drive up to the north lakes of Wisconsin, close to Michigan's Upper Peninsula, where Ruth's uncle had a cabin. One time we stayed through the week to distance ourselves from the city and its congealed memories. We rode around from one farmhouse to another, signing up farmers to donate produce to inner-city families. The connection Ruth had with people was automatic. No one could resist her. It was wonderful to watch her Farm to Fork program take shape before our eyes.

One weekend in mid-August, we went camping, something I hadn't done since my Eagle Scout training. I felt a certain pride in showing Ruth how to light a fire without a match. It took me a while, and I was seized with terror that I'd fail. But sure enough, a little fire began, first in the brush, then the twigs I'd placed on top of it, then the branches, and finally the logs. We watched the fire magically swell, mesmerized by its inevitability. As we sat gazing at it, Ruth turned to me and asked the question I'd dreaded.

"What are we going to do about the convention?"

"What convention?" I deadpanned.

"C'mon, Ray. We have to decide."

"Let's just keep the fire going and stay in the wilderness forever."

"I'm serious, Ray."

"So am I."

She smiled ruefully and stared into the fire. "Not sure we could ever do that, but we can dream of it."

"I don't want to go back."

"How can we stay in Wisconsin with the Democratic Convention in Chicago?"

"Daley is running it. He's a thug and it'll be ugly. That's how."

"Maybe you and Humphrey could talk?"

I gave a start. Ruth was doing it again: hinting at reconciliation with Humphrey. But my feelings were still raw, and there was always fresh news of the war and Humphrey's support of it to fuel my indignation.

"Ruth. You know that won't happen."

"The two of you have unfinished business," she insisted.

I grunted, hoping to put an end to the discussion.

"Maybe he'll finally make the break with Johnson at the convention," she said. "There's going to be a peace plank to the Democratic platform."

"I heard," I muttered blandly. "Won't pass."

She got up and extended her hand to me. "Ray. We can't

turn our backs on this. It's too big."

I nodded sadly. We got up, put the fire out, and drove back to her uncle's cabin in silence.

Chapter Forty-Six

ON THE MORNING of Wednesday, August 28, Ruth and I both woke up in a dark and anxious mood, bracing for a showdown at the 1968 Democratic Convention. In the living room, a half dozen college students—SMC leaders from around the country—wriggled out of their sleeping bags, assembled their gear, and fell in behind us as we made the trip downtown.

When we arrived at Grant Park, the comedian Dick Gregory was warming up the crowd, which was fifteen thousand strong. "So the secretary of state says not to worry about the Chinese. 'Oh, they got a nuclear bomb, but it's primitive,' he says. So I say, 'Primitive? Hell, man, you call some kinda nuclear weapon primitive when you scared of my switchblade?'"

The crowd howled encouragement.

"So he says, 'I don't mean that. I mean their delivery capability is primitive.' So I say, 'Man, do you realize with six hundred and eighty-eight million people, they don't need delivery capability? They can hand-carry the bombs over here.'"

The crowd roared with laughter. Protesters were streaming in with signs demeaning Humphrey: keep america hump-free and humpty dumpty sat on his balls.

Across from the park, in front of the Chicago Hilton, hundreds of Chicago police poured out of trucks, waves of blue flooding the streets. White-uniformed police captains conferred with great solemnity. Then they exploded into action, giving orders to underlings who started flinging barricades along city streets surrounding the giant hotel. They were joined by thousands of national guardsmen decked out with rifles, helmets, and nightsticks or "batons," as some called them. This "City of Broad Shoulders," had been transformed into a narrow fortress. Mayor Daley even sealed off the city's sewers so that protesters couldn't hide there.

A barbed-wire fence surrounded the International Amphitheater where the convention was taking place. Gathered inside was a remarkable collection of Americana that only a political convention could yield. There were schoolteachers and corporate executives, laboring men and scions of wealthy families, evangelist preachers and atheists, labor bosses chomping on cigars and lobbyists in elegant suits, movie stars with gleaming teeth and farmers from the heartland—and, for the first time, Southern whites and Negroes in the same delegation. But this was not the breezy boardwalk assemblage of the 1964 convention. This would be a brawling street fight that war had wrought and Mayor Daley's brutish nature inflamed. And I knew that, somehow, I would be in the middle of it.

Protest leaders gathered inside the command tent behind the band shell at Grant Park, as varied a group as the delegates inside the amphitheater. There were the hardcore war protesters like Students for a Democratic Society, Ruth's old group; David Dellinger's National Mobilization Committee to End the War in Vietnam; the moderate Women for Peace; assorted religious, civil rights, and labor groups; and the Yippies, who had galvanized public attention with their daring street burlesque the day before, nominating a pig, Pigasus, for president. The Yippie leaders and Pigasus were arrested.

As an SMC founder, I was invited to the command tent, and so was Ruth as a former SDS leader. We entered, hoping to help guide this massive protest, if it could be guided, in a peaceful direction. One step inside the tent dashed that hope. David Dellinger, Rennie Davis, Tom Hayden, and a dozen other leaders were tensely poring over maps, flipping wildly through charts on a clipboard, gesticulating, shouting, and pacing.

Hayden spotted Ruth and walked over to us. He offered a thin smile, and an apology for not showing up at our rally.

"That was two years ago, Tom," Ruth said casually. "We forgive you."

"Is there a plan?" I asked gravely.

"Not really," Tom grumbled. "The police have us penned in. We're working on a route to the amphitheater, but we have no idea if they'll let us out of here. We're just waiting for the delegates to vote on the peace plank. If that passes, things might cool off."

Unfortunately, that wasn't the case. As the vote on the peace plank lurched toward defeat, a woman charged in suddenly, yelling, "Come quick. There's trouble."

We ran outside and watched a boy scampering up a flagpole, grabbing at the American flag. Police charged in, tossing aside anyone in their path. They pulled the boy down, clubbed him, and dragged him off. Scores of demonstrators retaliated by pelting the police with rocks. Rennie Davis hastily assembled his "student marshals" and set up a defense perimeter between the police and the demonstrators. The move neutralized the rock throwers but provoked the police further. They plowed through the line yelling, "Go get them, fellas. Have some fun." Others yelled, "Kill Davis." Ruth and I watched helplessly as Davis was thrown to the ground, clubbed unconscious, and carted off.

David Dellinger rushed to the band shell to quiet the incensed crowd. "Sit down, sit down," he pleaded. "They want us to start a riot. Don't let them do it."

Dellinger's plea struck a chord with the fifteen thousand of us gathered in the park. The prospect of uncontrolled violence was frighteningly real, and everyone knew it. Since Sunday, the police and protesters had been taunting each other, each incident pushing the other side closer to confrontation, and the flagpole incident lit the fuse. Dellinger was trying to prevent an explosion. "We're going to march to the amphitheater," he said. "If we stay peaceful, we'll get there safely."

A blanket of calm settled over the crowd; a peaceful march to the amphitheater could work. It was inconceivable that such purity of purpose would be mistaken for violence by the police.

Then, out of nowhere, Hayden leaped to the stage, yanked the megaphone from Dellinger, and yelled, "No, no, no! They're not going to let us out in any organized way. Go out in small groups. Break for the streets."

Incredibly, Dellinger and Hayden, the country's leading pacifists, were dueling over tactics in front of fifteen thousand witnesses. Hayden had broken Dellinger's hopeful spell.

"Who do we follow?" Ruth asked frantically.

"Tom," I said without thinking.

"But Tom looks like he's lost it."

"I know, but he's right. We'll be less of a target in small groups."

Dellinger began his march to the amphitheater. Following Hayden's advice, Ruth and I collected a band of SMC members, hoping to head north on Michigan Avenue and join Dellinger's group. But every route out of the park was blocked.

All of us—our small group, some others, and the thousands following Dellinger—were blocked and funneled toward the Hilton, facing thirty rows of police in riot gear behind barricades.

I grabbed Ruth's hand. "Let's get out of here. It's going to blow." But it was no use. The crush of the crowd pushed us forward with suffocating momentum.

Police lobbed cannons of tear gas into the crowd. A low gray fog descended on us. Out of this eerie, depressive twilight, men came forward like apparitions with helmets, billy clubs, and gas masks—a grotesque reproduction of the hellish trench battles of World War I.

Chapter Forty-Seven

INSIDE THE HILTON, I was huddled with senior advisors in my hotel suite. An aide read the draft of the "peace plank," a bombing halt tied to negotiations. This was my chance to break out of Johnson's chokehold, I thought. "I like it," I said to my campaign manager, Larry O'Brien. "But have we heard from the president?"

O'Brien shook his head. "No, but Walt Rostow called. He said the plank will fly with Johnson."

"Okay, tell Walt I need to hear directly from the president."

"But Mr. Vice President, this is a good plank," O'Brien said. "We need to accept it right away."

"Yeah. I just need to check with the president."

My aides looked at each other and then dropped their eyes to the floor.

"Call the president, Danny," I commanded.

As we waited, I walked to the table, grabbed a slice of cold pizza, and wolfed it down. Danny handed me the phone. "Good evening, Mr. President," I began in a light-hearted tone. "I'm sitting here in Chicago looking over this plank on Vietnam. I was told it was cleared with your people."

"Well, goddamn it," Johnson boomed, piercing my eardrum. "It was never cleared." I yanked the receiver from my ear. Everyone in the room could hear Johnson's eruption. "I've never seen such shit in my life."

"Mr. President, we need to try something."

"What do you think Harriman's doing in Paris? Playing with himself?"

"No, sir. Of course not. With all due respect, we've got to

stop the bombing in the meantime. It will unify the party. I can't run for president without a unified party."

"I don't give a goddamn about you becoming president. I care about my two sons-in-law fighting in Vietnam whose lives you're so willing to jeopardize."

I glanced at my advisors, who were hearing everything and staring at me. I put the phone back to my ear for one more try. "Sir, this is a modest proposal."

Johnson continued to rant. I slumped in my chair, listening yet again as the president of the United States berated me.

"I never thought I'd be ashamed of my own vice president," Johnson concluded. He hung up.

I put the phone down and looked into the eyes of my stricken aides. "That man is going to destroy me."

After news of the defeat of the peace plank came in, I sat impassively in my room high above the street, listening to the chanting below—"The whole world is watching . . . the whole world is watching"—as if I needed to be reminded of this painful reality. The defeat of the peace plank had sparked outrage on the convention floor, pitting delegates against each other, all in plain view of nearly ninety million Americans watching it on TV.

A contingent of Secret Service arrived with a directive to stay in the room until the lobby could be secured.

"I want to go down," I said defiantly.

"Sir, that's not advisable. It's unsafe to enter the lobby."

"I'm not going to remain a prisoner in a hotel room," I snapped. "Let's go."

My entourage filed out of the room and moved silently through the corridor to the elevator, then down to the lobby. As we arrived, a walkie-talkie crackled to life and a garbled voice said, "Do not move the vice president through the lobby. Repeat, do not move the vice president." A Secret Service man clamped an arm on me and held me tight.

Chapter Forty-Eight

BREAKING DOWN their own barricades, the police commenced their attack, clubbing, pummeling, and pounding us in a frenzy of swinging clubs. There was no place to go except deeper into the teeth of the savage assault.

Shielding my face from the blows, I lost hold of Ruth. I heard her voice dissolve into a sea of screams. I tried to force my way back to her, but it was hopeless. The press of the crowd drove me into the police gauntlet. Demonstrators were falling everywhere. Still, the throng kept jamming me forward. Dozens of us were squeezed through a narrow opening in the police line, within feet of the hotel's plate-glass windows.

Encircled by demonstrators, frantic police officers ratcheted up their ferocious barrage, striking our heads, stomachs, backs, and knees with their clubs. It was simply impossible to shield ourselves from the assault. Some of the demonstrators dropped to the ground to avoid being pushed through the hotel windows. The rest of us were forced forward, trampling them. I pulled my jacket over my head to protect my face from impact with the glass, but others in front of me took the first hit.

Shards of glass went flying as we burst into the lobby. Somehow, I stayed on my feet, but within seconds a police officer appeared with a raised club aimed at my head. I ducked and threw up my arms to shield the blow. I was hit on the shoulder and fell in a crumpled heap, but I was still conscious. I started to get up and another police officer charged me, but at the same time, a man in a suit, a delegate, was also running toward me.

I covered my head, but there was no blow. When I looked up, the police officer was on the floor and the delegate was standing over him, screaming. The police officer got up, faced the delegate, and raised his club against him. With agonizing slowness, I got to my feet and hurled the weight of my wounded six-foot frame into the officer, blindsiding him and knocking him to the ground before he could hit the delegate. I fell, exhausted.

But the police kept coming. One of them charged at the delegate, poised to strike. Out of nowhere, a tall man in a business suit intercepted the officer, lifted him in the air, and threw him to the floor with such force that the officer lay on the ground, moaning. More men in business suits appeared and surrounded the delegate, protecting him as a fresh contingent of police ran toward them.

With a bolt of stupor-shattering recognition, I realized that the man I thought was a delegate was Hubert Humphrey. His eyes were flashing wildly behind the cordon of Secret Service. The police officers came to a dead stop, frozen at the sight of six armed men in business suits. Silence enveloped the room. Protesters, police officers, delegates, and hotel staff all came to a halt.

A white-shirted captain started screaming at the police. "What do you think you're doing? This man is the vice president of the United States. There'll be hell to pay."

Humphrey charged at the police captain. "Now see here!" he shouted. "No one is to be removed from this lobby until they receive medical attention. Do you hear me? And no one is to be arrested."

The captain gave Humphrey a look of stunned disbelief, amazed that anyone, even a vice president, would challenge his authority. The cops paused, like snarling dogs momentarily bewildered by a master's command, but when the captain did nothing, they resumed dragging demonstrators out by their shirts, legs, and hair.

Humphrey grabbed the commander with one hand and poked him in the chest with the other. "Did you hear me? I'm the vice president of the United States, goddamn it, and I just gave you an order."

Brought to his senses, the captain ordered the police to back off.

Humphrey shouted at the Secret Service, "C'mon, help these people."

Secret Service agents started hauling bloodied protesters to the elegant chairs of the hotel lobby as police officers stood motionless, like bystanders at a neighborhood fire. The protesters were strewn everywhere, commingling with glass, torn chairs, broken vases, and busted restaurant tables.

Humphrey helped me to a chair and ordered a police medic to dress my wounds. I saw the faint impression of a smile and a flash of affection on his face.

The moment was broken when an aide rushed up to him. "Sir, you've got to go. They're nominating you for president."

Humphrey looked at him wildly, as if trying to decipher what in the world he was talking about. He summoned the police captain and pointed to me. "Make sure this man and all the others are cared for. I want your word on that."

The captain nodded.

"Say it."

"Yes, sir."

Secret Service agents assembled around Humphrey to escort him out. He took one more look at me. "Are you all right, son?"

"You're the only one who can stop this," I whispered.

"I'm sorry, Ray." He moved closer and bent down. "I didn't hear you."

"Tell people the truth about Vietnam," I said. "Stop this now, or they will never follow you."

Humphrey rose with a quick, stiff breath, and agents

rushed him out of the hotel to a waiting limousine.

As Humphrey left the hotel, he started coughing. It was the tear gas. Then the Secret Service hustled him into the limousine and off he went.

I rose slowly from the chair and headed for the door, leading a bedraggled and bandaged contingent of demonstrators out of the lobby and onto the street, escorted by the police captain. We walked through a gauntlet of police showering us with venomous looks. But no one touched us as we dragged ourselves back to Grant Park.

I scoured the park. This was where Ruth would come if she could. It took me an hour and a half to wade through the survivors of the siege. My shoulder and arms were aching fiercely. Finally, I made my way back to the command tent and yelled, "Does anyone know where they're taking the wounded?"

"Michael Reese," someone shouted. "It's the only place that can handle so many."

I walked into the Michael Reese emergency room, flooded with young people in bloodstained shirts and makeshift slings. Two police officers barged in, almost running me over, one with a gash over his right eye. Nurses rushed over to him, ignoring the wounded protesters. My rage boiling up, I marched to the intake desk, where the partner of the wounded officer was bantering with the nurse.

"I'm looking for Ruth Torricelli."

The nurse looked at me contemptuously. "Sit down and wait your turn," she said, then resumed her chat with the officer.

I grabbed her arm. "Are you going to tell me where she is, or do I have to look for her myself?"

The portly police officer suddenly transformed from

fawning flirt to violent hulk. He lunged at me, but I expected it and skirted him. Another officer standing by the emergency room door spotted us and came running. Before he reached me, dozens of wounded protesters got to their feet and blocked his way, forming a defense cordon to protect me.

The intake nurse cried out, "Ruth Torricelli is in E-6, for God's sake. Please."

The uprising subsided, and the wounded took their seats. The police officer rose from the floor, dusted himself off, and headed for the door. The injured stared at him with hate-filled eyes.

I moved down the corridor to E-6, pushed lightly on the door, and walked in. Ruth sat limply in a chair. Her puffy eyelids lifted to greet me, and a faint smile passed across her swollen lips. I kneeled down, cradled her head, and stroked her hair.

Chapter Forty-Nine

I OPENED THE WINDOW in my room at the Hilton and looked out. Muriel watched me nervously from a couch nearby. Hundreds of police officers were sifting through the carnage. Snatches of sound floated up to my room: sirens, epithets barked by police, and the clacking of barricades. The smell of tear gas, too.

"I saw him tonight, Muriel."

"Who, Hubert?"

"Ray. Beaten up by Daley's storm troopers."

Muriel walked over to me and placed her hand on my arm.

"His eyes . . . they used to convey hope," I said. "But all I saw tonight was anguish. Tomorrow I will tell millions of Americans I'm ready to be their president. But I've given them no good reason to vote for me."

"Hubert, stop. That's not true. This is a dreadful situation . . . Lyndon still pulling strings. But you'll get through it. We always do."

"We both know it's deeper than that."

Muriel stared at me, her eyes hollow with fear, as I walked us back through time.

"I'm reliving the chapter at the drugstore. When Dad held me responsible for the outcome of his life."

Muriel lowered her head and started to cry. "I remember," she said, trying to stifle her sobs.

"'I felt ashamed for wanting my own life.'"

Muriel gripped my arm. "Hubert, come away from the window."

"That's what Lyndon said on the phone tonight. He said, 'Don't make me ashamed of my own vice president.'"

"Oh God. Hubert."

I started to weep. Tears of sadness mixed with those from the tear gas. "That young man, Ray," I whispered. "He showed more courage protecting me tonight than I ever showed protecting young men from this god-awful war."

Muriel closed the window, took me by the hand, and led me to the couch.

"Muriel, I've lost my way."

Chapter Fifty

AS I LED RUTH from her hospital room to the taxi, strains of Humphrey's acceptance speech drifted through the hallway. He was reciting St. Francis's prayer.

"'Lord, make me an instrument of your peace,'" he quoted. "'Where there is hatred, let me sow love; where there is injury, pardon. Where there is doubt, faith; where there is despair, hope. Where there is darkness, light.'"

"Those are the words of a saint," Humphrey continued, "and may those of us with less purity listen to them well, and may America tonight resolve that never, never again shall we see what we have seen."

The words were gallant and the sentiments noble, but from him at this time, they struck me as tardy and tedious. As the taxi neared Hyde Park, Humphrey faced reporters' questions.

"Mr. Vice President, you spoke of reconciliation, but have you seen what's going on in the streets? Don't you think the police overreacted, sir?"

"Anybody who saw this thing would be sick at heart, and I am. But no, I don't blame the police. I'm sorry to say, I think these demonstrations were premeditated and planned by people so full of anger and hate that they'd rather destroy our nation than work to heal it. I have no time for them."

Ruth and I looked at each other, shaking our heads. What reconciliation was he invoking in his speech? He was tied to a senseless narrative and could not escape, nor could we escape from its fallout.

I guided Ruth out of the taxi and held her arm as she

walked unsteadily toward her apartment. Her roommate, Julie, rushed out to greet us. "Oh my God, Ruth. Are you all right?"

Ruth nodded.

Then Julie turned to me. "Ray, you need to call your mom right away. She's been trying to contact you all evening. It's important."

I refused to leave Ruth's side, but Julie urged me to go on ahead. "Go call your mom, Ray. I'll help Ruth upstairs."

I was on the phone when Ruth and Julie entered the apartment. I glanced at Ruth and shook my head. She walked over and sat next to me.

"I understand, Mom. I'll catch the first flight to New York. Okay, see you tomorrow." I hung up the phone.

Ruth gasped. "Tomorrow? What—"

"Dad had a stroke. It's bad. They don't know if he's going to make it. I gotta go home."

PART SEVEN

Fall 1968–Spring 1974

Chapter Fifty-One

I SPENT MUCH of the fall of 1968 in Rockville Centre. There was little to do except visit Dad in the hospital. He was paralyzed by the stroke and didn't respond to me or Mom. At first, his doctors offered optimistic assurances, which gave way to pessimistic predictions, and gradually descended into hints of hopelessness. Finally, there was resignation. There was nothing to do but wait and hope, in eerie symmetry with the countdown to Election Day on November 5.

Humphrey's presidential campaign hobbled along; to most Americans, he was Johnson's puppet with nothing new to offer. Whenever it seemed like he might make a break, he slipped back into his old pro-war rhetoric. Humphrey simply could not escape the deadly magnetism of Johnson's hard line. Incredibly, even with the presidency on the line, he was stuck in Johnson's orbit.

Then, on the evening of September 28, Humphrey delivered a nationwide broadcast live from Salt Lake City. The speech was highly publicized, raising expectations of a policy shift on the war. Sitting by Dad's bed, I tuned in to watch.

The speech began with the worn phrases Americans had heard countless times, like "de-escalation," "de-Americanization," and "bombing moratorium." But now there were new terms, like "cease-fire," "supervised withdrawal," and a pledge to "review our commitments." The shift was subtle, almost undetectable. But it was something. Humphrey might be digging free.

I glanced at Dad, as I did every few minutes, so he'd know—if he could know—that I was paying attention to him.

There was never any change, but this time he took a labored breath; there was a swelling in his throat, and a forced exhalation. His upper lip curled slightly inward as if he were trying to launch a smile. He had moved—I was sure of it—and I smiled back.

The next day, the papers reported Humphrey's "break" with Johnson. They made more of the shift than was really there—perhaps they were just trying to create a story. But the nation caught on. Humphrey began to surge in the polls. His personality was reignited. He looked ten years younger and ten times happier.

Even Johnson, watching Humphrey regain his natural role as champion of change, began to shift. On October 31, five days before the election, Johnson ordered a bombing halt to promote peace talks in Paris. But for some inexplicable reason, the South Vietnamese refused to attend, dooming the initiative.

Early on Election Day, before heading to the hospital, I walked by an old brick firehouse near my home. The stars on the American flag seemed to shimmer in the early November sun. A Dalmatian stretched lazily across the entrance. Norman Rockwell could have painted this scene, as he had so many simple but inspiring moments of American life. A sign on the firehouse door read: official polling place.

Though still too young to vote, I watched a line of neighbors waiting to enter the curtained confines of the voting booth. I was moved by the majesty of the process, by which unimaginable power passed from one person to another in an orderly and bloodless manner. It was a miracle of human ingenuity and cooperation, but a fragile one, vulnerable to the weaknesses of good men and the deceit of evil ones. I secretly hoped that Humphrey would beat Nixon.

I returned to the hospital just in time to sit with Mom at Dad's bedside as he passed quietly from this life. He had steadily declined after that remarkable moment of communication with me. When I told the doctors about it, they doubted it had happened. Mom believed me and regretted that she hadn't been there to share it.

A few days later, in the town of Farmingdale, Long Island, not far from the Catholic cemetery where Gerry was buried, I stood with my mother and Diane at my father's gravesite. My best friends and early Humphrey confederates—Ronnie, Marc, and David—were there, and others, too.

A rabbi led us in prayer. As he concluded, we each picked up a few small stones from a pile on the ground, placed them over the gravesite, and made our way silently back to the cars.

Chapter Fifty-Two

ON ELECTION DAY, there was nothing more to do, not until the returns came in. There were calls from well-wishers, but not that many. Friends seemed to understand that there could be few more solemn days in a person's life than waiting for the judgment of 110 million of your countrymen.

I ambled out to the barn, picked up a rag from the work bench, and began the gentle rhythm of polishing my old Model T., long neglected during the feverish months of the campaign. Every so often Muriel stepped onto the porch, braced herself against the fall chill, and strained to see me through the half-open barn doors. For the first time in months, I felt in control of my pace, following a tempo of my own making, free from the judgments of others and the assault of private doubts.

As night descended on the Midwest, we made our way to the Leamington Hotel in Minneapolis. The crowd outside was enthusiastic, yet for some reason I couldn't feel it. Inside the hotel suite, I wanted only my family, but friends came by; it was hard to spurn lifelong supporters, people who loved me and who had inspired me. Normally I draw energy from the love and enthusiasm of others. Not this time. But I let them in anyway.

And the cameras, too. I was a man who might, in a few short hours, become President-elect of the United States. They had to record the moment. So I was compelled to be the public man, in a moment when I wanted so very much to feel the sheer ordinariness of being a private man. Yet I was seeking the most public role in the world. I could not connect these two longings.

The TV was on, but it became just so much chatter, as if the commentators were talking about someone else. I was that person, but I felt more like someone with no past. Or rather, a person whose entire life was congealed into a single moment; a moment of coming into new life in the shadow of shattering defeat, or one spent in the bright light of ultimate power. That such a formidable chasm of fortune awaited one man was outlandish. I marveled at the sheer improbability of the moment.

I didn't dare believe I could win, but couldn't bear the thought that I might lose. I felt the familiar stomach pains. Deep down, I knew the fate that awaited me. A win in New York engaged my spirits, but New Jersey was faltering. Even Illinois, the bright spot for Kennedy eight years ago, was fading; Daley would not come through for me as he had for him. Democratic leaders in California had, like Johnson, deserted me, and that electoral jewel was lost.

I came so close to winning—only 500,000 votes away— but I saw in my electoral defeat the reflection of a greater loss: of my own identity, not only through Johnson's mistreatment, but also by the turn in the American character. The progressive structure I had painstakingly built lay splintered and crumbling. Americans had become a fearful, narrow, and pessimistic people, and I was, as pundits had pronounced, out of step. I was a stranger to my own people.

Back home in Waverly, in the early hours of the morning, I got up and made my way to the bathroom. In the partial light, I noticed a dark splotch in the water in the toilet. For an instant, I thought I was in a dream—some bizarre image conjured up that would dissipate in the light. Then I saw thin streaks of red radiating out from the splotch in the bowl.

In an instant, the obsessions of the campaign dissolved, replaced by terror. My knees buckled, but I grabbed the vanity and caught myself. I wobbled to the toilet seat and sat down, listening to my heart pound like a train roaring down a track. When it finally subsided, I got up, prayed that I would not wake Muriel, and called Dr. Berman.

"Edgar," I said, "I'm peeing blood."

Chapter Fifty-Three

IN JULY 1969, two Americans walked on the moon. That same year, five hundred thousand Americans trudged through the mud at Woodstock. An equal number plowed through the jungles of Vietnam, six thousand of whom had already died that year. Under Richard Nixon, the war wound into higher gear; yet, ironically, it had ground down the sensibilities of most Americans, the so-called silent majority, into numb indifference at the mounting deaths.

As the nation drifted, so did I. After returning from New York, I took a full-time job at Head Start. Then Nixon cut its funding, so I fell back on my volunteer work with Philip. His father soon landed a good job with a tool and die company in Detroit, thanks to the widening employment opportunities offered to Negroes by the auto industry—a result of the civil rights movement.

On our last day together before he moved to Detroit, Philip looked me straight in the eye and handed me a little white sheet of paper with his new address. "Write to me, please," he said, each word measured. His father beamed, and his mother burst into tears. Philip looked bewildered, as if he said something wrong.

I picked him up and kissed him. "Thank you, Philip. I will."

One of my friends from the council started a baseball encyclopedia and thought my skill at detail might be helpful, so I joined him. It turned out to be just plain boring. Assembling all those facts and figures was mind-numbing. Baseball statistics are entertaining to read, but not to compile. I wasn't helping someone get elected or changing minds; it was just a way to pass time.

Unlike me, Ruth had found her calling: the Farm to Fork program took off, delivering over a ton of produce each week from the farms of Wisconsin to the tables of inner-city Chicagoans. I had loved helping Ruth start Farm to Fork, roving the byways of rural Wisconsin, so I signed on to work with her. But at the office, she was so busy. I never really saw her, and I had to take direction from one of her lieutenants. We agreed that it wasn't a good fit, and I quit.

I went home to visit Mom in late '69, and as luck would have it, it was the week that *The Making of the President 1968* was shown. As with *The Making of the President 1960*, which had aired four years ago, Humphrey lost, this time to Nixon. I sat with Mom silently, each of us reflecting on what the tumultuous passage of time had wrought.

When I got back to Chicago, I added a few occupations to my string of failed jobs: writer for an educational film company, freelance proofreader, even taxi driver. I hoped to find some temporary meaning in these stints as I awaited clarity about the next chapter in my life. I wanted to be part of something big, as I'd been with Humphrey, and then with Kennedy. But the truth was, I couldn't trust anyone else's dream, and I was incapable of creating one myself.

I considered applying to law school and even took the law boards, but then thought better of it. *Is this really what I want to do?* I asked myself. *Toil away at the margins of injustice rather than confronting it head-on?* That's the way I explained my decision to Ruth. But as Ruth knew all too well, I wasn't confronting anything head-on anymore, least of all my own discontent.

My decline perplexed everyone. Taking time to heal, or even drift, was understandable to most people after a death, a devastating personal disappointment, or a national tragedy. I fell under all three—but a year and a half felt too long.

"Indulgent," "aimless," and "selfish" were some of the labels I could imagine my father using to describe it. Worse, I knew Ruth was thinking them.

But in a bizarre way, my descent was calculated, almost comfortable in a cold, ironic way. It was as if, by reaching my lowest point, I could take the full measure of detachment from everything I had once relied upon to motivate me. There was a kind of satisfaction in falling to the bottom and starting over; you could observe every step out and assess its authenticity. Somehow, though, I couldn't manage a single step without doubting its value. My comfort zone had become disengagement, disinterest, and timidity. And nowhere were the effects as devastating as they were in my life with Ruth.

Moments that had been so commonplace began to irritate me. If she asked me to pick up something from the store for dinner, my defensive mind transformed it into: *You're not as busy as I am, so it's your obligation to do the shopping.* If she referred me to some article about a college friend accomplishing something, it became: *See what so and so is doing; why can't you make something of yourself?*

Then we started fighting. All of my energy was spent on defending myself and mounting imaginary arguments before saying them out loud to Ruth.

Finally, it all exploded on a spring morning in 1970, seventeen months to the day since Dad died and Humphrey lost the election.

Chapter Fifty-Four

I WAS DOZING IN BED, vaguely aware of clanking sounds in the bathroom as Ruth moved through her morning routine.

"Hey, get up," she said, as she ran over to nudge me out of bed. "You'll be late for your interview."

"I'm not going to the interview," I said groggily and rolled away from her.

She grabbed my shoulder and turned me toward her. "What are you talking about? We've been through this. You said you were interested in that union job."

"I was never interested. But you were, so I went along with it."

"That job is perfect for you. It's organizing!"

"It's perfect for *you*. Perfect for what you want for me, not what I want."

"Okay, fine, Ray. Only, I called in favors to get you that interview."

Ruth grabbed her briefcase and headed for the door, then shouted back at me, "Did you at least call the business agent to cancel the interview?"

"Hmm," I mumbled.

"Is that a yes or a no?"

I growled back. She stomped out and slammed the door behind her.

I got out of bed and dressed listlessly. I called the union with some phony excuse, and then left the Drexel Avenue brownstone Ruth and I had occupied without roommates since graduation. I braced myself against the crisp April air and headed east, making my way through the Gothic arches and crisscrossed walkways of the quad.

I paused in front of a poster announcing Stanley Kubrick's film *2001: A Space Odyssey*, which was showing at the student film center in Ida Noyes Hall. Ruth and I had enjoyed it together when it came out two years ago. Remembering our closeness then, a thought flickered: *Hey, we could see it again together!* Then the gloomy truth seeped in that Ruth was too busy to see a movie. We hadn't done anything together for weeks. Maybe longer.

A few passersby recognized me and nodded. I kept walking southward across the midway to the law school. I entered it like an intruder. I had no invitation, no aspiration, and no direction, the exact opposite of what law students were supposed to have. I felt like I stood out with my long hair and beard, wearing Gerry's St. Agnes varsity soccer jacket. But no one seemed to notice. *What are they thinking?* I wondered. Maybe they weren't thinking anything about me. Maybe I was the one doing the thinking, being critical of them.

I made my way to the admissions office. At the counter, an older lady with reading glasses dangling from a gaudy necklace was shuffling through a stack of papers. She peered at me as if I had just landed from another planet. "May I help you?" Her voice trailed off in a cloud of distraction.

"I may be interested in an application," I said mechanically.

She narrowed her eyes. "An application? We don't usually get walk-ins from people who 'may be interested.'"

"Could you tell me what the minimum standards are to get in here?"

She shot back derisively, "The University of Chicago Law School is one of the top law schools in the country. You don't just 'get in here.'"

"Ma'am, with all due respect, I'm sure everyone attending this school managed to somehow 'get in here.'"

"Well, I never—"

"What do I need to get . . . to be accepted here? Bottom

line, please?"

"Top ten percent of your class."

"And the boards?"

"Seven hundreds. But really, young man, this is most unusual—"

"I'll take an application."

"Who are you?"

"Nobody. But I graduated cum laude from the college here."

"Oh. I see." She handed me an application. "Well, the deadline is two days from now."

"I guess I'd better get started, then," I said with a sheepish smile. "Is there a place where I can sit and fill this out?"

She hesitated, then pointed to a small office adjacent to the admissions counter.

"Good," I said. "Thank you."

Inside the office, I dropped Gerry's jacket on a chair and started reviewing the application. It was impossibly long. I hadn't anticipated eighteen pages of questions about my interests, hobbies, community commitments, group affiliations, summer activities, jobs held, etcetera. It was endless. I looked over the references page—potentially my strongest suit—but realized that I couldn't use Humphrey's name. How impressive would *that* have been? A reference from a former vice president of the United States. But it was out of the question now.

I pondered the other famous people I'd known who might have written a recommendation. Robert Kennedy would have praised me, but he was dead. The mayor of Chicago, having portrayed himself to the world as a brutal and vindictive man, was also out of the question. Tom Hayden might have written something, but he was viewed as too radical. Here I was, an honor student, Eagle Scout, and youth leader, and I had to hide my past to enter this sanctuary of legitimacy.

I froze for an instant, gnashing my teeth. What was

I doing? This was insane. Did I have to deny who I was to gain entry here? I looked up, worried that the admissions lady would observe me panicking. But she didn't. I stared down at the application and waded into the questions.

I knew I had to move fast, and that I couldn't make mistakes. It was like the stencil I'd used for my first Humphrey flyer in high school: one mistake and I'd have to do it over. But there was no time to start another application, and I wouldn't be accepted with crossed-out words; I had to get it right the first time.

I labored over the application for five hours straight. When I finished, I politely asked the admissions lady if she would review the application to make sure it was complete.

"Well," she said hesitantly, "we don't usually do that."

"I know," I said. "Please."

She bit her lip. Finally she took the application from me and began looking it over. "I must say, I've been here fifteen years and no one has ever filled out an application in this office in one sitting. You must be a very committed young man."

"I hope so. Thank you. But I need your help to make the deadline. Can you call the registrar at the college to get a transcript of my grades?"

She smiled at me. "Yes, I know the people over there. I can probably get it today." I smiled back at her. I had an ally. Maybe that was a good sign.

"Great. Thank you. Thank you very much." I extended my hand.

She took my hand and shook it. "Looks like you made the deadline."

I left the office with a pulse of optimism—until I realized that I had to explain all of this to Ruth.

Suddenly, I heard a voice call out: "Hey, Ray, wait up." It was one of my volunteers from the Student Mobilization Committee. "What are you doing here?"

"Just looking around, I guess."

He scrutinized my beard, my soccer jacket, and my diffident bearing, like a lawyer would. I waited for the incongruity of it all to hit him, and then it did. "Wait a minute. You're not thinking of applying *here*, are you?"

"Maybe."

"Are you kidding me? Ray Elias, anti-war activist, going to law school? Wow."

I nodded sullenly and turned to leave, but he yanked me back with another question. "You must have lucked out in the draft lottery. Otherwise you'd be, you know . . . in Vietnam."

"I would never go to Vietnam," I said, taking a step toward him. "You should know that."

"Sure, Ray. Well, welcome to the establishment. It's not so bad here. Hell, if you can't beat 'em, join 'em."

Chapter Fifty-Five

RUTH WAS SITTING at the sawhorse kitchen table, drinking tea and going through the next day's Farm to Fork schedule.

"Where have you been?" she asked coldly.

"Nowhere."

"Nowhere, huh? Okay."

"I went over to the law school."

"That's interesting." She got up and reached for another tea bag from the shelf. "Any reason in particular?"

"Well, what would you say if I told you I applied?"

"I would say you're kidding, because it's too late to apply."

"Well, no, there are two days left," I said lamely.

Ruth prepared her tea. "No, seriously, what were you doing there?"

"Well, actually, I applied."

Ruth gave me a cold stare. "What are you talking about? Two months ago you said law has nothing to do with justice."

"It was kind of spur of the moment."

"Spur of the moment!" she repeated, incensed. "No one applies to law school on the spur of the moment."

"Really, I did."

"You blow the interview this morning while you're hiding this . . . this . . . this law school scheme of yours?"

"No," I said. "It wasn't like that, Ruth."

"You know, Ray, you go from job to job, wasting your talents on stupid things. I get that. You're going through . . . whatever. But keeping secrets from me? That—"

"Ruth, you're wrong. I didn't keep it a secret."

Her face was so red, I thought she might burst into flames.

"I don't believe you. All your rhetoric about how lawyers can't change a thing. 'Handmaidens of the status quo,' you called them. You said they were 'cop-outs.'"

"I never said that," I snapped.

I got up, moving awkwardly around Ruth in the small kitchen to get tea for myself. "I thought you might be pleased."

"Pleased? Law school would be great—if you really wanted to be a lawyer. But frankly, this just sounds like another stalling act. Your heart isn't in it. Your heart isn't in *anything*. I can't stand to watch this."

"I don't know what to do, okay?" I replied angrily. "You just said you could handle my . . . my . . ."

"Procrastination."

"All right, procrastination. Well, I don't think you can. You act like it's my responsibility to save the world, like I owe something to 'the movement,' to do something useful. Why? Because I used to? Well, it just doesn't interest me now. I don't want to be tied to my past. If you've found your mission, that's great. I don't owe anybody anything."

Ruth exploded. "Who do you think you're talking to, your father?"

I glared at her, then stomped off to the bedroom and slammed the door. My mind was like a railroad switchyard, thoughts moving around like trains seeking a way out. *Don't come in*, I prayed. I needed time to figure out what forces were conspiring to drive me away from the woman I adored.

Then she walked into the room. "Ray," she began in a detached yet pitying tone, "you resented your father because he didn't believe in you, and Hubert Humphrey because he abandoned you, and now me because I don't understand you. Well, you know what? None of it's true. Everyone's not against you. You made up all that crap so you don't have to trust anyone. Haven't you lost enough people in your life?"

I felt a fierce wind rush through me, grabbing my spirit and whisking it away. The emptiness was bleak, brittle, and horrid. At that moment, I hated Ruth. No one had the right to render another person so bare.

"Get out," I raged. "Get out!"

"No, you get out. I'm going to Wisconsin this weekend. Don't be here when I get back."

She whirled around and stomped toward the door. Then, softening, she said, "I'm sorry, Ray. I think we need a break."

And that was it, like thunder following lightning: a flash, then a storm, then the damage. I knew it would take a very long time to sift through it.

Law school was a three-year odyssey in suspended animation. I drifted through it, sustained not by interest or even curiosity, but by raw will. Survival, not the prospect of a rewarding legal career, became an end in itself.

My labor law professor, James Morewig, was a classic egghead, with thick tortoiseshell glasses that embedded his eyes in a sea of glass. He spoke ponderously, as if his utterances were divine oracles—perhaps they were, in his mind. His sentences were so long and convoluted, I often thought the man was genetically incapable of exiting the same sentence he entered. Like most law professors, he had carefully calculated an off-putting demeanor to instill fear in us. His sarcasm reminded me of Mr. Francis in high school, but he lacked an underlying affection for his students.

Not that I dwelled on such questions, or any questions relating to law school. I spent most of Morewig's class, and all my classes, lost in thought. Occasionally, I felt a pulse of admiration for the elegance of the National Labor Relations Act, the cornerstone of American labor relations. But my excitement was short-lived. My thoughts soon turned to familiar obsessions, like why I'd ever entered law school in the first place, and how in the world I'd managed to lose Ruth.

Unfortunately for me, one afternoon Morewig caught me immersed in these errant thoughts.

"So you see," he said, using the same phrase he began nearly all his sentences with, "the National Labor Relations Act effectuates a delicate balance between the inherent right of management to maintain order in the industrial process, and the right of employees to express dissatisfaction with those processes and engage in activities that further their collective interests. I wonder who might volunteer to comment upon this profound tension. Anyone? Mr. Elias, you seem engrossed in some weighty topic. May I deign to hope that it is this one?"

I panicked. I hadn't grasped his cumbersome question, so I blurted out something nonsensical, confirming to the class, and to Morewig, that I had no idea what I was talking about. He glared at me and moved on. "Anyone care to expand on Mr. Elias's woefully inchoate formulation?"

And with that, I slipped back into my thoughts, with even more fuel to ponder my inadequacies.

Chapter Fifty-Six

WHEN EUGENE MCCARTHY announced that he wouldn't run for reelection in 1970—he had become bored with politics and the Senate—I saw my chance to get back to Washington. After two years of college teaching, here I was, a freshman senator again, being welcomed by the chairman of the Senate Agriculture Committee.

"Before we proceed with our agenda this morning," the chairman began, "I would like to acknowledge the newest member of the committee, certainly no stranger to any of us. Hubert, I congratulate you on your election to the United States Senate. Gentlemen, I present the former vice president of the United States, Hubert Humphrey, and happily, our colleague again."

"Why, thank you, Mr. Chairman," I responded. "It's a pleasure to be back."

"Hubert, although I may regret this, I yield the floor to you."

The senators chuckled, acknowledging my reputation for long-windedness.

"Thank you, Mr. Chairman. As you know, the subject of agricultural infrastructure is near and dear to me. The interior waters are critical to the agricultural well-being of the nation, and therefore we must spare no effort to revive and renovate our infrastructure to support crop irrigation systems, over-the-road transportation, and related scenic byways."

The senators nodded good-naturedly.

"My bill would—" I stopped abruptly. I had suddenly felt a sharp pain in my side.

My colleagues looked up, alarmed. "What's wrong, Hubert?" the chairman asked.

"I'm all right. I just . . . never mind. As I was saying . . ."

Chapter Fifty-Seven

HIGH ABOVE CHICAGO, on the sixty-eighth floor of the Sears Tower, the elevator doors rumbled open and I stepped into the lavish lobby of the Baker, Bates & Stanton law firm. I was the very image of a young professional: a stylish three-piece suit, the *Chicago Tribune* tucked under one arm, and a rich leather attaché case, a graduation gift from my mother, in the other. The receptionist handed me a message, and I headed to my office.

My office commanded an expansive view of the west side of the city. Homes stretched for miles, like tiny toy structures placed in neat rows in an architect's mock-up. I took off my jacket and hung it carefully behind the door as the intercom barked out, "Mr. Elias, Mr. Stanton is on his way."

William Stanton was the only original partner of the firm still alive; Baker and Bates had died years ago. Stanton had started with the firm forty-six years ago, right out of law school. At seventy, he was dean of the Chicago legal community and one of the most well-known people in the city. I was less impressed with his standing than I was fearful of his haughty demeanor.

Stanton sailed into my office and stated his question without pleasantries: "Do you know anything about labor law?"

"Why, yes, sir. I took that class in law school."

"Very well. Take a look at this." He handed me a file. "Tell me what you think. I've set up a meeting for you with the company president tomorrow. This is an important client. I need this done right."

Stanton departed as briskly as he'd entered, and I dove

into the file.

Early the next morning, I drove up to a nondescript building on the Near West Side. As instructed by Stanton, I went to the back door and punched the buzzer. A small sign read: Master Plastics.

Inside, a receptionist sat behind a thick glass window. "Name?" she asked with practiced disregard.

"Ray Elias from Baker, Bates & Stanton, to see Mr. Dougherty."

She made no move, so I stood at the window, waiting. "Take a seat," she said without looking up. "He'll be right out."

I'd barely sat down when the door swung open and out came a large and finely dressed man flashing a broad grin and extending a huge hand. "I'm Ralph Dougherty, president."

Dougherty led me through the plant, along a yellow-painted path winding around the production area. A collection of workers with sweaty faces were bent over a line of antiquated punch presses and metal lathes. Women pushed large bins through the crowded aisles, collecting completed lamp harps.

Dougherty motioned toward one of the operators, a small man who stared at us with deep-set, brooding eyes. "That's him," Dougherty said. "The union troublemaker."

I locked eyes with the man, trying to fathom what kind of trouble someone so unassuming might cause.

"Don't stare at him," Dougherty barked. "I don't want him to notice you."

It was too late for that, but I averted my eyes. Dougherty led me into a paneled conference room and motioned for me to sit down. "Can I get you anything?"

I shook my head.

Three men walked in and took seats around the table. Dougherty didn't acknowledge or introduce them.

"Okay, we're all here," he began. "Look, Elias, I treat my people right. Wages are fair, and when someone needs a little help, I give it to them, no questions asked. For instance, just last week, Mary Wagner needed money for her daughter's tuition to the parish school, and I advanced it to her." He turned to one of the men sitting at the table. "Tell him, Jake. I'm good to my people."

Jake seemed unsure whether to simply nod acquiescence or pipe up in support of Dougherty's boast.

"So," Dougherty continued, "I don't want any union screwing things up around here. I built this place from nothing, and no union's going to tell me how to run it."

"Mr. Dougherty," I said, "if you're fair to your people, you'll have no trouble winning a National Labor Relations Board election."

Dougherty slammed his fist on the table. "I don't want any damn election."

"Sir, the union has filed for an election, and the labor board has ordered one. There's no getting around the election."

"Now wait a minute. Bill Stanton said you'd be cooperative."

"Cooperative, sir?"

"I mean, he said you'd explain how to beat the union. So tell me how we beat the union."

"Well, sir, you have a lot of options. You can hold meetings with the workers on company time and talk about why life would be better without a union. In other words, you can campaign, and I can guide you through that. But an election is inevitable."

"Then I want that troublemaker fired. That will slow things down."

"Excuse me?"

"Stanton said we could fire the union leaders as long as it didn't look like we were targeting them."

"Mr. Stanton said that?"

"Well, not in so many words, but he said if we had grounds to fire him for work-related offenses, it would be lawful."

Dougherty nodded to another man at the table. On cue, the man produced a sheaf of papers and shoved it at me. I looked at Dougherty for an explanation, but there was none. I reached for the file and thumbed through it. All eyes were on me.

Dougherty finally broke the silence. "As you can see, he's been stealing from me for years."

"Mr. Dougherty, were these disciplinary notices written up contemporaneously?"

"What do you mean?"

"I mean were they written up at the time of the alleged offenses and given to the employee?"

"No. We just kept a running record here in the office."

"Then even if these charges are accurate—"

"Of course they're accurate."

"Okay, they're accurate. You still have to show that others who committed the same acts were similarly punished. If you can't show that, this termination would be discriminatory."

"I see what you're getting at," he said, turning to the third man. "Pauli, pick a few other guys, white guys you don't mind losing, and we'll fire the lot. Then they can't say we discriminated." A smirk unfolded across Dougherty's face. "I'm sure all of them have been stealing from me anyway."

The three company men flashed obliging smiles.

I beat a hasty retreat to my car, my briefcase bulging with the phony documents. A group of workers on their break hovered around the coffee wagon, staring at me.

Suddenly, a younger worker rushed up to me. "Ray Elias? I'm Jack Gould."

I nodded coldly.

"Maybe you don't remember me. I worked for you on the Student Mobilization Committee."

"Of course I remember you, Jack," I said, fumbling for my keys.

"You're probably wondering what I'm doing here."

I shook my head, hoping to discourage him.

"I dropped out of college when things got crazy—you know, with the war—and one thing led to another. Anyway, I'm here to make a little money so I can go back."

"I see," I said curtly, opening the car door and waiting for an opportunity to get in and leave.

"But what are you doing here? Are you from the government or something on this union thing?"

I said nothing and got into the car.

Gould kept talking. "You know, it's really bad here. No insurance, unsafe conditions . . . and Dougherty? He's a son of a bitch. I'm sure you know that, right?"

"Jack, forget it," I said. "I'm the company lawyer, for Christ's sake."

Gould backed away in disgust.

I closed the door and peeled out.

Chapter Fifty-Eight

I WAS SITTING AT THE BAR in a Near North tavern, gripping a Jack Daniels and staring into space, when a guy walked by and bumped my stool. It was innocent, I knew, but my drink splashed on my suit. I whirled around and said, "Hey, watch it." To myself, I muttered, "Jerk," but the guy heard it.

"Who are you calling jerk, asshole?"

I realized instantly what a fool I was—drunk enough to get into a fight but also too drunk to survive one.

"Hey, I'm talking to you," he said.

"Sorry, not in the mood for a conversation, buddy."

Then he put his arm on me, which I threw off with a brisk pivot. He backed off for a moment; I thought he might simply walk away. Instead, he lunged at me, but I was quick. I leapt off the chair, and he stumbled into the bar.

A barroom brawl . . . how ridiculous, I thought. With pathetic accuracy, this stranger and I were enacting a scene from a bad movie. I half expected a director to pop out from behind the bar with a megaphone and yell, "Cut."

Instead, Ruth appeared out of nowhere. She gave me a blank stare. "It's all right, Bruce," she told my assailant. "I know this man." She turned back to me. "Ray, this is Bruce Medford, transportation coordinator for Farm to Fork. Bruce, Ray."

Bruce and I stared at each other for a minute, and then Ruth took him by the arm like a schoolboy and walked him away from the bar. "Bruce, why don't you grab a table? I'll be right there."

Bruce nodded stiffly and trudged off. Ruth approached

me, staring.

"You didn't have to rescue me, you know," I said.

"No," she said, motioning to my half-spilled drink. "It looks like Jack Daniels is taking care of that."

"You should know that I can't be rescued. I'm a lawyer."

"Yes, I heard you're with Baker, Bates & Stanton."

"Uh-huh," I grunted.

"Why do the names of law firms always sound so musical? Baker, Bates & Stanton." She repeated the name, half singing. "At least the firm has that going for it."

"Okay, go ahead—say it. Union busters. I know."

"I didn't say that. You did. Ray, seriously, you don't look good."

"I'm okay. Just a bad day, or maybe a bad year . . . let's call it four years if you include law school."

Ruth glanced back at Bruce, who was staring at us from his table. "Ray, did you ever consider that maybe you're just on the wrong side."

"The wrong side? Ha. How would I know the difference?"

"By starting fresh."

"I'm not sure it's that simple."

Ruth glanced again at Bruce. He was waving her over to the table.

"You'd better get going," I said, motioning toward Bruce. "Thanks for the advice."

Later that night, I sat behind the desk in my apartment, staring at a blank page in the typewriter. I had managed only one line, the title: *Response by Master Plastics to the Union's Charge of Illegal Termination.*

I got up and paced around my living room, a large space with modern but sterile furnishings. A few contemporary prints hung on the wall, but nothing with any personal connection.

My string bass stood uncomplainingly in the corner, covered and idle, indifferent to years of abuse I'd heaped upon it by not playing.

I sat down, trying one more time to write. I told myself that if I couldn't write this damn thing when I was drunk, I'd never be able to stomach it when I was sober.

The phone rang. The answering machine clicked on and I heard the gentle voice of my mother. "Ray, it's Mom. Are you sure you're not home?"

I raced to the phone. "Hi, Mom. Sorry."

"I'm worried about you. I haven't heard a word in two weeks."

"I'm fine. It's just . . . busy, I guess."

"You're working too hard. I can tell."

"It's all right, Mom."

"Listen, honey. I was thinking maybe you should come home for a few days. Maybe we could go to your father's gravesite."

"I can't. Things are just a little up in the air right now. What if I come home around Labor Day? Things should be settled by then. Can we plan on that?"

"All right, Ray. That sounds fine."

"Okay, Mom. I'll let you know the dates."

"Do you ever see Ruth?"

"No, of course not, Mom. But, well, actually, I did run into her tonight."

"Really? Ah. You see, it's fate that I should call the same night. Such a nice girl. Your father liked her, too, once he—"

"I know. It's just, I don't know . . . it's complicated."

"Maybe it's not so complicated."

"Mom, really—"

"Just go back to the simple things, Ray. You used to be good at seeing things clearly. Just think about what you were meant to do."

"Meant to do? I have no idea."

"It may be staring you right in the face."

I glanced at the blank page in the typewriter. *That* wasn't what I was meant to do. At least I knew that. "Okay, Mom. I'll try."

"I love you, Ray."

My lip stiffened to stave off tears. "I love you too, Mom."

I hung up the phone and walked over to the window. A ribbon of cars moved steadily along Lake Shore Drive. I looked into the blackness of Lake Michigan, studying the blinking lights of the large ships on the water. I wondered what the vessels were doing stationed in the dim light so close to port, yet still stalled in the vastness of the great lake.

I walked back to my desk, picked up the phone, and dialed.

Ruth answered. "Hello . . . who is this? Ray, is that you?"

I hung up.

The next morning I went into high gear, moving quickly around the office, yanking papers from files, certificates from the wall, and books from the shelves. Young lawyers filed past, exchanging whispers.

Stanton elbowed his way through. "What the hell is going on here, Elias? Where's that report on Master Plastics?"

I handed him the blank page.

"What kind of joke is this?"

"It's not a joke, sir. That's all I managed to get done."

Stanton stared at me, incensed.

"I'm leaving, sir."

"Leaving? Without notice? This firm afforded you a remarkable opportunity, young man. Is this the way you repay us?"

"Mr. Stanton, I'm grateful. I am. But . . . a remarkable opportunity? I don't think so. The opportunity you afforded me was to commit an injustice against four innocent men."

I picked up the box with my belongings and walked out into the gaggle of lawyers staring in wonder at the scene.

"There will be consequences, Elias," Stanton shouted after me. Then, turning to the gawking lawyers, he said, "That's enough. Get back to work."

I rode the elevator sixty-eight floors down to the street, pondering the uncertainty I had just hurled myself into. I had no idea what to do. I had no new office to take my belongings to, no cause to commit to, no person to share it with, and so many lost years to make sense of. But before I could get to that, I had one more thing to do.

Chapter Fifty-Nine

A LITTLE AFTER 9:00 AM on August 9, 1974, I entered the Capitol. People were talking in whispers; rather than facing impeachment, President Nixon had resigned the night before for covering up the burglary of the Democratic Committee Headquarters at the Watergate complex. I could not help thinking that the many sins of this man had finally caught up with him.

My secretary greeted me urgently. "Senator, Vice President . . . I mean, President Ford's office just called. The president would like to see you right away."

I raced to the Old Executive Office Building across from the White House—my old stomping ground as vice president—to heed the call of a fellow vice president who was now president. I was wading through the crowd hovering around Ford's office when one of the president's aides spotted me and gestured for me to enter.

Gerald Ford and I were friends. He was a decent, respectful, and modest man. And, of course, he and I were two members of a small fraternity: living vice presidents. The only other one was Richard Nixon, who had just resigned as president twelve hours ago. Two other vice presidents—Harry Truman, who was Franklin Roosevelt's vice president, and Lyndon Johnson, John Kennedy's vice president—had died within the last eighteen months. Of the five vice presidents in the thirty years since World War II, I was the only one who had not become president.

"Hubert, I'm going to need your help," Ford said.

"Of course, Gerry . . . Mr. President."

"I mean on Vietnam. We're losing there. It's obvious. I'm determined to get out. You'll help me, won't you?"

"Yes, Mr. President." I said instantly, jarred by how swiftly I retreated from years of public support for the war. "You can count on me."

Walking back to my office, I tumbled into the well of memories about what might have been. I was glad Richard Nixon was gone. He was a peculiar man, a corrupt man, and a disgrace to the office that I had coveted. In the years following my defeat, I learned that, days before the election, Nixon had secretly contacted South Vietnam's President Thieu and persuaded him to boycott the peace conference Johnson called for, promising a better deal if he were elected. Thieu went for the gambit, refused to attend the conference, and caused it to collapse—and with it, my bid for the presidency.

Johnson learned of Nixon's back-channel treachery but refused to make it public. Such is the tenuous foundation upon which American elections, and democracy itself, rests. Still, my role now was to build trust again in the office that Nixon had violated.

I arrived at the Senate Office Building but kept walking, entering the surrounding neighborhood. I watched a group of Negro children skipping rope, oblivious to the momentous passing of power occurring just blocks away. I waved, but they didn't see me. I kept walking deeper into a world so foreign from the power exercised nearby.

I noticed a long line of men standing outside a drab storefront office. As I got closer, I saw the sign on the office: District of Columbia Department of Employment Services.

"How long have you men been waiting?" I asked a group of them.

They shrugged. "Two hours, and we ain't even in the door," one of them said.

"They don't move too fast," another added. "You know, the government."

These men reminded me of the gaunt faces of my South Dakotan neighbors forty years ago, standing motionless outside homes laminated with dust in a silent testimony of desperation. I remembered that the only sound was the grasshoppers gnawing at the fence posts after they had chewed up the crops.

I strode to the head of the line and marched into the office. The place was packed with Negro men poring over forms. Some were sitting in old metal chairs, but most were standing and waiting like the men outside. Clerks stood at the counter, chatting with each other, taking their time.

"There are people waiting," I said to one of the clerks. "Can't you move any faster?"

"Sit down, sir," he shot back. "Wait your turn like everyone else."

I charged over to a man in a suit with a badge. "See here, sir. You'd never know this was an employment office from the way this staff works."

Every eye in the place was on me.

"Just because these people are out of work," I shouted, "doesn't mean they don't deserve respect."

A look of shock burst across the supervisor's face. Then, turning to the employees at the counter, he said, "Get moving. Have a little respect. This man was vice president of the United States."

"Hubert, this is too big," Danny shouted as we strode down the halls of Congress to the Senate Bill Intake Office. "You've got to talk to leadership about it first."

"This *is* leadership, Danny," I replied, slapping a document down on the counter.

"But you don't have anyone on board. Labor, economists, industry people."

"They'll come on board, eventually. Everyone will."

The man behind the counter, an old-timer, drifted lazily to the desk and then jumped to attention when he saw me. "Senator! I didn't expect you. I mean, er . . . logging in your own bill?"

"Never mind that. I just want to make sure it gets in. We're thirty years too late on this thing as it is."

The clerk nodded and recorded the bill, reading the title out loud: "The Full Employment and Balanced Growth Act." Then he handed me a stamped copy.

"Just imagine, Danny," I said. "A nation where no one needs to suffer the indignity of unemployment."

Chapter Sixty

THERE WAS A RUMBLE of subdued conversation as I entered the courtroom. A handful of Master Plastics employees were gathered in the gallery near the defendants' table, talking with the four men Dougherty had framed for stealing. They had no lawyer, just a business agent the union sent, a beefy man in a brown polyester jacket with no tie. The defendants looked resigned and helpless.

Jack Gould, the former SMC volunteer, was there supporting his four coworkers. He spotted me but looked away. Dougherty sat at the other table, handsomely attired, exuding confidence and chatting with his lawyer, William Stanton.

I found a seat in the gallery, but Dougherty caught sight of me and tugged on Stanton's arm. Stanton turned and squinted at me, trying to discern what danger my presence might pose. As the judge walked in, a bailiff gaveled the room into silence and commanded all to rise.

Stanton charged to the bench. "Your honor, there is a preliminary matter of some urgency."

"Yes, Mr. Stanton. What is it?"

"A former associate of my firm who worked on this case is present in the courtroom. We request that the court inquire as to his purpose here."

The judge looked at Stanton quizzically. "Did you say former associate, Mr. Stanton?"

"Yes, your honor."

"As far as I know, there's no law that restricts lawyers from entering a public courtroom to observe the proceedings in a case they were once involved in. Usually, they have better things to do, I'll certainly grant you that, but—"

"This is different, your honor. We have reason to believe that he may be assisting the union in the prosecution of their case."

"Reason to believe, Mr. Stanton? Please, state your reason."

"He was terminated from the firm, your honor."

"Terminated? Did he quit, or did you fire him?"

"He quit."

The judge frowned at Stanton. "Unless you have proof that he's using information obtained while working on the case, I can't chase him out of a public courtroom. Do you have such proof?"

"Your honor, may I have a moment to confer with my client?"

"Yes, of course, Mr. Stanton."

After a minute with Dougherty, Stanton approached the bench again, whispered something to the judge, and then walked briskly through the swinging gate into the gallery toward me. "Let's talk outside," he snarled.

In the corridor outside the courtroom, Stanton demanded, "What's the meaning of this? Showing up in court, for heaven's sake!"

"Everyone in this courtroom," I began pointedly, "except the judge—at least for now—knows that these charges are fabricated. I'm here to make sure that he learns it, too."

Stanton started turning red; I had never seen him so angry. For an instant, I thought he might hit me. Was his veneer of respectability so shallow that he'd lose his cool dealing with a rookie lawyer?

"I'll have you disbarred if you betray my client's confidence."

"Mr. Stanton, I'll ask you to calm down for a—"

"Don't you tell me what to do, young man."

"Let's get to the heart of the matter, then. As you know,

a lawyer may breach a client's confidence if he learns that the client is about to commit a crime. I've researched the matter, and Dougherty's imminent perjury is such a crime."

"All right, all right. What do you want?"

"Take the men back—full reinstatement—and let the union election proceed."

Stanton was furious. His eyes widened like two pools of fire. "Wait here," he said and stormed back into the courtroom.

Seconds after Stanton left, I was startled by a figure emerging from behind a partition in the corridor. "Ruth!" I said with a start. "What are you doing here?"

"I have the same question for you. You just threatened one of the city's most powerful men! I thought you worked for Stanton, not the other way around. What's going on?"

"First, tell me what you were doing standing behind that partition."

"I tried to sneak quietly into the courtroom, but when I spotted you in the gallery and saw Stanton steaming toward you, I ran out and . . . hid!"

I shook my head and released a tiny smile. She smiled back.

"Honestly, Ray. The other night. You didn't look too good."

"No, I didn't."

"I thought you needed someone on your side."

"I didn't think I deserved anyone on my side."

"Ray," she said, taking a step toward me and touching my arm, as she had done so many times with stunning tenderness, "everyone deserves someone on their side." I was frozen in place by words of affection I had not heard in four years.

Stanton came storming through the courtroom doors. He gave Ruth a deprecating look and she stepped away. "Fine," he said angrily. "We'll do it. I'll advise the judge. But I never want to see you again."

"You won't."

He spun around in an indignant flourish and headed back into the courtroom.

I turned to Ruth. "I need to go back in, to make sure this happens right. Can you wait a minute?"

"Sure."

Stanton eyed me hatefully as I approached the bench.

"Your honor," he began, "an accommodation has been reached and the company is dropping all charges against these four men."

The judge looked curiously at Stanton and me. I suppose he was trying to figure out what a young lawyer might have on one of the city's leading attorneys. The judge turned to his clerk. "Did you get that?" he said. "Write it up." Then he banged his gavel. "Case dismissed."

The four defendants and their coworkers cheered wildly. The union agent looked around, bewildered, and then smirked. He'd managed to win a big case without opening his mouth! Jack Gould nodded at me, knowing I'd made it happen.

I hurried outside the courtroom to meet Ruth. "Miss Torricelli," I said, assuming an air of mock formality, "I have one question. How—"

"Jack Gould," she chirped.

I threw my head back in recognition. "Of course. But—"

"He called me. He said he couldn't believe what had happened to you."

"Yeah, well, neither could I."

"So what made you change?"

"I'm not sure. But I figured I'll never learn what I'm meant to do if I keep doing things I shouldn't do. That's all."

"That's all? That's a lot."

"I should have seen it sooner."

Ruth smiled. "I've got an idea. Do you have a few minutes?"

"I guess so. I'm unemployed. Why?"

"There's someone I want you to meet."

"Who?"

"You'll see. Don't worry. Follow me."

I fell in behind her as she hurried out of the courtroom. We raced across the Federal Plaza and down Dearborn Street into the South Loop.

"Ruth, where are we going?" I called out.

"Shush. Trust me." She gave me a seditious smile, the same one she'd given me on the way to the bookstore many years ago.

We arrived at a nondescript building on West Adams and walked up three flights of stairs and down a narrow corridor to an office marked coalition for worker democracy.

"Hello, Ms. Torricelli," a receptionist said cheerfully when we stepped inside. "Nice to see you. What can we do for you?"

"I need to see Stan, right away."

The receptionist got up, knocked on a nearby office door, peeked in, and then motioned us inside.

Behind the desk was a tall, skinny blond man with wire-rimmed glasses. He rose from his desk stiffly, as if his lanky frame barely hung together and he was afraid of breaking it.

"Stan, I want you to meet a friend, Ray Elias. Ray, this is Stan Roberts, executive director of the coalition."

Stan gave me a suspicious look. "Don't you work for Baker, Bates & Stanton? That firm hasn't been too—"

"Never mind that, Stan. Ray quit the firm, and he just did the most amazing thing I've ever seen in a courtroom. Without ever calling a witness, he made old man Stanton reinstate four union sympathizers."

Stan emitted an awkward smile.

"Don't you get it?" Ruth continued. "You need to talk to Ray. He needs to be your director of organizing."

"What?" Stan and I said in unison.

"Be quiet, both of you. Stan, let's face it. You need an experienced organizer to get this place off the ground."

"Off the ground? I don't need a director of organizing."

"Nonsense. The organization will flop unless you start sharing responsibility. Organizing is not your strong suit."

Stan hung his head. "Well, that I agree with, but not the part—"

"Ray is a brilliant organizer." She turned to me. "And Ray. You need to put those skills of yours back to use."

"Yes, I do. That's true, Ruth, but I don't know anything about this job. Two weeks ago I was a management lawyer."

"That's right," Stan said. "He was."

Ruth was like a freight train; she kept coming. "Yes, and years before that, you mobilized an entire university against the war."

"He did?" Stan exclaimed.

Ruth gave an emphatic nod.

"Well, okay, Ray," Stan said, softening. "Do you have any ideas about mobilizing labor?"

I looked at Ruth for encouragement. She nodded me on. "Well, yes, I believe I do," I said. "From what I can see, unions concentrate on getting a little piece of the company pie. There's nothing wrong with that. But it keeps them perpetually dependent."

Ruth was nodding furiously, urging me on.

"If working people—not necessarily unions—could actually get their hands on the levers of power, then the whole dynamic would change."

"But don't they do that through electoral politics?" Stan asked.

"I'm talking about economic levers, not political influence. Is there any reason why, for instance, a union pension fund couldn't invest in office buildings or residential housing, even build factories with their billions in pension money? What if every worker put two dollars a month into a group legal fund?

There would be millions of dollars to fight the companies that abused their employees. Things like that."

Stan stared at me, impressed.

"You see?" Ruth said. "Now I'll leave you boys to talk. I've got to get back to work. In an hour I expect to see plans for a full-blown national workers' conference."

I rolled my eyes, but Stan looked dumbfounded. "What? A national workers' conference?"

"Stan, I'm kidding."

I took a step toward Ruth as she turned to leave. "Ruth, wait. Can I see you?"

She paused. "Sure. What is it?"

"No, I mean later."

She smiled. "Call me after you get done talking to Stan."

PART EIGHT

Spring 1975—Winter 1978

Chapter Sixty-One

I STRODE OFF the Senate floor with Danny into the teeth of a dozen reporters peppering me with questions.

"Senator, estimates of your employment bill are as high as thirty billion!"

"If we can spend three times that on some military adventure eight thousand miles away," I shot back, "we can find a way to fight for the dignity of working people here at home."

"How can you put a whole nation to work?"

"We did it in World War II."

"Economists are calling your bill inflationary."

"Economists say a lot . . . and prove very little."

"But sir, even your Senate colleagues are calling this 'crackpot idealism.'"

I stopped walking and turned around. "Well, that's what they said when I pushed for civil rights in 1948, and Medicare in the fifties, and a nuclear test ban treaty in the sixties. And we passed every one of them. This is the issue of the seventies."

"But Senator," another reporter shouted, "organized labor is against the bill. They just issued a statement."

"That's it, fellas," I replied. "Gotta go to work." As Danny and I walked away, I murmured to him, "Did the unions really come out against this?"

"Some of them, yes. I'm afraid so, Senator. Protecting their turf. They think their guys may lose out if you put everyone else to work."

"These men are dinosaurs. We're going to have to convince them or go around them."

"Well, I've been thinking about that, Senator," Danny said as he handed me a press clipping. "Here's someone who can help."

The article was about Ray Elias and his work with a worker coalition in Chicago. Ray had dropped off my radar years ago. When I learned that he went to law school, I wished I could have given him a reference. He was making a name for himself on his own, but frankly, I thought some of his ideas were unusual and unrealistic.

I handed the clipping back. "I saw this, Danny. He'll never get anywhere with it."

"Ray is speaking your language, Hubert."

"Telling unions to build factories with their pension money? That doesn't make any sense to me."

Danny stared at me. "What makes sense is that he's a labor lawyer and one of the best grassroots organizers you ever knew. And frankly, things don't look too organized at the moment."

Danny never spoke to me like that. Not in twelve years. But he was right. We weren't making headway with the bill.

"All right, Danny. Give him a call."

Chapter Sixty-Two

WHEN DANNY CALLED, I knew Humphrey's bill was in trouble. The bill was vintage Humphrey: idealistic, optimistic, and, as always, aimed at reducing the pain and suffering of his countrymen. But requiring the government to create temporary jobs in tough economic times was seen as a throwback to the era of big spending. After Watergate and Vietnam, Americans seemed to lose faith in their government as a force that could transform lives. Even the momentum of the civil rights movement had stalled. Hubert Humphrey, the champion of government innovation, was seen as an anachronism.

I followed Humphrey's activities the way someone follows newspaper accounts of a person from their hometown who had gained notoriety in the outside world: through the slender thread of idle curiosity.

I think Danny sensed this. On the phone, he was blunt. "Hubert needs you."

It was true. He did need me. I had been mentally cataloging the flaws in Humphrey's bill. Yes, I could help. But should I?

I had a hundred excuses to hurl at Danny. But his words acted like a match on a fuse leading to a part of myself I kept hidden—a place of isolation and defensiveness—and his plea detonated it. I needed to run this by Ruth.

Ruth and I had begun seeing each other again, but not frequently and, frankly, without intimacy. A veil of politeness hung over us, a safety net to prevent tripping over the frayed nerves of past tensions. We rarely strayed beyond talk about work. But even in that confined space, there were reminiscences that brought smiles to our faces and the hint of a deeper connection.

After all those years of urging reconciliation with Humphrey, I expected her to support Danny's overture—but I was taken aback when she said, "Have you talked to Stan about taking a leave?"

"A leave? No. Danny invited me to a meeting. That's all."

"Sure, Ray." She laughed. "Do you think Humphrey's going to risk losing you again? Or vice versa?"

"I'm not leaving Chicago, Ruth. Not when you . . . I mean, we . . ."

My words trailed off, buried in a long silence. Then she set my course: "Ray, go see your old friend. He needs your help. I'll be here."

Chapter Sixty-Three

AN ACCIDENT SLOWED TRAFFIC on the way from the Washington National Airport, and I arrived late at Humphrey's office. When I walked in, he was addressing aides, who were arrayed around a conference table.

"The bill hasn't caught on, even with organized labor," he was saying. "They say they have other priorities. It's hard to understand how they could have a bigger priority than putting people to work. Be that as it may——"

Then Humphrey spotted me and sprang from his seat. "Ray!"

"Sorry, I'm a little late," I said, still out of breath.

"That's all right, Ray," Humphrey said gently. "We're just getting started. Someone get Ray a seat." Pointing to the huge stack of papers under my arm, he added, "Looks like you have a few things to share."

"Thank you, Senator. Yes, I have a few ideas."

"Well, go ahead then. Let's hear them. You're among friends."

I took a chunk of documents from my pile and started passing them out. Humphrey shot Danny a look, smiling. They must have been thinking, as I was, of our first meeting at the Capitol eleven years ago, when Danny had passed out my mimeographed campaign leaflets and song sheets.

"First," I began, "I think there are a lot of misconceptions about Senator Humphrey's bill, and the press isn't helping matters. So I put together a fact sheet, a Q and A to explain what the bill is and what it isn't."

I handed out another document. "Second, we need to

consider amendments to the bill that would expand support without diluting its provisions. I made a list of seventeen points I think we could give on."

"Seventeen points!" someone exclaimed incredulously. "President Wilson only had fourteen."

It was a good-natured reference to Woodrow Wilson's peace plan after World War I, and everyone laughed. I was glad; it lightened things up.

Picking up steam, I passed out another document. "This third document is the most important. To get labor support, we don't really need to rely on unions."

"What?" a half dozen voices exclaimed.

"The most we can expect from labor is lip service, but that won't be enough."

"What are you suggesting?" one of the aides asked. "How can we go around labor?"

"By appealing directly to the rank and file," I countered, "building support from the ground up. If we can do that, the leaders will follow." I waited for the idea to sink in, and then punctuated the point. "They have to. They'll claim it was their idea, but it doesn't matter as long as they support it."

Humphrey nodded ponderously. "How do we do that, Ray?"

"The old-fashioned way, Senator. Get out on the road and hold hearings, a dozen of them in cities around the country, with you as the keynote speaker at each one."

Humphrey brightened, so I kept going. "Imagine town meetings all over the country where working people can tell the personal stories that are behind the cold numbers. Let the politicians know the cost of their inaction."

Humphrey slapped his knee. "I love that. What does everyone think?"

There were a few hesitant nods at first, then voices of concurrence, and finally agreement. Humphrey got up and declared, "Weh-eh-ehl, let's get started. C'mon, Ray. Have lunch with me and we'll kick this thing around."

Humphrey and I charged out of his office and down the wide stairways of the Senate Office Building to the basement, where the underground tramway whisked us to the Capitol. Humphrey flew down the corridors with me beside him. Senators paused to gawk at Hubert Humphrey, living up to his old nickname, the "Happy Warrior."

Humphrey led me to an office off the beaten path. The room wasn't small, but it was dingy with faded walls, drooping shelves, and battered wooden desks scattered around the room.

"I know it isn't much," he said. "But it's right here in the Capitol. I guess you could call it a perk the majority leader gave me for old time's sake. Anyway, can you make this work as your office?"

"My office, Senator?" I said, startled.

"Yes, Ray. Let's get this thing rolling."

I looked around, recalling the old council office that Ruth and our friends had transformed together.

"What is it, Ray?"

"Nothing. It just reminds me . . ."

"Of course," he sighed. Then, shifting moods, he said, "C'mon, let's get some lunch."

Humphrey led me down the Capitol corridors to the Senate Dining Room. Spreading his arms, he said, "Wait till these guys hear what we have in store for them. That'll shake things up a little."

Humphrey's smile was, as always, infectious. Time had passed, mistakes had been made, awful things had been said, and sadness had magnified over time. But relief was overtaking us, along with the consolation of working together again.

Chapter Sixty-Four

I TOOK MY SEAT in the gallery of the Senate Committee on Labor and Public Welfare as the chairman gaveled the meeting to order.

"Gentlemen of the committee," the chairman said, "we resume consideration of the Humphrey-Hawkins Full Employment and Balanced Growth bill. The question is whether we should hold hearings throughout the country on the bill that Senator Humphrey and Representative Hawkins have sponsored. Senator Humphrey? You have the floor."

"Thank you, Mr. Chairman. As you know, I have advocated for hearings in selected American cities. However, I want to make it clear that these hearings shouldn't be restricted to experts with statistics. Sadly, I'm familiar with how charts and numbers have a way of obscuring reality. No, we need to hear from workers directly affected by unemployment, so its devastating impact can be plainly demonstrated."

"Mr. Chairman," one senator said, "I think this committee is well aware of the impact of unemployment. The focus should be on the budget impact of the bill Senator Humphrey is proposing." The other senators grumbled in agreement.

Humphrey was bristling, eager to meet the argument head-on. "Yes, Mr. Chairman, but we also need to look at the impact of not passing this bill. I'm talking about social unrest, the widening disparity of wealth in this country, and the impact on medical care, education, and decent housing."

A chorus of skepticism sprang from the members. Undaunted, Humphrey met the storm. "The only way we can understand the true measure of distress in this country is to hear from the people who actually suffer it, not statisticians citing numbers."

The chairman, deferential to Humphrey, asked how many hearings he had in mind.

"Twelve," he said boldly.

"Twelve!" the senators muttered.

"My God, Hubert," the chairman exclaimed. "It's not like we don't have other things to do."

"None more important than this, Mr. Chairman."

"All right, all right," the chairman said. "Hubert, you're passionate about this thing. Anyone who knows you should have expected that." Turning to the other senators, he said, "Let's take this under advisement." With that, he gaveled the meeting to an end.

Humphrey walked over to me. "We'll figure out how to get through to these guys."

I nodded but wasn't so sure. I knew he wasn't either. I started thinking of an alternative plan.

"Say," he continued, "I need to head over to Walter Reed Hospital. Getting some things checked out."

"Oh?"

"Nothing to worry about, Ray. Just routine. I'll see you tomorrow morning."

The next morning, I was sitting at a desk in my Capitol office, along with several college students just arrived from Minnesota, when Humphrey walked in. He brightened when he saw that the place was now clean and freshly renovated, thanks to funds he secured and office furniture retrieved from the bowels of the Capitol.

The young Minnesotans sprang to attention, and Humphrey greeted each of them with a personal touch: "Oh yes, Mankato State is a fine school. My son Robert went there.

What do you study?" Humphrey invested time with every one of them, reveling in their youthful energy.

Then he turned to me, all business. "Ray, we need to talk for a minute. The committee isn't going for the hearings. The chairman called me last night. They say it's redundant and costly. Do we have an alternative strategy?"

"Yes, Senator. I anticipated this."

"I had a feeling you did. So did I. Are you thinking what I'm thinking?"

"Bypass their committee and convene the Joint Economic Committee instead?"

"Exactly." Hubert laughed. "They stuck me on that fossilized outpost instead of the Foreign Relations Committee. Now I'll show them what we can make of it."

"That's right, sir. That committee was created to look at labor and economic issues, even if it's been dormant for a decade, so no one can argue that you're exceeding the committee's jurisdiction."

"And some of my old Republican allies are on it," Humphrey chuckled. "Like Javits and Percy. I'll talk to them."

"Full speed ahead, then?"

"Yes, Ray."

I sat down, about to dive back into my work, but Humphrey lingered, a somber mood overtaking him. "Ray, I was wondering if you remembered what day it is today."

"Of course, Senator."

"Good. There's a church north of here where I sometimes go. Do you have time to accompany me?"

"With pleasure."

"Let's go."

Humphrey and I entered the 19th Street Baptist Church, the oldest black church in Washington. Inside, congregants were listening to the pastor's tribute to Dr. Martin Luther King Jr. on the seventh anniversary of his assassination. An usher walked over to Humphrey and gestured to follow him to the front. Humphrey shook his head, and we took seats in the back.

It wasn't a large group or a long service—just one of thousands quietly taking place across America.

As we left the church, Humphrey said, "Let's walk a few minutes. There's a little park up the street where we can sit."

We walked up 16th Avenue and entered the park. A few people sat on benches, gazing dreamily into space. Several others were walking dogs, patiently attending to their unpredictable movements. A solitary vendor parked his wagon in the center, waiting for customers. Everyone was in their own world, none of them recognizing Humphrey.

As we sat down, it struck me that the last time he and I had been alone, just the two of us, was in my dorm room years ago.

"Ray, during the service I was thinking about Atlantic City, when I introduced you to Martin. I still remember the look of awe on your face, meeting such a great man."

"That's right, Senator. But I also felt that way three months earlier in your office."

Humphrey smiled. "Thank you. I'm flattered. But no. Martin? If I had to pick one day in my public life when I felt most encouraged that democracy worked, when my spirit soared on the winds of the American dream, it was the day Martin gave his 'I Have a Dream' speech. Kids will be reciting it long after I'm gone and forgotten."

"But many of those kids will study history and learn that Dr. King's speech might never have taken place without yours in Philadelphia fifteen years earlier."

Humphrey stared into the distance.

"I don't think I ever thanked you, Ray, for what you tried to tell me that night in your dorm room."

"I was too angry—"

"No, you were right, just the same. You said people wouldn't follow me if I lacked the courage to tell them the truth."

"They're following you now, Senator."

"I wasn't listening then, and it cost me the presidency."

He drifted off again, squinting into the distance, as if straining to hear a distant voice. "There were just some things I couldn't see about Lyndon. I owed him loyalty, that's true, but he crossed the line with his demands. I just couldn't see it. Muriel saw it. She lived through it once, and tried to tell me. I kept giving Lyndon more and more."

"Senator," I began, "I also wasn't listening that night."

Humphrey slowly turned his head toward me.

"My heart was closed. I refused to trust you. I let bitterness overtake me, just as you said. It cost us years, Senator. It cost me the love of the woman I adore . . . and it cost me the chance to make real peace with my father."

At the mention of my father, Humphrey took a sudden breath. His eyes shut and he tilted his head skyward.

"Some lessons are learned late," he said. "They take time. And time is not something I can count on."

My body shook in a thunderclap of panic.

"I couldn't tell you yesterday. But seven years ago, on election night, I saw blood in my urine. They found nonmalignant bladder disease. Dr. Berman's been watching it. There are painful tests every six months. But there have been changes . . . I'm going to need x-ray therapy."

"Oh," I said softly.

"It's okay, Ray. With a little luck, it should be fine." Hubert popped up from the bench. "Besides, I have too many chapters to write before they close the book on me."

He wanted to leave and get back to work to dispel the mood, but I was tossed off balance. My mind was astride my body, looking in—like the day Kennedy died, when I stared at the big oak tree from my bed in Rockville Centre. But I was a boy then, with a one-dimensional understanding of time, conscious only of how it flowed as a linear progression of events.

Now, facing Hubert's loss, I saw time as obstinate and unforgiving. The pace of reconciliation with this wonderful man was threatened, not by my inflexibility as in the past, but by imposed interruptions. I saw that time did not flow in a steady line but was asymmetrical. It was shaped into segments, with definable beginnings and ends. Then we judged them: good or bad, fair or unfair, lucky or unlucky, all vain efforts to manage and make meaning of events.

Now, the time with my friend Hubert could be coming to an end. It was unfair and unlucky. I felt suddenly catapulted to the stark terrain of adulthood, aware of "the press of time" that could cut aspirations short and curtail the imagination.

But I couldn't dwell on that now. My task was to fall in with Hubert's enthusiasm. So I, too, jumped up and said, "All right, Hubert. Let's go back and write another chapter."

With a belly laugh, Hubert slapped me on the back. "That's the spirit."

Chapter Sixty-Five

THE REGIONAL CONFERENCES that Hubert and I put together throughout the nation brought out hundreds of witnesses. Not just traditional laboring men like truck drivers, factory workers, and office workers, but dual-income working couples, single women, and part-time workers, both Negro and white. All bore witness to the uncertainty of employment in an age of unpredictable global economic forces.

The message was getting through. Hubert's colleagues in the House and Senate were conceding that the time had come for his bill. At the hearing in Chicago, crowds were dense, anticipating a showdown between Hubert and the famous University of Chicago economist Milton Friedman.

At a long conference table with a bank of microphones, Hubert and I were conferring when Ruth entered the room and walked over to us. I stood up to greet her, and Hubert followed suit.

"Senator, I'd like you to meet Ruth Torricelli. She . . . well . . . she got me back on track."

Hubert shook her hand vigorously. "Weh-eh-ehl, then I have a lot to thank you for, young lady."

"Senator, it's such a pleasure to see you men working together again."

"I'm pleased, too, Ruth," Hubert said warmly.

"Ruth is from Wisconsin," I gushed, "and still remembers the words from your 1960 campaign song. That's kind of how we met."

Hubert exploded into laughter. Ruth blushed and gave me a look of mock irritation.

"Well, Ruth, perhaps sometime I'll ask you to sing it for me."

"Yes, sir, I'd be happy to."

They shook hands, and Ruth waded into the audience and sat down. I watched with unabashed admiration.

"Is that the young lady you were telling me about?"

I nodded.

"Well, Ray, it doesn't look to me like you lost her."

That night, I knocked on the door of Ruth's apartment, the same one we'd shared five years ago. I carried a bottle of wine in one hand and a box of pastries in the other. She opened the door, smiling and radiant. She kissed me on the cheek and led me by the hand to the kitchen, the scene of so many productive plans and not-so-productive quarrels.

I looked around, taking measure of the years of change. Buddha was still staring down from the living room ceiling, but a brand-new couch had replaced the old one. The kitchen table made of planks and sawhorses was gone, a handsome sturdy oak block in its place.

What hadn't changed was the aroma of Ruth's spectacular Italian creations. How she'd managed to make a lasagna after working all day was beyond me. She pointed to the bottle of wine; I opened it and poured two glasses. Neither of us said a word, letting the silence stir old affections.

Ruth suddenly looked up at the clock and broke the stillness. "The news! Grab your glass."

A report on the hearings led the news. A reporter was interviewing Hubert.

"Oh yes," Hubert said, "you'll hear President Ford lamenting the plight of the unemployed when it's convenient politically. But when it comes time to take aim on the problem, with money and real commitment, the president is nowhere to be found."

The television camera panned the room, showing an overalls-clad worker testifying as I whispered in Hubert's ear. Ruth shook me by the shoulders excitedly, nearly spilling the wine.

"These nationwide conferences," the reporter resumed, "are reviving support for Humphrey's full employment bill, a legislative endeavor that congressional insiders considered all but dead six months ago."

Ruth and I clinked our glasses.

"And, inevitably with an election year approaching, the spotlight is again on Humphrey and speculation that he may throw his hat into the 1976 presidential sweepstakes."

Ruth looked at me expectantly. "Is he really thinking of that?"

I shook my head. "I don't know."

"The idea of a Humphrey candidacy," the reporter continued, "has attracted a wide spectrum of Democrats seeking an alternative to Georgia governor Jimmy Carter."

The screen shifted to footage of President Gerald Ford. "I fully expect that Hubert Humphrey will be my opponent this fall."

Ruth studied my worried look. "What are you thinking?"

"I just don't know if it's a good thing."

Ruth got up, clicked off the TV, and sat down again. "When do you go back to Washington?"

"Tomorrow."

She nodded.

"Ruth, I was thinking. You remember the idea you mentioned in Stan's office?"

"About you guys working together? Of course."

"No, I mean the idea of a national workers' convention?"

"What? No, I don't."

"As you were leaving Stan's office?"

"Oh. I wasn't serious about that."

"Well, Hubert likes it. As a way to cap off these hearings."

"Oh, Ray, that's huge."

"I told him it was your idea."

"You didn't have to—"

"And he insisted that you and I organize it together."

Ruth smiled indulgently, then looked away.

"He said we'll do it in Chicago so that you—"

"Ray . . . it's not the conference."

"What? What is it?"

She took my hand. "If we work together on a conference, well . . . we have to be clear on where we stand with each other."

I lowered my eyes, as I always did when I had to grapple with tough emotions.

She lifted my face with two fingers and turned me toward her.

"Where do we stand, Ray?"

"I made a mess of things, Ruth. I know that. I'm just . . . afraid."

"Of what? To try again? To trust me?"

"No. Not you. I'm afraid to trust myself. I turned my back on the people who loved me. My father, Hubert, and . . . I battled all of you in the name of principle, but it was just an excuse not to trust anyone. I lost everything."

"You didn't lose anything. I never stopped loving you, and neither did Hubert or your father."

I stared at Ruth disbelievingly. Then, as she had done so many times, she stopped me in my tracks. She lifted my face to hers and kissed me.

"Tell Hubert yes," she said.

Chapter Sixty-Six

THE MINUTE I RETURNED to Washington, Danny intercepted me. "Glad you're here. There's a group waiting. Top Democrats. They're talking to Hubert about running for president."

I winced.

"I know. I feel the same way. Hubert wants you in there."

One of Hubert's Senate colleagues was laying out the political terrain. "The deadline for the Pennsylvania primary is next Tuesday. And you'll have only seven days after that to enter in New Jersey."

Hubert listened in arched-brow concentration.

Another senator joined the argument. "We think you can easily beat Carter in New Jersey, then gradually pick off his soft support."

"Does he have any other kind?" another senator chimed in.

Everyone laughed except me, Danny, and Hubert.

Then it was Senator Walter Mondale's turn. As Hubert's fellow Minnesotan, his word counted the most. "The beauty of this situation is that people are coming to you, Hubert, asking you to run. The nation knows it made a mistake. If you give them a second chance, I think they'll rectify it."

"It will reopen old wounds," I said, breaching protocol, but Mondale wasn't offended.

"Who better to heal those wounds, Ray?" Mondale answered.

"What if he's remembered for causing them, Senator?"

Mondale nodded. He knew. We all knew. It was a risk.

"I think Americans are ready to forget the war," someone said. Others seemed ready to echo the sentiment, but Hubert brought an end to the discussion, raising his right hand slightly.

We all got up to leave.

"Ray, Danny," Hubert said. "Can you stay a minute?"

Hubert thanked everyone as they filed out, then turned to us. "You don't think I should do it?"

Danny shook his head. "Senator, we're making strides on the bill. Maybe that's your legacy."

Hubert looked at me. "Ray, do you agree with Danny?"

"Yes, Senator. Americans aren't looking for idealism right now. Not after a decade of disenchantment with government. They're turning to outsiders like Carter and Reagan, and . . ."

"Yes, Ray. Go on."

"I'm afraid those men will mock you, call you a liberal, and make it sound like a dirty word. I don't think I could stand to see that."

"The nation will catch up to you," Danny added, "but I'm not sure it's the best time for a presidential campaign."

"Time is something I may not have a lot of," Hubert responded.

Danny and I glanced at each other, alarmed.

"Have things changed, sir?" I asked.

Hubert walked to the window, staring out over the magnificent buildings ringing the Capitol. "Not for sure. But I need to go to Sloan Kettering in New York to have it looked at."

I closed my eyes. That infernal mental switch clicked on again; the agonies this man had endured rolled through my mind like a memory reel.

He walked over and put his arm around me. "It's okay, Ray. It'll be fine. Let's finish our work here. That's what counts."

A crowd of reporters and photographers pressed against the podium in the Capitol press room, waiting for Hubert to address them. Ruth had flown to Washington for the announcement. Hubert had called her directly; he wanted her there.

We stood together near the front of the room as Hubert walked out with Muriel. "Are you sure you can let it go?" I heard her say to him as he approached the microphones.

"You bet," he said with an enormous smile.

"Well, then. I'm with you."

Hubert kissed Muriel on the cheek.

Ruth and I looked admiringly at this devoted couple, partners and best friends for over forty years. Ruth wrapped her hand around mine as Hubert walked to the podium.

"Ladies and gentlemen, this has been an exceedingly difficult decision. You know I have figured in every national campaign since 1960. But I will not do so this year."

With those words, the mounting expectation that Hubert Humphrey would run for president in 1976, and finally win, was crushed.

As the media filtered out, Hubert motioned to Ruth and me to follow Muriel and him into the office behind the press room. He looked at me solemnly. "You know, whoever is elected, Democrat or Republican, they're going to need frequent and loud reminders of what my bill is all about. Will you pledge to do that, Ray, no matter what happens to me?"

"Of course, Hubert."

"And Ruth, will you help?"

"I will, because . . ."

"Yes, Ruth?"

She glanced at me with a wistful smile, then gently touched Hubert's arm. "Senator, your inspiration set the course of Ray's life."

Hubert smiled. "I'm afraid, dear, that I've been like a

small craft drifting on the open seas much of the time. I think you've been the steady hand that's guided his ship."

"Still," Ruth said, "I always knew he would return to you."

"To both of us, Ruth."

Muriel smiled. "C'mon, Dad. Time for us to go home."

Chapter Sixty-Seven

THE DOCTORS AT Sloan Kettering in New York advised surgery to remove Hubert's bladder, but even after the procedure, he still felt pain. He looked fine and kept working, but a follow-up biopsy revealed that his cancer had spread. The words "inoperable" and "terminal" were now used freely by his doctors.

The nation now accepted the inevitable: Hubert Humphrey was dying. An outpouring of affection flowed from every quarter. Friends and colleagues, allies and foes, leaders of nations, and even President Carter—who hadn't been charitable when he viewed Hubert as his rival—found eloquent words to honor him. The nation seemed to collectively acknowledge that it had missed the opportunity to be led by a truly decent man.

Among the unprecedented tributes—the renaming of buildings in his honor, medals, and fine speeches delivered in gilded halls—what meant the most were his last appearances before the constituencies he loved and had served so long: blacks, labor, teachers, and the elderly. Still, it must have been a special moment for him to stand before the House of Representatives—the only senator in United States history invited to do so—and speak from the podium where presidents of the United States delivered their State of the Union Addresses.

For me, it was a time of gratitude more than sadness; the winding path of reconciliation had led me back to an old friend, mentor, and hero. In the closing days of his life, I found myself reflecting on my good fortune as a boy to see in Hubert the inspiration of a lifetime. And despite the events that obscured that vision, I had found my way home through openness of the heart, as Hubert called it that night in my dorm room.

Ruth and I stood at the stage of the Chicago Auditorium, reviewing seating charts for the convention, when a teenager approached us. We looked up and took stock of the boy. He was holding a drawstring sack, just like the maroon one I hauled around as a student at the University of Chicago. He had a mop of stringy black hair swept to one side and deep-set eyes. He looked uncomfortable in a sport coat a size too small for his tall frame and a wide tie that was no longer in fashion.

"Mr. Elias?" he said faintly.

"Yes, I'm Ray Elias. Can I help you?"

"Um, well, sir, I've been reading about the convention you're organizing. I thought maybe the attendees would be interested in an informational packet. I've prepared some charts."

"Really? What kind of charts?"

The kid started rummaging through his sack. Ruth nudged me to pay close attention to him, smiling at his eagerness. He pulled out a folder holding a thick sheaf of pages and handed it to me. As Ruth and I began reviewing the documents, he launched boldly into describing them.

"Each of these reports shows an aspect of the social effects of unemployment," he said. "For instance, the impact on children, economic data proving that full employment does not cause inflation, statistical alternatives to the way unemployment is currently measured, and the impact of rising health-care costs on middle-class families."

Ruth and I looked at each other with matching expressions of surprise and admiration.

"You see, Mr. Elias," he continued with high-pitched

sincerity, "the government is sweeping millions of people under the rug through statistical sleight of hand." He pointed to the chart Ruth was looking at. "For instance, that one shows—"

"I'm sorry," I interrupted. "I don't think I got your name."

"Michael. Michael Talbott."

"Michael, this is Ruth Torricelli."

"Oh yes, I know," Michael said, smiling diffidently. "Everyone knows about your Farm to Fork program, Miss Torricelli."

I smiled at Ruth, then said to Michael, "Do you have time to go over this more closely?"

"Oh yes, sir."

Ruth looked at her watch and gave me a quick hug. "I've gotta run. See you tonight." Turning to Michael, she added, "A pleasure to meet you, Michael. I'll see you soon."

"Thank you, Ms. Torricelli."

At the Coalition for Worker Democracy, I introduced Michael to the staff, now five times larger than it had been three years ago when I joined. Stan had taken a job with a national union in Washington, and I headed the coalition.

"Everyone, this is Michael Talbott," I said. "He's prepared some charts, some great stuff for the convention."

The staff greeted him warmly. I motioned to Michael to stick with me as I moved swiftly through the office, fielding questions and instructing staff in the frantic run-up to the convention.

"Ray!" one of my staff called out. "I've had WMAQ on hold. You've got to talk to them."

"Tell them I'll call back in thirty minutes." Turning to Michael as we walked down the hall, I said, "That chart depicting unemployment levels adjusting for part-time work and underemployment . . ."

"Yes, Mr. Elias?"

"I was thinking. Let's reduce it to a one-page document. We'll run off two thousand copies for the convention."

"Yes, sir."

We entered my office and Michael drifted over to the wall, a look of ingenuous delight overtaking him as he surveyed the photos of Hubert and me. I watched with pleasure as he read the inscription on my favorite one, the first he ever gave me: *"To Ray Elias, my campaign manager and good friend, Hubert Humphrey."* A puzzled look came over his face.

"What is it, Michael?"

"There are a lot of photos of you and Senator Humphrey when you were, well . . . my age, and then more recent ones. But there's a big gap."

"We had a falling out, Michael," I said matter-of-factly. "Over the Vietnam War. But it went deeper than that."

Michael looked at me expectantly; he wanted more, so I obliged. "There were things he did that I could not understand. That I couldn't respect—"

"About the war?"

"Yes. He didn't believe in that war, but he forced himself to publicly support it."

Michael wore a puzzled look. Then, he looked away.

"There were pressures on Hubert I didn't understand, and I judged him harshly."

Michael nodded, but I doubted he could understand. I didn't want to go any further. I had just met this young man, and now wasn't the time to describe the twisting pathway that lay ahead—from inspiration, through disappointment, and finally to reconciliation. Michael would have to learn that for himself, and mistakes would be made. But I might guide this young man, smooth out some rough spots, help him avoid the worst pitfalls.

"Michael, take a seat. I want to show you something." I opened my desk drawer and pulled out a letter written in rough script, with four signatures scrawled at the bottom.

Michael read the letter. "Who are these men thanking you, Mr. Elias?"

"Ordinary working men abused by a selfish boss. The world is full of people using their power to hold others down. Every person must decide for themselves the role they're willing to play to take on injustice. I came back to Hubert because I realized that few people in this country had done more to fight it than he did, despite his flaws."

"I understand, Mr. Elias."

"And that's what you're doing, Michael."

"Thank you, sir."

"Let's make America pay attention to its working people again."

"I want to."

"I can see that."

Just then, a secretary barged in. "Ray, Dan Gleason is on line three. He said he needs to talk to you about news reports that you're running for Congress."

Michael lit up.

"What?" I snapped. "Tell Dan those reports are news to me. I'll see him at the convention."

"Ray, I'm afraid he really insists on talking to you."

"All right. Tell him I'll be right with him."

Michael was staring at me in wide-eyed anticipation.

"I'm sure there's nothing to it. What are they thinking? I'm twenty-eight years old."

Michael broke into a smile. "That's what labor needs. Someone young instead of . . . well . . . maybe I shouldn't say anything."

"I know. I know, Michael. Let's meet again in the morning?"

"Yes, sir."

"Ray is better. Call me Ray."

"Okay, Mr. . . . . I mean, Ray."

Chapter Sixty-Eight

RUTH STOOD WITH HUBERT offstage, steadying him, as I introduced him to a thousand working men and woman crowding the Chicago Auditorium.

"I've learned from Hubert Humphrey that a government without compassion cannot succeed, that a community without forgiveness cannot endure, and a person without love cannot trust. He is my hero. *Our* hero. An American hero. Ladies and gentlemen, Hubert Humphrey."

Hubert moved toward the podium unsteadily. I walked over to help him, and then stepped back to stand with Ruth.

"I may be moving a little wobbly right now," Hubert began, "but I am going to end up damn strong."

Tears began to stream down Hubert's face. The cameras flashed.

"I've always been accused of being too emotional. My wife, Muriel, said, 'They'd take your picture if you wipe your eyes.' Well, that's all right—take the picture. Because if you've got no tears, you've got no heart."

Ruth clutched my hand as tears came to her eyes and mine, too.

"You see," Hubert continued, "we have work to be done. Throughout our great land, there is a war on. A war against man's ancient enemies of idleness and hopelessness."

The crowd roared.

"And a war against government leaders who have become like political morticians, counting millions of jobless like so many dead, pleading for more time to let the structure of our free enterprise system work. Well, I say it isn't working, and I'm going to fight to make it work. As long as I can stand, I can fight, and I'll fight with you."

A few weeks later, Dan Gleason, president of the Chicago Federation of Labor, sat me down at the bar of the Blackstone Hotel to talk about my candidacy for Congress. Dan was a burly man, a former teamster, with a wide face and a barrel chest. His white hair was slicked back, giving him both a distinguished and ominous look. Everything he said sounded gruff, but you always knew where you stood with Dan.

True to form, he got right to the point. "You interested?" he asked.

"Dan, the thing I don't understand is, why me? You've got tons of guys looking to run who are more experienced, have paid their dues, and have lots of money."

"And lots of baggage."

"I don't have the money for a primary against those guys."

"There won't be a primary," Dan said laconically.

"Oh?"

"I'll see to that."

"Look, Dan, the truth is, if I did this, I couldn't be just labor's man in Congress. I know other men would do that for you. That kind of loyalty is . . . well, I've seen it."

"Do you really think we expect that?"

"I'm not sure I know exactly what you expect."

"What we expect is what you learned from Hubert Humphrey," he shot back.

I stared at him, startled, unsure what he meant.

"Look," he said, "we expect you to fight the fights that need to be fought. We know that some of those aren't going to be labor's fight and then you'll tell us. But we figure enough of them will be. And when they are, we know you'll never give up."

I stared at Dan with unblinking admiration. He had described Hubert perfectly. True, Hubert had faltered in a colossal way; his weakness clouded his vision, crippled his drive for the presidency, and diverted him from his path. But it couldn't erase the commitments of a lifetime, because he never gave up.

"All right, Dan. I'm flying to Minnesota tomorrow. I'll call you when I get back."

"Give my best to Hubert."

"I will, Dan. And thank you."

"You're welcome, Ray."

"I mean, for reminding me what Hubert Humphrey taught me."

"Yup. None better than him."

"None better. That's right."

Chapter Sixty-Nine

MURIEL OPENED THE DOOR, smiled, and hugged me. "Welcome, Ray. He keeps asking if you got in safely."

"I'm sorry, Muriel. I should have phoned when I landed."

"Ray, it's fine."

She led me through the living room, introducing me to extended family members I had never met, then led me into Hubert's room. He was lying in his bed, lean and drawn, talking to the chief justice of the Supreme Court, Warren Burger, a fellow Minnesotan. Hubert smiled when he saw me.

"I'll let you go now, Hubert," Burger said, "but we expect to see you again soon."

"Thanks for coming, Warren."

As the chief justice departed, Hubert motioned me closer. A telephone and an overstuffed address book sat on the bed beside him, with newspapers strewn about.

"My family got me this WATS line for Christmas. Now I can talk as long as I want."

"Since when did you need a WATS line for that, Hubert?"

He let out his trademark belly laugh, but it was thin this time and dissolved into a convulsive cough. He recovered, took a deep breath, and stared into space.

"Hubert?" I waited for him to turn and look at me. "Did you see that Washington correspondent's poll?"

He shuffled through some newspapers and picked one up. "I have it right here. Let's see. What did they say about me? Oh yes, 'The most effective senator of the twentieth century.'"

"It's an understatement, Hubert."

He emitted another weak laugh. "I'll probably catch holy hell from Lyndon for that, too," he said, pointing upward. "You know, when I get upstairs."

I nodded, suppressing a laugh; I did not want to make Hubert laugh again. He closed his eyes for a moment, then turned to me with an arched brow, pursed lips, and a labored cadence.

"Look, Ray. When Humphrey-Hawkins gets to President Carter's desk, I won't be around for the signing. I've arranged for you to be invited. No foul-ups this time."

We both smiled, sharing this memory of the aborted rendezvous at the Benton dinner years ago.

"Come sit here," he said, with two quick slaps of his hand on the blanket.

I sat down on the edge of the bed. Hubert reached behind the stack of papers, pulled out a small rectangular box, and handed it to me. I knew instantly what it was.

"Go ahead, open it."

I opened the box. It was one of the pens Hubert had shown me when I first visited his office.

"President Johnson signed the Civil Rights Act of 1964 with that. The greatest legislative achievement of my life. I want you to have it."

"Oh, Hubert, no, I . . ."

"Go ahead. Take it. It's not a memento. It's a reminder to never shrink from a challenge. Like running for Congress." He smiled coyly.

I looked up, startled. "How——"

"I have friends in Chicago, you know."

"Hubert, how can I do it? How can I ask the trust of so many when I've let others down?"

"Don't be afraid, Ray. Even when you disappoint a whole nation, if you find your way to the truth, they'll understand and forgive and trust you again."

Hubert's wisdom was a prescription for the peace I had

been chasing. It was so simple, but stubbornly unattainable. He had reached the end of the journey and received the love of a nation, while I was still sifting through dark routes and blocked pathways.

"I've always admired you, Ray. From the beginning. Even in anger, you showed me the way back to . . . to . . . being someone who deserved to be followed."

The tide of sadness overwhelmed me, and a tear broke loose just as Muriel walked in. On that cold January day in central Minnesota, I leaned over and hugged Hubert Humphrey for the last time.

Chapter Seventy

RAY LEFT MY BEDSIDE holding back tears, and then let them flow as he embraced Muriel. I always saw in this young man's eyes the majesty of long-term dreams. Many of my colleagues in Congress had dreams of their own, but no vision, values, or aspirations for their countrymen—just the rousing of ego they liked to think was virtue. Politicians like that have no heart, so they can never truly fight for people beaten down by economic circumstances or subdued by prejudice.

I was a fighter for justice, that was true, but I was afraid of confrontation when it mattered. Muriel was right all along. I was bound to Lyndon as I was to my father. The simple truth, she said, was that I couldn't stand to be unloved. Lyndon knew that, and made it a weapon of domination. He exploited my weaknesses and stifled my strengths. But the truth is rarely simple. My loyalty was not blind. I took an oath of office and felt duty-bound to fulfill it. I was blind in another way: to the means of maneuvering past Lyndon's psychological grip to win the presidency and end the war.

Still, I lived a life with purpose, devotion, and service. Stadiums, streets, and office buildings were named after me to honor my contribution. But my most enduring contribution was the inspiration I instilled in the young people who sought my guidance, in whose eyes I saw the promise of America and who carried the future of the country with them.

In Congress, Ray would face obstacles that would vex the most committed optimist, but his willingness to plod on was a more vital resource to this nation than all our industrial might or agricultural bounty. If we couldn't trust our young men and women to shape government as a force for fairness and opportunity, then all the words spoken in Congress and all the elections held would not save our republic.

I planned to write to President Carter to set up a council to revive this collective spirit of America, and restore faith in its future. I would tell him to put Ray on it when he got to Congress later in the year. Why didn't I think of that before?

"Where's my Dictaphone," I whispered to Muriel, who was standing by my bed in solemn vigil to my silent reverie. "I need to send President Carter an urgent memo. God, there's so much work to be done."

I closed my eyes, and I was a boy back in Doland, in my bedroom with the old wallpaper filled with bluebirds. I heard Dad call, "Pinky, get up. We're going for a ride." I got dressed and ran outside. He was standing still, with his hand outstretched. Everything was perfectly quiet. Only the wind seemed to move. Then we were driving along backcountry dirt roads. A deep-purple cloud rolled across the South Dakota flatland, growing darker as it built up with dust. But as it gave way to the Minnesota farm country, there were only green fields, and fresh water surging in rivers rolling wildly through the countryside. I was riding on a magic carpet, snapped clean of its prairie dullness by the Good Lord, flying high over a land of inexhaustible lushness. Beckoning me was the promise of a new beginning in a great city not far from the headwaters of the Great River.

Chapter Seventy-One

ON FRIDAY, JANUARY 13, 1978, Danny announced to the world that Hubert Humphrey had passed from this life. The president of the United States sent Air Force One to bring his body back to Washington. The president had rows of seats removed so Hubert's coffin would fit in the main cabin, not below with the luggage. Arriving in Washington, he lay in state under the dome of the Capitol, as President Lyndon Johnson had five years earlier and President John Kennedy fifteen years before that.

At the service in the Capitol rotunda, I stood with Muriel and the family, surrounded by hundreds of the nation's most well-known and revered citizens, and others not so well-known but revered by Hubert. "He was never elected president," said Edmund Muskie, his vice presidential running mate in 1968, "but now he is being treated like one."

President Carter's words were poignant in their simplicity. "When he first visited me in the Oval Office, I felt that he should have served there. Hubert may well have blessed this nation as much as any president."

It was Vice President Mondale who spoke the most memorable words. "He taught us how to hope and how to love, how to win and how to lose. He taught us how to live, and finally, he taught us how to die."

The next day, Hubert was flown home to Minnesota, where more than three thousand people, including half the members of Congress, jammed into the House of Hope Presbyterian Church for the final service.

Once again, Vice President Mondale fashioned the most

poignant tribute: "Hubert never found a person who was not worth his time and, like Abraham Lincoln, he could not be separated from his people."

The service ran well past schedule, just like so many of Hubert's speeches. *He would have gotten a kick out of that*, I thought, smiling.

On the flight from Minneapolis to Chicago, I closed my eyes, summoning the scenes of the last two days and pressing them into memory. *Unbelievable*, I uttered to myself. Yet it was believable. It had been the story of my young life. I had come to know something about the truth of things and the truth about who I was. I saw what goodness was in a public person. I learned how to aspire to it and I learned to never presume that I permanently possessed it. Our nation had just suffered two presidents without humility, who turned their arrogance into weapons.

Hubert's flaws were failings of an exuberant spirit, not an embittered heart. He was a man with a rare gift for empathy, and from it flowed the greatest social legislation of the second half of the twentieth century. But he also had the capacity to forgive others, even the men who deceived him. From Hubert, I learned the kindness of patience.

But I had been an obstinate student. With such resistance, what chance did I have to succeed in Congress? I was lured by the satisfactions of service, but fearful of my defensiveness, rigidity, and mistrust. What would Hubert say to help me constrain these flaws?

I imagined him saying, "Don't be afraid if you lose your way. Listen to the people who love you, because they're the ones who can trim your pride and guide you back to understanding, forgiveness, and trust." Even though I had failed to understand Hubert, and to forgive him and trust him, he understood, forgave, and trusted me. If I could guide Michael and young men and women like him the way Hubert guided me, then I could truly serve my country.

I made my way through the arrival gate. Ruth embraced me, and Michael waited dutifully behind, waving shyly.

"I saw you on television," Ruth said. "You were smiling."

"Hubert wanted that—a celebration."

"Have you decided?" Ruth gestured toward Michael. "He can't wait to hear, and frankly, neither can I."

I walked over to Michael and shook his hand. "It means a lot to me that you came, Michael."

He nodded, his eyes sparkling.

"I'm going to run for Congress," I said, looking at Ruth and then at Michael. "That is, if you'll help me."

Michael was beaming. "I'm ready, Mr. Elias."

I embraced Ruth. "It's good to be home. There's so much work to be done."

The three of us walked out of the airport, heading back into the city to begin again.

Author's Note

THE SAYING THAT "truth is stranger than fiction" poses a challenge for writers, and an opportunity. Truth is not credible when it lies outside customary experience. Fiction can suspend usual expectations and offer alternatives so authentic that we are led gently into unfamiliar terrain where truth often resides.

Standard historical accounts of Humphrey's total submission to Johnson barely graze the surface of the compelling psychological factors that drove Humphrey. These factors are hiding in plain sight, and my job was to coax them out and render them credible to elucidate and humanize not just Humphrey's struggle, but Ray's, and all of ours.

I believe that Humphrey's fealty to Johnson cannot be explained by either loyalty to a demanding president or the calculated pursuit of the presidency. Rather, these motivations were blended with another potent factor: the persisting impact of his father's dominating personality. Recapitulating his protracted submission to his father's will as a young man, Humphrey could not escape the pull of Johnson's raw and brutal domination, even with the presidency at stake.

Ray is under a similar spell. He transformed his father's overly critical manner into twin infirmities: doubt of his considerable talents and difficulty trusting others.

Yet, despite setbacks, neither boy nor man was felled by these limitations. They found redemption in each other and triumphed together. The characters in this novel, like most of us, push their way through the fog of psychological constraints to a place of understanding, forgiveness, and reconciliation.

Alignment with who we know ourselves to be is a deeply psychological journey, not an exercise in logic, and its course must run through unwieldy emotions. I wrote this book to portray that pathway.

I sought also to revive an awareness of what goodness looks like in politics. Hubert Humphrey was an eminently good man. Readers may rightfully protest that it is not the novelist's job to press a claim of goodness in one of the novel's characters, but rather, to illuminate the building blocks of character so that readers may assemble their own structure.

However, as an American who lived through the tumultuous events of the '60s and '70s and who sees perilous challenges in contemporary events, I feel an urgency to make a case for virtue in public life. Humphrey was a man with a rare gift for empathy, from which issued the greatest social legislation of the second half of the twentieth century.

Human nature lies most compellingly in our capacity to understand our own failings and forgive the flaws of others. This quality is, or used to be, a dominant feature of the American character. "Everyone deserves a second chance" is a distinctly American mantra. Without empathy, we wade through the mire of our limitations and inevitably weaponize them, blame others, and create political movements out of bitterness. Humphrey had the gift of empathy; he could forgive and reconcile. His flaws were those of an exuberant spirit, not an embittered heart.[1]

A third purpose of writing this novel was to portray the value of idealism to young Americans. Both Ray and Hubert are flawed, but they are idealistic. Their idealism doesn't serve self-interest, but something bigger than themselves:

---

1 The description of Humphrey's flaws as the excess "of a generous spirit, not an angry or embittered heart" appeared in David Broder's *Washington Post* column on June 6, 1972. This column was included with a group of his others that won the 1973 Pulitzer Prize for commentary. (https://www.pulitzer.org/article/hubert-h-humphrey-man-who-really-wanted-be-president)

contribution and service.

In our country, itself the creation of flawed men, we depend on idealism even as we witness the unraveling of our institutions by men and women who purport to serve them. Still, believing in the nobility of the endeavor is ballast against cynicism and ignorance, the extremes that constitute a vise grip on a nation's character and subdue its resilience.

These two men found their way to such understanding, as a nation must. I sought to instill in young readers an appreciation for the nobility of such a journey, the necessity that they undertake it, and how they must activate their potential to lead others.

STUART H. BRODY
New York, 2023

Acknowledgments

EVENTS IN THIS NOVEL were drawn from my real-life relationship with Hubert Humphrey or otherwise document-ed by credible historical accounts. Certain events, dialogue, and characters were fictionalized in service of the story, but might well have occurred as depicted.

My thanks go to several readers who helped guide the final product: Marc Snyder of San Francisco, California, Katherine Brewster of New York City, James Lonergan of Woodstock, New York, Evan Kory of Nogales, Arizona, Katherine Reinhardt of Willsboro, New York, Paula Groo-thuis of Long Island, and Caroline Kaiser of London, On-tario, who so carefully edited a first draft of the book. And to other early readers: Sue Regan, David Browdy, Howard Bernstein, Sy Rotter, Bill Giruzzi, and Kaitlin Meyer. A spe-cial thanks to David Alpert and Katie Shepard, and my nine-ty-eight-year-old neighbor and former piano teacher Bernice Pomeroy and her daughter, MaryAnne, who listened with such joy to my weekly readings by her side in the final weeks of Bernice's long life.

Thank you also to the award-winning young adult writ-er Steve Sheinkin, who encouraged me to write this story as a novel for young people and provided many insights along the way. And to the late Forrest Church, pastor of All Souls Church in New York City, who did the same.

Of the many materials I've reviewed over the decades, including Hubert Humphrey's two autobiographies and the account of his devoted physician, Edgar Berman (from whom I borrowed passages for the chapter on Humphrey's visit to

Vietnam), the source that stands out is Carl Solberg's 1984 biography, *Hubert Humphrey*, a comprehensive work displaying clear affection for its subject without compromising objective evaluation. A recent biography by Arnold Offner, *Hubert Humphrey: The Conscience of the Country*, is a timely corroboration of Solberg's account that offers fresh insights as well. And the most recent, *The Price of Loyalty* by Andrew L. Johns, focuses incisively on the Vietnam War and the many ambiguities surrounding Humphrey's attachment to President Johnson.

Above all, my gratitude to the late Ruth Ann Malato, who offered me her open heart, however unable I was to grasp the magnitude of her gift.